Sara Maitland was born in 1950. In 1979 her first novel, *Daughter of Jerusalem*, won the Somerset Maugham award. Since then she has published three other novels: *Virgin Territory*, *Three Times Table* and (with Michelene Wandor) *Arky Types*, as well as several volumes of short stories, the latest of which is *Women Fly When Men Aren't Watching* (Virago 1993). Her other works include feminist theology and a biography of the music hall cross-dresser, *Vesta Tilley* (Virago 1986). Her new novel, *Home Truths*, is also published this year.

Sara
Maitland

Virgin Territory

Published by VIRAGO PRESS Limited, February 1993
20–23 Mandela Street, Camden Town, London NW1 0HQ

First published in Great Britain by Michael Joseph Ltd, 1984

*A CIP catalogue record for this book is available from the
British Library*

Printed in Great Britain by Cox & Wyman Ltd, Reading, Berkshire

Acknowledgements

This book seems to have changed considerably since I first started work on it. Many of the people who helped or advised me may not recognise my indebtedness, but I would like to thank them all, especially Jeanette Winterson, Michelene Wandor (again !), Nora and Rob Bartlett, Alan Baker, Jorge Santos, Pat Manthorpe, Angela Blanding, Peter Daly, Ruthie Petrie, Anne McDermid and Jennie Davies.

Also the sisters of the Society of St Margaret at the Haggerston Priory, with special apologies to Sr. Anna SSM who also came from America to London to test her vocation; I met her too far into the novel to change the characters' names, but there are, to the best of my knowledge, no other points of similarity between the two.

The religious order and the South American country described in this novel are entirely fictional.

The author and publishers would like to thank the following for permission to quote extracts: Virago (*Dreams and Dilemmas* by Sheila Rowbotham); Journeyman Press/Play Books (*Gardens of Eden* by Michelene Wandor); The Women's Press (*The Moon and the Virgin* by Nor Hall on p. 14); Picador (*Pilgrim at Tinker Creek* by Annie Dillard on p. 177) and Mitchell Beazley (*The Sign of the Tree* by Meinrad Craighead on p. 203).

For feminists the existence of universal and
ahistoric psychic patterns clearly has to be
contested because these inevitably confirm
and legitimate male power.

Sheila Rowbotham, *Dreams and Dilemmas*

I want to be my own jealous God, you see.

for the irony is,
I am made only too well
in thine image, the
image of a jealous God (see Psalm 35)

'the meek shall inherit the earth'?
I have not learned meekness from watching you.

*   *   *

you say you will hover over me
your wings
giving me protection
I've got news for you
I'm allergic to feathers

Michelene Wandor, *Gardens of Eden*.

I

At 8.45 one night, on the pitted track which led from the shanty-town to the house above it where the nuns lived, Sister Katherine Elizabeth was raped by two men, (probably) members of, or paid by, the National Security Forces. Quite early in the process, which was prolonged and painful, Sr. Katherine Elizabeth realised quite consciously that she did not share Saint Maria Goretti's vocation to die in defence of her virginity. So her resistance was more vociferous than physical. She shouted and yelled, and later on shouted and yelled in English so that people would know it was one of their American nuns who was being attacked, but no one came to help her. Nonetheless she was physically not severely hurt, and in fact Sr. Pauline who was with her sustained the more serious injuries. Trying to assist Sr. Katherine Elizabeth she was hit across the face; stumbling backwards she became entangled in her habit and fell heavily, knocking herself unconscious on the rocky road. This may have protected her from being raped too.

Afterwards, when the rapists had vanished into the noisy night, Sr. Katherine Elizabeth opened her eyes and saw the immensity of the tropical sky. Down the trail of the bright stars, distant spinning galaxies, she saw a last glimpse of the pure white unicorn disappearing and she was afraid. She was not a virgin any more. All over the world, with and without choice, women lived in poverty and obedience, but her virginity was the mark of her profession and a core of her identity. She had not known this before and it was in loss that she learned it. She was momentarily uncertain whether God would forgive her for not dying to defend the gift and seal of her relationship with Him. Tears rolled from the corners of her eyes as she lay quite still. The dirt on her face

1

muddied the tears and she knew that they clogged, broke up and were decrystallised. Then she thought about how much she hurt and started worrying about Sr. Pauline, who still lay inert, and the dark moment passed, a shadow across the sky fleeing as swiftly as the unicorn.

When everything had been quiet for a while, four women and a couple of men came up from the township. They were sheepish, embarrassed and fearful, but also not without a certain curiosity to see the American sisters in these unusual circumstances. With a heavy apologetic tenderness they ministered to the women whose job it was to minister to them, and helped them home. The other sisters were singing compline.

Sr. Katherine Elizabeth left Sr. Pauline, still groggy and confused, in the care of the women and slipped into chapel. She felt rather than saw Sr. Jo's irritation at her lateness, and was unexpectedly relieved by its familiarity. She felt a great need to be for the last time with her community normally. Until she told them, the rape had not really happened.

The chapel was a small plain room at the back of the house. It had simple rush-seated chairs and a small altar over which hung a cross made out of beaten tin cans, a present from Sr. Pauline's children's class. The room was whitewashed and supposedly 'as simple as the homes we work in.' It was not, of course, because it was clean, because it was used only for prayer, and because they were highly-qualified, middle-class women with good taste and impeccable manners. Sr. Katherine Elizabeth tried to lean on the repetition, the continuity of the Office, and not see or know their limitations, but she could feel something dripping down between her legs and she did not know if it was blood or . . . she would not even think of the word. She could deny it all, keep it hidden, secret, unnamed, unknown. That was a great temptation.

Sr. Jo said the blessing: 'The Lord grant us a quiet night and a perfect end.' With her sisters Sr. Katherine Elizabeth said 'Amen', but she said it with a pang of guilt and a flavour of restorative irony: they were not going to be granted a quiet night, poor lambs.

The anthem cut deeper, finding a new place in her.

> *Mother of Christ, hear thou thy people's cry*
> *Star of the deep and portal of the sky,*
> *Mother of God, who thee from nothing made*
> *Sinking we strive and call to thee for aid:*
> *Oh by that joy that Gabriel brought to thee,*
> *Thou Virgin first and last let us thy mercy see.*

She felt a sudden surge of pure anger, sweet and frightening. Their thin little women's voices bleated on; far out to sea and high over the menacing jungle hung the fierce hard stars. Star of the deep. Sr. Katherine Elizabeth was forty-one years old and, she thought peevishly, not nearly as pretty as Sr. Pauline. Under her dirtied and torn habit was a great hole which cried to heaven for vengeance. Thou virgin first and last let us thy vengeance see. Sr. Katherine Elizabeth foraged in every place she knew for recollection and calm, and she found none. She felt a blush begin deep down somewhere just below her navel and rise up towards her face.

It worked its way into their flesh, the hard fact of the rape. Sr. Jane Clare, who was a nurse, examined Sr. Katherine Elizabeth and reported starkly that she did not think there had been any serious or permanent damage. Her hands had been so tender and careful and loving, but she woke in the middle of one night with the image of Sr. Katherine Elizabeth's bruised and swollen vagina magnified in her mind. She was disgusted to observe her own prurient curiosity, she had extended her medical cross-questioning into areas that had not been necessary because she had wanted to know how it felt, and if somewhere she had missed something, something that Sr. Katherine Elizabeth now knew, and had been able to learn without blame or loss of status. She wanted to know and watched the women in her ante-natal clinic with a new fascination, a concealed envy. Her horrible dreams woke her up in the night, and sensing the other sisters' soft breathing around her she sweated with shame. She found it hard to risk going back to sleep again for fear of waking with those thoughts again. She was tired all the time and her temper was short.

She snapped at Sr. Pauline, whose headache went on and on.

3

Sr. Pauline was weepy and feeble; she caught herself wondering why everyone was making such a fuss of Sr. Katherine Elizabeth when really, when everything was looked at sanely, rationally, she had been much more seriously hurt. No one seemed to care about her.

Sr. Jo, as their sister-in-charge, felt guilty and responsible; she could not clear from her head her moment of irritation when Sr. Katherine Elizabeth had arrived late in chapel that evening. It had been unfair of her and she knew that of them all Sr. Katherine Elizabeth was the least likely to be late without good reason. She felt she should have known, should have been more sensitive, more in tune with her sister. And she was irritated with herself for feeling so pointlessly guilty, and gradually irritated with all the others for making her feel guilty. She began to think that it was all too much for her to have to cope with and she wired her Mother Superior in the USA for advice. Mother replied promptly by asking if Sr. Katherine Elizabeth wanted to come home. Then Sr. Jo had to cope with Sr. Katherine Elizabeth's hurt that Mother did not trust her to bear all things in Christ and with Sr. Katherine Mary's furious anger that she should have run the risk of sending any such message over the telegraph without consulting the rest of them. Sr. Jo was fed up with both of them and began to worry about whether she was suited to be a sister-in-charge, and whether she should be doing more to hold the situation together, more to give a supportive and loving leadership. She wanted everyone just to get on with their work and try and forget this unfortunate incident, and then was she irritated with herself afresh because her own mind refused to leave the matter alone so easily.

They could not escape, could not get away from the physical reality of rape. Each morning they looked at each other over the breakfast table, unwilling to tell their dreams, to expose their unholy images, each isolated in her own fearful and violent responses, each curious about the others' silences. Discovering in themselves new and nasty things. Not naming them. Tidily each morning they walked down the hill together in the damp dawn to hear Mass in the huge rotting cathedral, and received together the pain of the crucified Christ who had also been penetrated, broken and bleeding, but who had afterwards died and been resurrected. Sr. Katherine Elizabeth would remember again the thoughts she had had immediately following the rape and wonder, sadly, if God had loved Maria Goretti more than He loved her. She had shouted and shouted and no one had come.

Eight days after the rape, Sr. Katherine Elizabeth — whom they usually called Sister Kitty, to distinguish her from Sr. Katherine Mary whom they called Sister Kate — rushed into the oppressive atmosphere of breakfast, her face lit up with joy. 'It's OK,' she squeaked, 'It's all right; I've got my period.' She hugged Sr. Jo spontaneously and beamed at them all. There was a silence in which they each felt stabbed with contrition because it had never occurred to them that Sr. Kitty might have been enduring that fear too. Not one of them had thought about pregnancy and its implications and they had left Sr. Kitty alone with that torment for over a week. Now in her relief they entered into her fear and were appalled. Sr. Kate said in a hard vicious undertone, 'We're all so bloody innocent it makes you sick.' Sr. Imelda innocently went into the kitchen and baked a cake, streaked through with strawberry jam from a precious pot sent from home and being kept for Christmas. They bought some wine and tried to have a party, but the taste was soured by their nervousness and their anger.

Sr. Imelda, unexpectedly, and Sr. Kate, inevitably, found it easiest to be open about their anger. Sr. Imelda was indigenous and possibly this made it easier for her to be angry, unfearful of white liberal guilt. It was a wicked shame, and a shame on her own people, moreover; things like rape she said should not happen to nuns and that they did was disgraceful. Disgraceful. She managed to use the word to express both a prim disgust and a sadness at the cosmic lack of godliness that she felt the rape manifested. She clucked and chittered at the children who hung around the house eager to lay eyes on this new curiosity, a raped nun.

Sr. Kate was equally angry, more angry; but her anger was less well directed and more lethal. Sr. Kate was easily the brightest of them all, and motivated by political and sociological perspectives which the others could not always understand. She did not feel that rape should not happen to nuns, but that rape should not happen. She was also the clearest in her own mind, and in her longwinded passionate diatribes on the subject, that this rape, like all rapes, was not a sexual but a political assault. She knew, of course, that it had been perpetrated by the Security Forces, an opinion she knew was shared in the shanty-town, and that now they had done this and got away with it, there would be more to come; hiding the incident was going to make the sisters still more vulnerable. And yet of course they could not report it; it had been stupid, criminally stupid of Sr. Jo to mention it to Mother directly like that. Didn't she know about phone tapping, censorship, monitoring.

And they could not report it. They had realised that the first morning, when walking down the hill they had seen the worried eyes, the deep fear in the slum community. If the sisters reported the rape the Security Forces would move in and arrest someone, anyone, would punish randomly, would take the excuse to deal with a community leader, a suspected opposition member, with someone they wanted removed. The government wanted the sisters out, anyway — not them especially, their particular little household, but their whole order and all the orders like theirs who, theoretically protected by the US Government and able to leave quickly if necessary, could be for the people a focus of resistance, a succour in the struggle for justice; who were at least able, as local Christians were not, to hold up the hope of a Church that would side with the poor against the establishment without risking the punishments that threatened the local community. It was only a little they could do, organise and observe and teach and heal, but it was better perhaps than it would be without. To expose themselves as needing the protection of the State would both undermine their credibility within the local community and put a question mark not only over just the one little house in Santa Virgine, but over the whole US-based Roman Catholic justice work in the country.

Sr. Kate's anger was for their impotence, their vulnerability, their inability to defend themselves or the community in which they worked, and for the pointlessness of everything they tried to do in the face of what had happened. She felt trapped. Her anger was biting and the sisters were afraid of her, sucking at her energy and clarity but isolating her cunningly for fear that her burning anger would spark off the dry tinder of their fears and irritations and explode them all.

They were all tired, too tired. In the midst of it all work had to go on. The cycle of prayer and visiting and teaching. They taught health care and catechism and literacy and the Gospel. They taught skills and survival mechanisms. They worked, they always worked, too hard in the face of the appalling conditions and they could not, in that endless soaking heat, cope with the new strain, yet they felt honour bound to cope with it. No one could give in, no one could opt out, because the poverty and the need were too present, too absolute, and because the others were still struggling on, brave and godly. The others, each of them felt, were the good nuns; the good nuns who could handle personal disaster and spiritual desolation, dedicated, disciplined, beloved of God. Each of them burned alone in an anguished isolation which they felt they could not contain and which they knew they had to contain.

Only Sister Anna felt nothing at all; she sat detached and distant; her eyes were sharpened by her feeling of distance and she knew all about the agony the others lived with — she watched it with something akin to distaste. She thought they were all rather pathetic, herself included: highly professional grown-up women in a place where even reading was a rare skill, trained and practised in giving out instruction and advice and wielding — yes, damn it, for all the poverty and humility business — wielding power, respected and admired for it, and they could not think of one single sensible thing to do about a day-to-day occurrence like rape. She watched herself as well as her sisters and wondered, without much real interest, if there was something wrong with her.

Five weeks later in the middle of her adult literacy class Sr. Anna burst into tears. No one could have been more surprised about this than she was and there was nothing she could do about it. In front of the weary, patient, harshly determined women who sacrificed their little leisure to try and learn a skill that Sr. Anna took for granted, she could not stop crying. They were baffled and kindly and they went away quietly, leaving her standing in the old cathedral porchway with the high crumbling arches reaching up over her and the tears flowed out of her body while

7

she observed them with amazement. She stood there crying for nearly an hour. Two days later she burst into tears in the middle of Morning Prayer, floods of tears that coursed down her face and shook her body. Not silent weeping but violent, disruptive sobbing. By the end of the week she was doing it three or four times a day. Then she stopped being able to eat. She would come calmly, even hungrily to the table, but as soon as she picked up her fork she would feel a sweeping desire to vomit.

After ten days or so of this she sought out Sr. Kate who was her friend. It had always seemed a strange friendship even to those who knew both of them well. Sr. Kate so wild and brilliant and perverse; Sr. Anna so disciplined and determined and constant. They had been in the novitiate together which often made bonds between women, but when Anna was professed, a year before Kate, and sent to her first mission, their superiors had assumed, sadly since they were both in need of friendship, that that would be the end of it. Eleven years later they were together again in the white house above Santa Virgine and it was clear to both of them that the friendship remained. They laughed sometimes, knowing that twenty-five years ago their Mother Superior would have disrupted every sister in the order rather than let two people who loved each other and liked to work together be in the same house. Friendship, close particular friendship was probably one of the most straightforwardly good things about the reform movement. But now they were not laughing. They were clinging to each other, scared and almost desperate. They took a walk together, turning deliberately and with accord away from the shanty-town and seeking fresher air higher up the hill.

'I think I'm ill; I think I'm getting ill,' Sr. Anna said. 'I'm never ill, it really is very annoying.'

' "Very annoying" ', parroted Sr. Kate, mocking, affectionate and careful. 'Come on, listen to yourself. If you thought you were ill you'd go to Sr. Jane and not drag me halfway up a mountain to make sure no one overhears us.' She was teasing but tender; Sr. Anna understood that balance in Sr. Kate perfectly well; it never irritated her as it did the other sisters, it comforted her as pity never could. 'You're not ill,' said Sr. Kate, 'you're cracking up.'

Sr. Anna was frightened.

'We're all cracking up as a matter of fact,' she went on, trying

8

to be calm, trying to pour out love, trying to feel the Sr. Anna-ness of her friend, trying to love and serve, not hate and burn. 'We're all cracking up except oddly enough Sr. Kitty, and she's a sort of saint. She's such a conscientious and competent forgiver that she has to face up to what's happened to her so she'll know who to forgive and how to go about it. But all the rest of us are cracking up and frankly you needn't look for too much help around here, because if you go all the way and have a good recog-nisable grand-scale crack-up, we'll all be secretly grateful.' She paused. 'Look at me, I'm so angry, I'm so angry that I lie awake at night with it, angry and powerless and angry and sick with it all.'

'But I don't feel that.'

'So? For God's sake Anna, go home. Ask for leave, go home, get the hell out of here and work out why you don't feel angry about it.' She turned away crossly while Sr. Anna registered abruptly that it was the first time Sr. Kate had ever left off Sister before her name.

Sr. Kate still had her back turned, but she was standing abso-lutely still and clearly meant to be heard even though she spoke quietly. 'Anna, I'm so angry that I want to kill someone. Because killing is I think the only damn thing that I know how to do anymore. I don't even care who. I just want to kill the bastards.'

Sr. Kate wanted to say, 'For God's sake Anna, don't go. Please don't go and leave me. The centre is falling apart. I need you and you need me. You need my anger and I need you to drain it off. We need each other. I'm frightened and I need you. To be nuns we must be sisters, we must use each other. Don't go away.' But the training was powerful, the thinking of others not oneself. And she was worried for Anna, by something in Anna she could sense but not name, something self-destructive, something somehow childish. She did not know what it was. And in herself she feared her own anger, feared that if she let Anna too near it it would tear her apart, would break her up. 'Please don't go,' she wanted to cry, but that feeling was not allowed so she said instead and again, 'For God's sake Anna, get out of here. You can't cope, and we can't cope with you. Have some pity.' She said this with a smile, and Anna knew that Kate had mentioned the rest of them to make her feel less selfish about asking for something. She should not ask for things for herself of course, she was trained and conditioned against her own desires, but if she could think it was for the good of the community that would make it all right.

Anna smiled a nervous little smile; part of her wanted Kate to want her to stay, part of her accepted the love and care she was being offered, and part of her was amused by Kate's transparency. 'Oh dear, isn't it a bore having such well-trained consciences?'

They both laughed. Standing there on the hillside they both felt a moment of freedom and delight. 'I'll tell you what we both need,' said Kate. 'We need another holiday like that one.'

Two years before they had taken their summer leave at the same time and had decided mainly because Kate could not afford the trip home to the USA that they would go exploring in the Amazon basin. Anna's father would gladly have paid for the flight but she had persuaded him to pay for the pair of them to go south instead. So they had left the high country not for the civilised lands of the north but for the dark sweaty jungle below them. There, held in the enormous cupped hands of the mountains they discovered the great river and the secret places of the vast forest.

They had booked a boat trip down the river, spending nights in assorted camping sites, primitive but reliable; a tame exploration they had thought before setting off, but it had turned out to be more than enough. They were devastated by the profusion of the jungle, by its excesses and extravagances; a steamy langour had attacked them, held them in its arms, rocked them like a mother and they had not been able to struggle against it. Everything was effort except the motion of the boat moving downstream, drifting placidly, and they had had to consent and drift with it. The rules were held in soft abeyance, all mental precision seemed eaten away, all the hard clarities and certainties gone. Despite the puffs of diesel from the stern of the boat and its orderly chugging noise they had realised that the jungle was untouched, unimpressed by the presence of the white people, the Europeans, it shrugged them off; hardly had they passed around the next bend than the great forest reasserted its isolation, its singleness, its chaotic, uncaring, corrupt fecundity. The sun seldom penetrated the overhead cathedral roof of branches, but it was not needed. The profusion of the jungle generated a heat of its own, and they crawled through the humidity like a dream. Around them they could hear but seldom see the signs of a dense secret life, animal, bird, insect and Indian. Huge butterflies and flashes of parakeet and humming bird broke the green dark light. The beautiful hard forest of New England had in no way prepared them for the richness of the tropical rain forest. There was no order, only infinite variety, even in the trees. Kate, courageous even against the impossible, had tried to count palms and rubber trees and laurels and rosewood and mahogany and steelwood and bamboos reaching to preposterous heights; and chocolate trees and silk cottons and figs and acacia; and purple hearts and cow-trees and cashews and balsa. She broke down defeated, poor Kate, when even their patient and competent guide admitted that there were more kinds of cedar tree than he knew names for. Here and there giant hard-woods broke through the roof and towered away out of sight, supported by their flying buttress roots. Creepers and great sprays of undreamed flowers, orchids, funghi and lianes sixty feet long burst flowering out of living wood twenty yards above their heads. Richness and rottenness beyond imagining.

In the evenings the beauty was claustrophobic; they had begun to desire dinginess. The sun setting behind them along the river sometimes managed to pierce the green cave. The dying light broke up the monotony of green and revealed the variety. There were no words for so much green, so many greens, like cool fire; moving, alive, consuming, green fire. And there seemed no point in all the many things they knew how to do. They had sweated off their dirt there; although the river itself seemed filthy they had come to feel clean, wrung out like clothes, wrung down to knowing their own tiredness. Under the mosquito nets in the hot dark night, when the physical jungle retreated back into itself and there was only the jungle of childhood fantasy in which snow white panthers and forty-foot boa constrictors crept ever closer, the hot muggy arms of mothers cradled them so close that they feared suffocation and desired it too.

And then they had talked, a new kind of talking because the sturdy walls of white stone and duty were so far away. During the nights Kate was impassioned, angry, with herself and with the the drifting idleness of the floating, although during the days she seemed less concerned about their passivity than Anna was. At night she ranted, leaping wildly, boldly, sometimes giddily from subject to subject. She was moved by everything as Anna knew she was not, moved by the beauty of the great river, and moved too by far away things: social conditions, imperialism, liberation theology, US so-called aid and the assumptions it made, the habits their order still wore, the restrictions and sexism of the Church even since the Vatican Council, the right to self-determination of all peoples, the splendour of the god of darkness, the humidity of the night, the viciousness of the jungle insects, the pillage of natural resources and the malice, the grinding biting soul destroying malice of poverty. When Anna spoke of the love of God and the redemption of creation she felt as though she was twittering, as old and as conservative as Sr. Amelda, as frozen and tight as the hills of the Hudson River valley. She knew the limitations of her life and did not know how to face them. But before joining the order Sr. Kate had been a student activist; she had been involved in the Civil Rights movements and had known the pain of not being wanted by the southern blacks with whom she had chosen to identify — no, not identify, and she knew it — whom she had chosen to serve. They had not finally wanted her service, she had liberated them into not wanting her. Now in the dark, insect biting night, old angers bounced around with new ones, all boiling together, but the bitterness that was certainly there was buried under a great enthusiasm, a wild lust for life, a huge joyfulness and a buoyant bubbling elegant wit — and a self-deprecating irony which scared Anna, for herself and for Kate, even while she delighted in it.

One night Anna had tried one more time to find the answer to something that she had never understood, despite the endless discussions among the other novices, ever since Sr. Kate had first arrived at the Mother House, mini-skirted, wild-haired and with blazing eyes. Why had she become a nun?

'I didn't think there was any choice, I suppose. I didn't want it, not particularly. God did. It came down to that or to stop being a Catholic altogether — tempting, always, but not practically possible.'

Anna had still not understood.

12

'Oh, you know . . .' Sr. Kate was irritated by Anna's stupidity almost. 'You know, it's about going all the way. I always was an extremist. Doing something crazy for God, something outrageous, because Christ on the cross is so totally outrageous and the very idea of God is outrageous and there is God with a belly laugh waiting for the clowns to do their act. No, I should not mock, really, I wanted to go beyond sense and sound argument. Can't you understand that. Going all the way, going too far. The Counsel of Perfection, that's what I wanted.'

'Manichee, Gnostic,' Anna had teased. Sr. Kate was the only person she was allowed to tease and it was fun, especially in the dark where no one was the wiser. 'Gnostic, just wanting perfection, special insider stuff, secret knowledge. Heresy.'

But Sr. Kate had refused that bait. 'Well yes, in part, of course. You know what trials I have with those particular heresies — each to her own heresy, and I'll leave yours aside for now, but the Gnostic lot, even the Manichees, well I have to say they've always seemed most sensible — though luckily I've also abandoned good sense and so am orthodox. And also of course, which may be a part of it, I was getting to a point socially I mean, where not wanting to sleep with all those eager heroes did need some sort of an excuse.' She laughed and then stopped laughing. 'But not entirely. I wanted to be free to take arms against a sea of troubles. I wanted some shape and order and control over what I seemed as an individual less and less able to control, to discipline. Oh dear, And where has it got me, I ask?' and she had slapped at her own arms, infuriated by the insects which continually attacked her despite all precautions. 'Down in some crazy jungle with a nice liberal maiden, being bitten to death by vampiric mini-monsters. Next holiday, Sister, let us find some decent desert. I'm not up to this. I don't like being eaten alive; and I never took vows in order to sit subdued in a mammoth-sized sauna bath.'

Anna had said, 'Well, Sister, I've lived in the desert, in several deserts as a matter of fact, and firstly they have biting insects too and secondly they're not all they're cracked up to be spiritually.'

'Well at least they must be chaste, unlike this rampant fertility around us here. Much more seemly for Holy Nuns.'

They had laughed. They had laughed, but at the end of the

holiday Sr. Kate had given Sr. Anna a present. In the face of their vows of poverty, many gifts between the sisters took the form of cards with what were called 'edifying texts' copied on to them. Sr. Kate's gift to Sr. Anna had been a quotation that Sr. Anna had never managed to locate and often felt irritated by:

> The virgin forest is not barren or unfertilised, but rather a place that is specially fruitful and has multiplied because it has taken life into itself and transformed it, giving birth naturally and taking dead things back to be re-cycled. It is virgin because it is unexploited, not in man's control.

They had laughed then, through the sultry holiday, laughed in protection and in joy and in defence. And now, standing together on the hill above their home, they strained towards each other, seeking again that warm intimacy; but they also pulled apart, frightened of themselves and of what they might do to each other. Sr. Anna knew she would be bereft, alone, without Sr. Kate, but did not feel the right to hang on to her seeking consolation. Sr. Kate felt she would burn away, burst into bright destructive flames, destroy herself and others, without Sr. Anna's coolness and poise, balancing her flight, tethering her dangerous darkness. But they had not learned, ever, to ask for what they needed. They leaned towards each other, their cheeks close and soft for each other. For a moment they resembled a High Renaissance painting of the Visitation, two women strong for each other, when they have no one and no space to be weak for; an embrace of need posing as generosity. Then the moment passed. The bell rang. They turned back to the discipline of their Office, two sisters both in their thirties, both clever and desiring love, both struggling with a difficult community experience.

Sr. Anna did not ask for leave, because she felt too guilty about needing it. But she could not stop herself sobbing and starving. In the end Sr. Jo had had enough. Although she too felt guilty and a failure, she also felt too strongly that it simply was not fair — she just could not cope, on top of everything else, with a weeping anorexic nun.

'I'm not *sending* you,' she said, covering her own sense of inadequacy somewhat desperately, 'because you know we don't

14

do things that way, but I think you need help and I know we can't give it to you here.'

Sr. Anna took a deep breath; sixteen years of training in the religious life really did help with some things. 'I'm afraid you're right, Sister, and I'm sorry, but really I can't help it; I can't help myself and I know that we don't have the resources here. I'm no use here and if I'm going to be ill I'd better do that back at the Mother House.' Running away. Sister Anna is running away. Running away when the going gets rough. Sr. Kitty didn't need to run away. She'd been raped. Who do you think you are? What sort of nun are you, for God's sake? What sort of nun was she if she had to run away, run back to mother whenever something nasty happened? She was a grown-up. She was behaving like a child. Or, she had a duty to do whatever was best for the community. The life of the community was more important than the feelings of one individual and rather insignificant nun. They needed another sister out here, a real sister who could work and do her share. And underneath, underneath all the accusations and excuses, the sudden vivid and welcome thought of a real bathroom, really hot water and a very long bath.

'I want to go home.'

II

Six months later she was still not at home.

She was adrift instead in a huge city on the other side of the world. It was strange for her not to know her own place. Conventual life did, at the very least, make clear where you were meant to be and what you were meant to be doing. Was obedience meant to be the same as freedom from responsibility? She was here to find out. But she found it baffling and exhausting suddenly after so many years, not to know where her exact, where her own, place was. The sisters in Leyton were certainly good and kind and as helpful as they could be. She was the one at fault, she had to try harder not to be judgemental. The rich and the safe had to be ministered to, too. The centurion's servant, the raising of Jairus's daughter, Zacheus, up his tree, were all as important to Our Blessed Saviour as the healing of the lepers or the woman with the issue of blood. Sr. Anna knew that. And anyway she knew and struggled to remember that the people here in the East End of London were not rich, were not safe. They were poor, they were oppressed, they were raped and mugged and defeated. It was not them, it was her, it was her standards of poverty that were distorted. She was sick, she was ill, her judgement was poor. A poor judge. Who was she to judge them? The sisters here meant so much good, were so sane and busy and useful, just as they had been in Santa Virgine. But the volume of their not-understanding, of their kindly liberalism boomed in her ears, shutting out what had once been her certainties. She wavered; who was she anyway, who was she who could not cope, who had broken down when her ministry was most needed, who had not been able to handle a crisis; who did she think she was to judge these busy, competent, devout women?

16

Of course she wanted to be good and kind and self-denying and holy. Had not being all those things made her happy for years? Had not sitting round and weeping about nothing made her unhappy? What was happiness anyway? Did it matter? Did anything matter? But still she yearned for some sense of being at home, being consoled, being at peace. She had left Santa Virgine and the longed-for New World in South America because she had wanted to go home and now it seemed that there was, for her, no home.

She had never really had a home. Santa Virgine was the front-line, not home; too much attachment made more difficulties than it could solve and they had to learn that. During her child-hood they had not had a fixed home, travelling joyfully and crazily about the world, foot-loose and fancy free. Had she become a nun only because she had wanted a home? Certainly she knew that the Mother House had been home for her at least through the years of the novitiate. They had all liked that image: while you were growing up as a nun you stayed at home under mother's wing, then you spread your own and flew off all over the world, but it was there, it was promised, the big white house on the hill, the Mother House, home.

Certainly her sense of relief arriving there after thirty-six hours of travelling had been immense, but even then it had been clouded. The sister who had met her off the final bus had been, it seemed to Anna, quite incredibly, unnaturally clean: what did poverty mean when it did not mean being not-clean all the time? The physical cleanliness of the sisters in Santa Virgine had seemed strange and alienating to the people of the slum town, she knew that; their chapel, pure and chaste, had seemed not only oppressive and dull, but far away and meaningless to many of their people, precisely because it had been clean. Clean, dull and frightening. But this woman who drove the car and smiled, what could she know about dirt, about filth, about rape and violence and police searches in the night and about not having enough hot water. What was the point of her, of their, poverty?

The house seemed clean too, but somehow that was different. A huge white house wrapped around with the brightness, the flaming golden ferocity of the fall: yet that evening so much nature seemed not soothing but somehow excessive and greedy to Anna, yet another lack of poverty and humility.

'This house is full of the ghosts of dead virgins.'

The statement was so clear that Sr. Anna started, turning her head in the car to see who had spoken. She felt, realising there was no actual voice, singularly foolish.

It was not the nuns who were the accused dead virgins; the sisters though virgins were alive and busy. The house had been the Hudson River summer home of a self-made Victorian magnate, built for opulence and leisure, even for happiness. But his son had died and his two daughters, who had in the end bequeathed the house to the order, had lived there alone for years, slight shadowed women whose money huddled round them like a blanket of guilt.

The Indians had sat so, on the outskirts of Santa Virgine, like the nuns. Huddled in blankets which had covered their despair. Their blank faces had scared Sr. Anna. They had probably scared them all. They would sit there, wrapped in their silence and their blankets, for days, apparently not moving, and then they would be gone. Sometimes they would be very drunk, sometimes they would beg, but normally they just sat. They scavenged off the scavengers of colonialism. Their poverty was absolute, it moved them slowly and undramatically towards the final solution. Their dumb outrage, their world-deep sulk, brought the hope of salvation crashing around even the bravest, but they were dispassionate, desperate and silent. Sr. Kate had once said, furiously, that they were wrapped in their blankets like the sisters were wrapped in their habits, keeping themselves apart as the only way of keeping themselves together. But Sr. Anna could not think now of Sr. Kate; the anger that had been smouldering in Sr. Kate's stomach was being fanned. It was dangerous, dangerous, and she could not reach out and extinguish the flames lest she got burned; or lest something in her was extinguished at the same time.

But here was the Mother House. She could lay all the rest down, she had come home. The ghosts of the virgin sisters were heavy here. The bustle of the nuns whom they had thought they shared enough to make them their successors could not lay these ghosts. The negative brooding quality of their virginity was

18

sucked into the positive feelings that the nuns claimed to have about theirs, but it was not exorcised, it was not laid to rest.

It had never occurred to Sr. Anna, until the car pulled up at the front-door steps, that sometime in the future this might not be her home any more. That it was conceivable even to think such a thought ravaged her. She burst into tears. The sister driving, switching off the ignition with a sharp little sound said, 'I know, it is good to get back, isn't it?'

Sr. Anna interpreted her own tears, gratefully, as those of relief.

But she had not been able to stay.

Anna had entered the novitiate within six months of graduating from a Roman Catholic girls' college. In 1967 things had already been in turmoil, in the Church and on every American university campus. She had thought, rather vaguely, of going south and working with the Civil Rights movement, or going to Washington and working with the Anti-War movement for a while before she joined the order; but both ideas sprang from individual conscience and not from political commitment or social involvement. Time passed without her knowing exactly why neither of these things had happened. After collecting her degree she had gone to Arizona, to find the place where she had been born. That had seemed just as important, no more no less, than the justice issues that pounded in her ears. She had made a private retreat among motels and desert. The desert had called her vividly. Among the cacti and the strange raised lumps, neither rock nor sand, she had felt a confusion of aims. But at Flagstaff, rather quietly one evening, she had realised that she would go back east to the white house in the Hudson Valley which she had first encountered two years before on a conference on Spanish American history. That day she had peered over the edge of the Grand Canyon, and, excited and scared, had known simply that she did not wish to go down to the wild water at the bottom, so she would become a nun instead. It was a moment of light, an understanding of vocation. Of both pride and a proper recognition of limitation. They spent so long in the novitiate poring over their own vocations, their sources and their

19

centrings, that it seemed to Sr. Anna that hers had become static, patterned, fixed, devoid of its own conflicts. Retrospectively it seemed that this, and this alone, had been the moment of self-knowing. She had flown east again two days later, carrying with her this burning passion: this was what she had to do and now was when she had to do it. Her father had been quite unexpectedly in New York and she had spent the week with him and one of her sisters who lived in Queens with her growing family. Her sister had looked tired, fat, and bad-tempered. Mass in the nearby church had been ordered, gracious and decently modernised. Everyone had been pleased for her, pleased and touchingly sad.

Of course it had not really been as sudden as that. She had already applied to the order, been tested and interviewed and accepted. But she had not known. She had not had that certainty inside herself. Her father took some extra time off work and drove her up-state. She had made him happy.

He liked the idea of one of his daughters becoming a religious; and especially Anna, his baby. It justified him. It contradicted all those voices which had told him that you could not bring up children like that, particularly daughters, and expect them to turn out stable and well-adjusted, good. He had been pleased with Anna, and had demonstrated his pleasure to her. They spent her last night in an expensive intimate hotel, which seemed otherwise full of honeymooning couples, and they had laughed together about this. He had driven her to the Mother House and with a splendid flourish handed her over to the Mother he had never provided her with before. He was, in many ways, a very unusual man.

It had been a fall day then too, not different from the day of her return. Her father would be furious when, or if, he heard that she had not been tough enough. He wanted his girls tough in head and heart, as he said, 'Nothing frilly about my girls. Good, sensible hard-working girls. Obedient too. But clever with it, able, competent. All five of them.' He got what he wanted, expected from them: sweetness and submissiveness which were his touchstones of femininity, left over from his own immigrant childhood, and the drive for perfection that he would have wanted from his sons had he had any.

20

Self-contained, self-controlled, self-disciplined, detached too, because she had never had anything to attach herself to, and at the same time used to the demands of a community life, to living with others and accommodating to them, her childhood had served Sr. Anna well in the convent, made her unexpectedly well suited to the life of the religious. An exemplary novice, a bright useful young sister, could-go-far. The furore, the crazy days of the seventies did not seem to upset her unduly; by and large a moderate, willing to take on the renewal, but not giddy with it, sensitive, skilful and committed to getting on with the work. Interested in theology without wanting to rush off into speculation. Capable of forming friendships, and capable of submitting them to the needs of communal life. A very valuable and properly well-liked member of the community.

So what had gone wrong? 'What is it, my dear?' Reverend Mother had, as it happened, been her own novice mistress. 'What happened? It doesn't sound like you; can you tell me about it?'

But Sister Anna was lost in a blizzard, a wild blinding storm. She could not speak about it because she did not know what was happening or why. Her prayers fragmented around her, crashing into splintered images or worse, dislocated words. This was not, she felt sure, a classic arid patch; there was no aridity, no sense of an absence of God. God was there all right and waiting. She had failed Him, He would punish her. In her fear she tried desperately to hold on to the thread of prayer, but it led into, not out of the darkness, the labyrinth. She retreated despairingly into the verbal prayer of childhood, rosary beads and measured incantations, repetitions. She leaned on the Office but it would not support her weight. Everything was broken into fragments, everything was gone, all the old defences, the simple certainties.

Incoherent dreams, half-formed tigers pouncing with the whole power of morning, but then not there. She was lost in a fog, dense, blinding, her groping appearing risible, grotesque, monstrous to the invisible God.

Jacob wrestles with the angel.

Jacob wrestles with the angel and is wounded for ever.

Jacob wrestles with the angel and is wounded in the thigh and he defeats the angel.

Perpetua treads down the head of the Egyptians. She is warrior. She is victorious. But in her power she dreams herself to be male. Is this her weakness or her glory? Perpetua is not a virgin. She is wife, mother, crone. She is in a different movement of the cycle of the moon.

The unicorn drinks the milk from the virgin's breast. Virginity tames the fierceness of his purity. Virginity breaks the wildness of his lusts.

Sr. Kitty lies on her back and watches the white unicorn vanish. But the unicorn is unique and is male. In the dark lands of the interior the conquistadors thought they would find El Dorado, the city of gold; but not only of gold, the city of the boy king, the city of untarnishable purity. They had broken the hard pessimistic purity of the Aztecs, the high mountain purity of the Incas. Did they seek the city which offered all they thought they sought, knowing with a doomed certainty that they would not find it?

In their dark interior they built enormous cathedrals, proclaiming the power of Spain, the power of their King Emperor, the power of their King God. They built them with despair because the jungle, the great virgin forest just stood aside waiting, laughing, undefeated, and always beyond, over there, not yet, a little further, was the city of El Dorado. The dream of eternal joy, of life without end and richness without deserving, of judgement and redemption.

Sr. Kate's anger surged in Sr. Anna's dream world. Anna reached out to her, but she turned her back. She ran off through the jungle, her anger cutting a clean way through the underbrush. When Anna prayed for her the prayers broke up and could not pierce her hide. Sr. Kate was furious with Sr. Anna in the dreams. Sr. Kate was alight with anger. There was a cloud of flame, a dark nimbus round her head, but her own anger delighted her. She nursed it in her bosom like a child, she used it as a weapon to wound things, destroying them. She leapt out embracing her anger, keeping it glowing with the fuels of her heart. Sr. Anna was afraid of the heat that Sr. Kate emanated. Sr. Anna knew that if she would only go into out into the hot fire and embrace Sr. Kate and put their two angers together, something magical might happen, something terrible and powerful, but she

22

knew that she did not dare. She could not reach Sr. Kate with her prayers, and Sr. Kate could not reach her with her anger.

Sr. Kate had been Artemis once, powerful in purity, giving nothing away, accepting no gifts, generating her own. The bold huntress. But now she was inclined towards Kore, the black blank side of the moon.

Sr. Anna was Pallas Athene, the virgin created by the Fathers. A creation of the Fathers and virgin only because they liked it that way. She was at the beck and call of the Fathers who ranted in her head, in her dreams and in her private spaces.

'Behave yourself,' said the voices of the Fathers. 'Pull yourself together. It is all right, we will not desert you. Keep the rules and we will take care of you.'

But they were stern too. 'You are not making enough effort. You must listen to us. You must not listen to anyone else. You must not weep in public. We do not like scenes. You have failed us, you are failing us. You will have to be punished. We will punish you.'

And worst of all, 'Do you think you are fit to be a nun? Do you really think so? Perhaps you ought to leave.'

Perhaps I ought to leave, thought Sr. Anna to herself, perhaps she should give it all up.

'You needn't think you can just leave,' contradicted the voices of the Fathers. 'We won't let you go. Oh no. You have promised us, we will hold you to that promise. You must be a good girl. You want to be a good girl, don't you.'

At first the voices of the Fathers had shocked her, terrified her. She had cowered before them, hiding under the bedclothes and trying to bolt them out; rushing out to work in the garden or the library. She could not tell anyone about them, they made that perfectly clear. She was not to tell anyone. If she did they would destroy her. If she did they would eat her alive. The Fathers wanted a good and obedient daughter; for a price they would offer her protection. But protection from what? She tried being bold with them.

'If you behave,' said the voices, 'we will protect you. We will take care of you. We will say, "This is our beloved in whom we are well pleased." If you behave we will protect you.'

'Protect me from what?' she tried to summon her courage.

They did not like such boldness very much.

'Don't be impertinent,' they said. 'Don't be uppity. We will protect you from yourself, from the mad woman inside you who is trying to get out. You are disintegrating. You know you are. Come to us, submit to us, and we will protect you. If, if you will behave yourself we will love you.'

She was suspicious of them, the Fathers. She was suspicious of them and frightened. They were not the childhood voices of her conscience. She did not know for certain whether they existed inside or outside her head.

'We hold all things together,' they told her. 'Without us there is nothing, nothing but chaos, a watery chaos that you will drown in. We will take everything away.'

She tried not to hear them. She tried to obey them too, pulling herself together as directed. She was frightened of the disintegration, of the formless void that seemed to be opening out beneath her feet. If she was not a nun, who was she? With what voice could she speak, could she answer their accusations? If she was not a nun there were no words.

Then there was a time of storms. Fall turned into a wild winter and the storms that beat against the white house were unprecedented in their ferocity. Sr. Anna knew that she was Jonah, that she had fled from Santa Virgine to escape from God and that now the Fathers were determined that she should have no resting place there. She was putting the sisters at risk, the house would break up under the weight of the storms, it would break up just as she was breaking up inside. She wanted to say to Mother Superior as Jonah did to the sea captain, when he fled from Nineveh to Tarshish, 'Take me up and throw me into the sea; then the sea will quiet down for you; for I know it is because of me that this great tempest is come upon you.'

'Mother,' said Sr. Anna, 'I think I want to request a dispensation.'

'What?'

'I want to give up. I'm not good enough. I can't seem to get myself together in any way. I can't pray, I can't work, I'm a nuisance to you all.'

'Anna, dear, that's nonsense.' Mother Superior was surprised but quick thinking. 'Look, dear child, this hardly seems like the right time. You think I underestimate what happened to Sr. Katherine Elizabeth and the effect that, inevitably, that had on all of you. I think you are in shock. I don't think that now is a good time to think about anything so drastic as leaving. I mean, you've been here, in the order, a good while, what is it now? about sixteen years, and this is the first serious wobble you've ever had. You have to give it longer.'

'I can't stay here, I can't.'

'It's your mother. Children should be with their mother in times of difficulty. I am your mother, I want to hold you.'

But there is a time when all good mothers should let go. Mother Superior knew that too. She could not fathom Sr. Anna. She offered her psychiatric help but Anna did not want that.

'Perhaps you do need some space. But I really don't think at this point you should even consider dispensation.'

Sr. Anna had no experience of mothers. Her own had run away. She had known only fathers. Lots of fathers. Mothers she did not know about; not about how they can hold you in the dark places of the night. Mother Superior and Mother Church of course, and Holy Mary Mother of God, but all of them very wedded mothers, mothers who were on the side of the Fathers, not on the side of the children.

Now Sr. Anna wanted to be held; she wanted to be wrapped up in a blue woolly blanket and held gently on someone's lap, but she did not know that this was what she wanted and she would not have been able to ask even if she had known.

'Sister, what does your director think, what does he say?'

She went of course to confession, but she had a diminishing sense of what was sin and what was not. You cannot tell even the nicest priest about voices shouting in your ears all day, nor about being Jonah and having to be thrown overboard. And, well, Father John had been her confessor and director for years, since halfway through college. She had loved him purely and simply and he had so loved her. She knew that. But now she did not think that he could hear her. He had invested in her being a nun; like her own father, it had pleased him enormously. He had caught her soul, played her on a skilful line, never pressing but slowly, slowly reeling her in and delivering her safe to the shore. She could not make him hear because he did not want to hear. He did not want to go all the way into the depths of her shadow places. He cut her short, he stopped listening, the clichés

25

swallowed his voice. She felt that he did not mean to neglect her needs. She felt that she should find now, in this place, a new confessor who did not have an investment. But it seemed like a betrayal; he would be hurt; she could not hurt him when she knew he loved her, when he tried so hard to love her. And she knew that she did not speak to him clearly, did not in all humility and sincerity bare her soul. She wanted now to be heard and understood without having to make the dangerous effort of speech. She knew it was unreasonable and she knew it was what she wanted. So it was all her fault, not Father John's, not the Church's, not anyone's but hers. *Mea culpa, mea culpa, mea maxima culpa.*

Her Mother Superior wanted to keep Anna in the order. She recognised this in herself and was humbled at realising how little she had minded about losing some of the others in the last ten years. She wanted Sr. Anna because Sr. Anna was a credit to them all, to the order, and because she had been one of her own novices. She sat at her desk thinking, remembering Anna and Kate together in the novitiate, an unlikely and a healthy friendship. Kate had woken Anna up, had touched some area of feeling that Mother had not been sure really existed in Anna, and Anna in her turn had steadied Kate — wild wonderful Kate, whom it was impossible to understand, but whose own clarity had been all that was needed. If Anna had become a nun to escape from the dangerous outside world, which was possible of course, quite possible, then why had Kate come? She was not afraid of the world. Mother remembered the two of them with a sudden enormous affection, so young, so eager, both a part of that last generation of sisters who had entered and been formed before the time of trial. Mother approved of the Renewal, with all her heart, but it did make, it had made the novitiate difficult. Now she prayed for Sr. Anna, and she summonsed many of her personal friends from the community of saints to pray for Anna too: St Joan, St Catherine of Siena, and Margaret Mary Alacoque.

Looking at Sr. Anna's files she realised that the girl, though not a girl now of course, past her mid-thirties, how strange, had never really been alone in her life. She had come from Catholic university straight to the convent with no real break. Was that good or bad? Was it worth a risk? She suggested to Sr. Anna that she take a sabbatical; that she go away on her own though still a full member of the community; she could do some research, get back to her academic roots. 'Perhaps you miss that more than you know, that sort of work. We are all very seriously concerned about the history of Christianity in the New World. We have to try and understand our pasts better. Go and work for a year on that, on the role played by the religious orders — presumably it will be the Jesuits mainly and the Dominicans — in the colonisation of South America. Take up the work you did for your Masters.'

Later she said, 'Aren't I right in thinking that your father is in Europe at the moment? In Scotland? Yes, why don't you go to London, use the British Museum. You can stay with our European branch. They're a bit different from us, you'll see. You could go after Easter. And Sr. Anna, in the meantime try not to worry. We can manage to look after you for a little, you know.'

So like Jonah she was thrown overboard and the ship could sail on in safety. 'At the end of the year,' Mother had said, 'at the end of the year you can decide what to do. There isn't any hurry. Nine months,' she smiled, 'like a pregnancy.' It was not a completely honest smile, it was a device, a device to draw Sr. Anna out, out of herself and in towards mother. But even as she spoke she knew that this was not the bait to draw Anna; some of them discovered that need in themselves, but that was not Anna's difficulty. Reverend Mother's mind dawdled off, unable to understand the lure of pregnancy, baffled as to why perfectly competent and intelligent women would rather croon over a baby from their own stomachs when they could have lives as religious and all the hungry babies of the world if that was what they wanted. Her mind shifted to other problems, of which she had all too many, too many daughters, too far flung around the globe, and this was just one of them, and however fond she might be of Anna, she must not, she could not have favourites could not pick and choose. She was mother to them all.

So like Jonah Anna fell overboard and into the cold dark sea and the great fish swallowed her up and she lay in the belly of the fish in the darkness. The life of the fish, its grindings and burblings and beatings reverberated with the voices of the Fathers. It was too dark inside, and neither the pain of Holy Week nor the empassioned brightness of Easter could reach her;

she had been sucked too deep into the black belly.

And when the fish spewed her out she found that she was not at home, but loose in a great strange city, uncertain what to do or how to do it. She was lonely and depressed and, as she began at last to feel again, what she felt was fear. She was frightened; she was paralysed with fear, a sickness of brain and spirit. She woke too early in the morning weighted down by heavy dreams that she could not recall. But . . . there was also a memory that she tried to dodge and refused to think about . . . she knew that when the aeroplane had taken off from Boston airport, splitting sea and earth and sky on that impossibly perilous runway, she knew she had felt a great relief, a lightheartedness, a freedom. Somewhere in her, untapped, untouched was a childish, almost spiteful glee; she had got away, escaped, she could do what she wanted, she was on her own. More than that, she had stolen time from the community, from her shared responsibility, she had slipped off with the swag. She did not want to deal with that feeling. It went away anyway; it had barely lasted longer than it took the pleasant air stewardess not to offer her a drink. It was of no consequence.

But some days, never when she expected it, never reliable or trustworthy, but occasionally in the cool pale London springtime she would catch herself prancing along the street. London was illuminated with memories of childhood, memories of holidays. They had been there more than once in the fifties, for her father to do that mysterious thing called business; but for the girl it had always been holiday time, they had never settled, never been to school or made a resting place there. She remembered particularly the odd mixtures, a very old city with Roman walls and ancient churches — all stolen from them by evil Protestants they had thought then — and the great holes left by the Blitz which had not to the children seemed threatening but more a promise of new beginnings. There had been so much construction work then, slotting the new buildings in among the old, with continuity but no unity, no sense of design, but a feeling of growth and inevitability. In these memories she was seized with delight and walked, rode the tubes, scrambled for the buses and rejoiced.

But the moments of lightness came and went, the fear remained constant, underlying everything, dogging her footsteps even when they were light and lighthearted. She found that it was terribly difficult to organise her day, her thoughts, her work. For seventeen years she had done what she was told, had known at all times where she was meant to be and what she was meant to be doing. Now she had no powers of self-motivation, no sense of controlling her time, no sense of direction physical or mental. She knew she was not really working when she sat each day in the library, ordering books and perusing them at random. Of course she had forgotten a great deal, but that was not fundamentally the problem. She had no purpose. Mother had been a bit vague; since she knew absolutely nothing about the history of Latin America, how could she have been otherwise. There was nothing in particular that she wanted to know, that she wanted Anna to tell her. Anna knew that this project had been invented solely to give her something to do, and to justify Mother in having the order support her while she did it. But her sense of duty was strong and when it wavered the voices of the Fathers were more than ready to pounce in and reinforce it.

They liked the move to London; they were free now of the restrictions she had imposed on them before, free and powerful, swooping down in the dark evenings and pecking at her.

'Direction,' they said. 'Narrow is the path and strait is the gate. Learn that well, it goes for everything. You need discipline, structure, rigidity. You need the discipline. Admit you need it.'

They made her memorise childish hymns, especially when the spasms of joy attacked her. She would travel on the tube trains muttering little rhymes, 'I will not fear the battle when thou art by my side.'

'Not "when", not "when",' they reprimanded her. ' "If", "if". Watch yourself, don't be so arrogant, don't assume we'll be at your side, you have to earn it, you have to earn us.'

> *I will not fear the battle if thou art by my side*
> *Nor wander from the pathway if thou wilt be my guide.*

'No wool-gathering permitted. No stepping aside from the narrow pathway to pluck flowers,' they told her.

'When little girls wander from the pathway, bad things happen to them. Little Red Riding Hood got *EATEN UP*.

'When little girls pluck flowers, bad things happen to them. Persephone went to *HELL*.'

29

The voices sucked her down, like Persephone down into the shadow land; if she ate anything there she would never get out. The Fathers were the gods of the shadow, of the heavy dark place. Or they were the only power that could rescue her from the dark place, and then only if she would promise to serve them all her days. But she did not know what the place was.

Was it hell or the labyrinth. Was it a place to be lost or a place to learn the way.

The Fathers do not provide a guiding thread. That is not part of their job.

'It is harder to enter the Kingdom of Heaven than for a camel to pass through the eye of a needle,' they bullied. She knew, even as they spoke so stern and ungiving, that there was something missing from the quotation, but she could not stop and catch at that thread because they drove her mercilessly. If thread is to be passed through the eye of a needle, it must be licked into shape.

'Purge yourself of these disordered thoughts. Stamp them out. Seek shape, order, discipline. We will lick you into shape. We will discipline you for the Kingdom if you will only repent. No anger, no struggle, don't resist us. Submit. Submit your foolish will. Work harder.'

She tried to work harder. She ordered volume after volume of meaningful books. She sat with them for hours, but she could not find a thread. And she did not like what she read. It gave her no comfort.

Fifteen years ago, when she had last studied Christian history, she had been a Catholic Apologist; they all had. She had struggled to keep separate the teachings of the Church from the activities of its members. It had not been Holy Mother Church's fault that in her name and the name of her glorified spouse, the Spanish conquistadors, greedy for private gain and in the service of a king desperate for hard currency to pay his German bankers and the cost of his Italian campaign, had destroyed, enslaved, robbed, cheated and violated whole series of cultures.

But now that did not seem to satisfy her. She could not flush out of her mind the memory of the Indians squatting beneath the mountains in silent sulkiness on the outskirts of Santa Virgine. The maidens of Caxos, the chosen women, the chaste and honoured daughters of the Inca state, had been raped in their sanctuary by men who claimed allegiance to Christ and travelled with the blessing of the Church.

She thought for a while that she might do some work on Antonio Vieyra, the charming and courageous Portuguese Jesuit, who was harassed by the Inquisition for advocating tolerance for the Portugese Jews and struggled all his life for the civil rights of Indians in the New World. Apart from his extraordinary and bold record for respect, admiration and practical politicking for the Indian tribes along the river, he also seemed a man of humour and balance, not stern and crazed but businesslike and sane. An expert at the art of the possible, but also at bringing more and more aspects of life within that scope. He was a splendid and effective and caring missionary. But she stopped dead; because the people among whom he was 'missionising' in São Luis and Belém and the other settlements were themselves Christians, as much a part of the Church as he was. He was charming only because he was abnormal. And in the end even he believed in the Reductions, the closed camps of hard discipline and Christian rigour in which the Indian converts were effectively emprisoned to 'protect' them from enslavement by other Christians and from relapse into paganism. In the end too he was defeated, driven out, and the Indians, who were Christ's children, used as slave labour by the men who had taught them they were Christ's children. It troubled Anna, too, that most of the later Catholic historians saw this as a conspicuous evil only because during their six months of compulsory labour their moral and spiritual training might be neglected.

Once a Brazilian Indian entered the Loretto Reduction dressed as a pajé, a witch doctor, accompanied by a young man and woman he claimed to have created. He claimed he himself was three in one, one God, the Lord of Death Seed and Harvest. The Jesuits had him whipped one hundred lashes, not once but three days running because he had blasphemed against the Trinity.

Fathers Montoya and Maceda had led a retreat from the Paraguay Reductions because their converts were always being dragged off by the Paulistas into slavery. They loaded their twelve thousand Indians on to seven hundred wooden rafts and floated them away from their homeland. All the rafts were smashed on the Parana cataracts, but nothing daunted the worthy fathers:

31

they marched them overland to their new home in Missiones, in Argentina. A bizarre exodus, which did indeed save the Indians from the Paulistas, but secured them as exiled slaves for the Jesuit priests.

In the end it was no more than that: a string of funny anecdotes about confusions and muddles and mistaken thinking, because the alternative was unbearable. The flourishing complex networks of tribes that had once inhabited the Amazon, maintaining a level of population never since reached again, had been destroyed, blotted out of history and material reality in the name of Jesus Christ.

Anna struggled to find some way to approach what seemed to her a mounting horror. They, the Catholic Church, had battered and impoverished an entire continent, a land rich in resources, in culture and in dreams; and then they had won sanctity by ministering to their own victims. The gap was too enormous: the teaching of the Church, however much it claimed to be based in the life of the one who died willingly, had been the instrument of oppression, and she could not believe it was her job to defend that, to make it sweet and acceptable. She tried: she read about the great debate in the sixteenth century, lost herself in the travails of the Reformation and the Counter-Reformation, of the careful prayerful humanists who had argued against slavery, against degradation and greed and exploitation. She turned with joy towards Dürer's marvelling at the Aztec treasure, not at the gold itself but at the spirit and genius of the society which had made the golden artefacts. And not he alone; there had been a great if gentle mourning across Europe when the treasures of Aztec and Inca were melted down for bullion. People who had known that something was being destroyed, more precious than all the gold of El Dorado. A valiant struggle carried on in the universities and monasteries, a struggle outside its time and place, to defend the rights of individuals of all races, and the cultural rights of people so foreign and far away that they must have seemed like a dream. But she knew it was not enough. It was not enough.

With the laughter of the Fathers in her ears, she could not escape the fact that it was in the name of the Church, with the blessing of the pope, by people who prayed and received the

32

sacraments that the golden lands of hope and promise had been ruined, despoiled, assaulted. Raped. No, they had not been innocent people, that would make it all too easy. The Aztecs had used live human sacrifice and had enslaved others in their turn. The great Inca himself had ruthlessly massacred his half-brother and three-quarters of his own family. Hard, harsh people, as violent but less resilient than the bearded hooligans who came against them. The cathedrals the conquistadors had built to honour the God of Victory with stones torn from the broken temples had been lovely, had been glorious, but they had stunk of carnage. Her flesh stank of carnage. The religious orders, the holy nuns of Latin America were not the rape victims but the rapists. She was overwhelmed with the brutality, yet the Fathers laughed and asked her, 'What did you expect? Did you want a sweet white liberal God? What came ye forth for to seek — a mealy-mouthed gentle-Jesus-meek-and-mild? We smote the Egyptians with the seven plagues and laughed when their boy children died in the night. Don't you know that when you eat the bread of the living sacrifice, it is not just the tissue of the carpenter from Galilee, it is also the power of the Living Word that commanded the earth to come out of the chaos, that broke the chaos, raped it, remade it. We make order. We decide. We control. Open, open out to us. Consent. Consent and you will enjoy it. If you resist us we will have to punish you. When Athualpa died he was smiling; he knew a noble opponent when he encountered one; in his gruesome death he met a stronger God than his own and he was smiling. Remember, we finished him and we will finish you if you do not consent.'

As a well-trained nun she knew that it was all right to ask questions, but not to come up with the wrong answers. She was eaten with pride, her skin stank not only of carnage but of the hellfire reserved for those who take God's prerogatives and dare to judge. She was sick and giddy with pride. Why else was she ill? She was too puffed up with self-love and judgement to get on with the simple business of doing her job and being a good nun. Who was she to to pass judgement on history, on her betters, on priests and popes and brave men. Who was she to pass judgement on anyone.

'Bless me, Father, for I have sinned.'

She wanted his forgiveness, even without knowing what for. She had been pleased when she got his letter saying that he would be passing through London on his way from Aberdeen to Brussels. She suddenly wanted him to put his arms around her, give her his hug, his blessing, assure her that she was his little girl and that he loved her. Waiting for him at Kings Cross Station, grateful that he should come all this way by train instead of flying, she had felt a rising hope in her stomach, a childlike excitement, left over from all the days when she and her sisters had welcomed him at stations and airports all over the world. One man, one safe good strong man who knew and loved her.

But even as she saw him walking up the platform, she felt her heart sink again. She would not be able to tell him. To gain his forgiveness she would have to repent, would have to tell him she had sinned; and she would not be able to do so. He did not want to hear it. He wanted to hear that she was happy and well, that she was doing well, that everything was well and that she was a credit to him. He did not want to hear hysterical rubbish about her not being able to cope, about doubting vocations or about Holy Mother Church's failures in South America. He did not want to hear and he did not have to. Because of course it did not really matter, everyone had difficult times in the religious life, and he worked so hard for her, for them, and he loved them, her, so much and why should he have to worry; what right did she have to worry him?

They threw their arms round each other.

'Baby,' he said. 'How are you? You look great.'

'Oh Dad, it's been a long time. You look pretty terrific yourself.' Even her vocabulary altered, became infantilised in his presence; and surely if he thought she looked great, given how much weight she had lost, he was not looking at her. But this was a heresy, something she did not want to think and would not permit herself to think.

'No, I'm getting too old for all this running around the world. Now come on, tell me what you're up to, what are you doing here, for heaven's sake?'

A deep breath, but not needed really, because she knew she was not going to tell him. It was not possible. She said, 'They've sent me here on a research project.'

'Is that good?'

'Well it's fun and it's interesting, and it makes a change. Of course I've got a bit rusty.'

'What are you researching then?'

He was not stupid, she would have to tell him something precise, something authentic sounding. She would have to move from simple suppression to outright lies now. 'It's about the role of the Dominicans in the early history of South America; another missionary order you see. It may turn into a book.'

He glowed. 'That's my girl. You know, one thing I've always liked about your lot is that they don't waste your brains, they use what God gives them. I approve of that. Come on now, I'll take you to eat.'

It was one of his favourite things, taking her to lunch somewhere expensive. She might belong to the order and live a life of holiness and service, he might not see her for years on end, but it was his privilege and no other man's to take her out for a meal and feel nourished by the quizzical looks that they would inevitably attract. He swept her into a taxi, taking control, making the decisions, feeling protective and powerful. She could think only of the fact that she was going to have to eat, that she was going to have to master herself and eat a whole meal. She would have to act sane, to be sane for him, so that he would not have to deal with her madness.

'How are the others?' she asked him (working through her whole family would use up quite a lot of time). 'Who've you seen?'

'Fine, fine. Everyone's fine. I guess they're all doing well at the moment. I saw Claudia in New York a month or so back. The kids were great; Amy's thinking of getting married, but I think she's a bit young, don't you?' Amy was her sister Claudia's oldest daughter and Anna had not seen her for at least six years; suddenly she could not even remember how old she was or what she looked like. She was not even sure that she cared. There really was something wrong with her, heartless and cold.

'Oh Dad,' she said, 'they all do exactly what they want to do nowadays anyway. You just have to face it.'

'Well, what's changed? You lot always did exactly what you

35

wanted to.' He smiled proudly. 'Hell raisers. Never paid a blind bit of attention to your poor old father. Well at least he's a Catholic. Her fiancé I mean,' he added, sensing that Anna had failed to follow him.

She had stopped even trying. There was nothing there. There was nothing between them at all. He was a nice enough elderly man who did not need to be burdened with the emotional life-crises of a nun in her late thirties. She even found now that she could eat perfectly normally, because it was so much easier to eat than to have him find out that she couldn't. And he would not notice anything he didn't want to. But of course he loved her; he loved them passionately, had refused to give them over to any of his sisters to raise, had with minimal assistance done it all himself, had taken such good care of them, never let them feel that they were a drag on his career though they must have been; he had been saintly really.

He ate and talked and ate. He glowed with confidence. He strode the world and plumbed its depths and brought up treasures from the deep. He had brought up five lovely daughters, too, even though people had told him he would not be able to. His baby was a nun and she had been sent half-way round the world to write a book, and that was just great.

He was charming to her now, charming and amusing, a fine companion for a lunchtime.

'Anna,' he said, when mutual acquaintances and family doings were all exhausted, 'I found a real gem for you. Listen to this. I'm going to have it made into a locket and wear it round my neck, like the Irish do.' He hated the Irish and what he called their sentimental religion. He came originally from a South German family and had pretensions about his connections. All his daughters had seen through them years ago, but they never disillusioned him because he enjoyed it so much. 'Listen, it's this poem thing.' They often swapped absurdities from their shared Catholicism; they liked the idea of being sophisticated grown-up Catholics. He had delighted in the Vatican Council and the putting of the sentimentalists in their place.

> *'Since to err is only human*
> *There's a whole lot on the slate*

> *That I'll have to give account for*
> *When I reach the pearly gate.*
> *But I'm not a-worrying*
> *About the deeds I've done;*
> *I'll just whisper to St Peter*
> *"I'm the Daddy of a nun."*

She laughed. 'Oh Daddy, that's terrific. I think you really believe that deep down, don't you?' She kept her voice light, teasing him. No, she realised suddenly, she wasn't teasing him, she was flirting with him, trying to gain and keep his approval at any cost, to be admired by him, loved by him.

'Well of course I do,' he laughed with her. 'Would I have given up my baby for anything except my own salvation?' But though he laughed Anna felt giddy, as though she was at a dangerous corner somewhere. High up and unbalancing towards a fall. But falling was not permitted.

They moved on to world politics; oddly he liked her to be a radical, it confirmed him as a man who had good sense, who could not afford but could appreciate the desires of others for a better world. Her politics reminded him of when she was a teenager. He explained in detail why larger Aid, real Aid as opposed to politically advantageous giving was not economically sensible and she could not argue with him because he knew all the facts and was so kind and so clear about the possible terms for the discussion. He ended up thinking that she really was on his side and he could allow her, the dear girl, the excitements of hoping for a more just society.

He was always in a hurry. She knew he would be in a hurry to go somewhere else; so, not too soon after lunch was finished, but soon enough, she said, 'Oh dear, Dad, I've got to rush. I have to be back at the convent. I've got some work to do.'

'Can't you take one day off holiness to be with your own father? What about all that honouring stuff, or has that gone out with the Council too?' But she knew he was relieved. Of course she had to say work or he would find it hard to justify his own desire to be moving on.

'Well, when will I see you again, sweetie?'

'I'm more stable than you are. I'll be here till the end of the year. When will you be back in London?'

37

'God knows,' he told her. 'The higher you get, the more you're at the beck and call of others.' He gave her a warm kiss and twenty pounds for 'her poor folk'. They got up and moved across the restaurant. 'How's that crazy Sister Kate?' he asked, more a courtesy than anything else. He had not liked Sr. Kate when they had met, but at a distance he was able to think of her as an endearing if nutty kid.

'She's fine, just fine.' Anna tried to think of a humorous Sr. Kate story but failed to find anything appropriate.

'Give your Mother my regards when you write her.' He liked the idea of incorporation into her conventual family. He always sent them a generous Christmas present. He walked Anna from the restaurant to the front door of his hotel. Crossing the luxurious foyer Anna felt embarrassed by its opulence and her fraudulence. He insisted that she took a taxi and paid the driver direct himself. He hugged her and she was driven off. A heavy gloom settled down on her. She had lied to him. But the Fathers were pleased with her. Apart from a fairly mild off-the-cuff remark about what had she expected and did she not remember she was to call no man father, they left her in peace. And he had made him happy. She had been a good girl, a good daughter. He could board his plane that afternoon with affection and satisfaction.

Quite suddenly and unexpectedly she had to ask the cab driver to stop. She stepped out of the taxi and was sick in the street, vomiting out the whole of the lunch so expensively produced. She leaned against the cab, retching, sweating and apologising. She could tell that the driver thought it was all a very rum show — driving a sick nun from that plush hotel all the way to Leyton. He was kindly about it though. Back in the taxi Anna felt the heavy weight of failure and defeat. And a great pool of loneliness which was best ignored.

'Bless me, Father, for I have sinned.'

'The Lord be in your heart and on your lips that you may make a true and full confession of all your sins.'

It always worked; Sr. Anna relaxed for a moment in the acceptance of the guarantee. But it was not so easy.

She hardly knew any more what her sins were. How could this strange and invisible young man help her find out. She was herself a sin; the guarantees might not work. She had promised God, she had promised God that she would be faithful, cleaving only to Him, His bride, His darling. She had made the promise. But God had promised her too and she was not sure that He was keeping His promises. That in itself was a sin. A covenant relationship, it was called; she had entered into a covenanted relationship with God and God was faithful. He had been faithful to His people in the desert and after the desert and always, although he had some odd ways of showing it — the exile in Babylon, the destruction of the Temple, the centuries of pogroms, the Holocaust itself, the endless Middle Eastern War. But she was not allowed to question the ways of God. God was faithful; it was she who lacked faith, who had not kept her side of the bargain, who had broken covenant, who had run away when the going got rough. God had withdrawn, whether temporarily or permanently, His passionate affection for her because she had not been faithful enough. But a covenant is a blessed commitment; you could not tell until the end whether it worked, that was its nature, its mystery, its power. God did not have to be nice to her, even if she deserved it, which she did not; that was not part of the deal. The small print had all sorts of tricky details. God would be faithful if she was; she could only be faithful if He gave her grace. No wonder the poor old Israelites had felt baffled. But was it a sin to doubt, to have doubts? If it was, then there was no hope; you cannot repent of what you cannot control, what is outside will and desire. She wanted to be faithful, and she was not.

She muttered through a list of technical sins, driven back suddenly to her childhood. She and her sisters had gone to confession every Saturday, wherever they had been. Well taught, she had known then what sins were, but often she had no sense of their sinfulness, her conscience had not indited her. What seemed to her grave and painful, bad, worthy of anger, never seemed to strike the confessor in the same way. And however impersonal it was meant to be, you soon learned that though all priests spoke here as Christ, they all had different priorities, different Christs in whose power they spoke. She knew she was missing something out. She had examined her conscience, a faithful daughter of the faithful Father, the faithful bride of the glorious son, and yet there was something missing and it was herself.

The priest absolved her. There was the sweet sense of relief of course; it did work and she was forgiven. She could let it all go. He gave her a hymn for her penance — nuns were not usually given hymns. He asked her to pray for him who was a sinner also. The routine was restful. Then as she was about to leave he added, 'This isn't a penance, not a formal one, but I think you should get out of yourself a little. I know you're in a foreign country, but I think you'd find it useful to seek out an occasion for good works. Visit an old lady. Something like that. Ask your sisters, I'm sure they'll be able to help.'

She bit down on a passionate resentment, for herself and for the poor old lady. She was appalled at herself. She said, 'Yes, Father.'

She knelt in a pew. Prayed first for him who was a sinner also. Thanked God for His holy priesthood throughout all the world. Prayed for this nameless young man, for his vocation and for his ministry. Gave thanks for the forgiveness, for the gift of the Sacrament of Reconciliation, a free gift through the sacrifice of Christ. She heard her own neat prayers from another place inside herself and was interested in them. They did not reach her grounding place and she knew they did not. But it must not be allowed to matter. You press on through the night of doubt and sorrow. You use the Will, the great powerful muscle that makes men different from animals. Emotions don't matter. You direct the Will to the project of holding on to God in the darkness.

The Fathers said, 'Stop complaining. Thérèse of Lisieux knew no sensible consolations throughout her whole life.'

'Is that', Anna asked without thinking, 'why she died of consumption at twenty-three? Dried out, eaten away with loving, loving, loving without any response, any delight. What sort of a marriage was that?'

'That will do,' the Fathers were loud and angry. 'That will do. Shut up and say your penance. Right now and mean it.' Like a child she obeyed.

Come down oh love divine, seek thou this soul of mine
And visit it with thine own ardour glowing. . . .
Oh let it freely burn, till earthly passion turn
To dust and ashes in its heat consuming. . . .

Let holy charity mine outward vesture be,
And lowliness become my inner clothing;
True lowliness of heart, which takes the humbler part
And o'er its own shortcomings weeps with loathing.

She was repelled. This time she could not arrest the feeling before she recognised it. She thought she was going to be sick again. What was wrong with the hymn, with her? She had a bright vision of the women in her illiteracy class, so lowly, true lowliness not of heart but of stomach, and the Magnificat Mary singing that in her all the poor and oppressed would be exalted. The enormous gap between their lowliness and the promises that God had not kept. But it was not just that. It was not Kate's passion for justice glowing and dancing furiously unquenched, no dust or ashes. It was something nearer. It was she who could not accept the God who demanded these things of her.

She felt the pain, but she could not use it. She was scared. There are some questions too painful even to ask. How could one avoid the questions, avoid the pain. What was God playing at?

Like a stubborn child she shouted at her own thoughts. She did not need the instructions of the Fathers now. She could punish her own sinfulness. 'I will be obedient, I will be good. Dear God, come and get me out of here. Please. Name your price and I'll pay it. Please. Merciful God, creator of all things, judge of all men. Tell me the rules and I'll keep them. Just keep me safely out of here. I can't stand it. Punish me. Make me good . . . . "For I, Except you enthrall me never shall be free, Nor ever chaste, except you ravish me." I need forcing, God, I need you to force me. Make me, break me, make me good and acceptable again.'

She craved it suddenly, physically, her belly melting, wanting, warming; greedy for her own humiliation, her own rape. Christ, she cried. She could not stay here in the Church with her head full of such filth. 'Rape me chaste.' She begged God and the Fathers sneered; they would consider it, they told her, if she was very good. If she deserved it.

I really am going crazy, she told herself firmly. Kate was right and I am cracking up. I am sick. That's all. It was an escape, and she should have known it, but her head described the problem as one of illness, needing rest and gentleness and getting-out-of-

herself. It made things much easier. All her doubts and difficulties came from that, that alone, came from the fact that she
was not very well. It was simple, a relief.

At Mass that Sunday they asked if there was anyone who could
spare some time to help a mother with a brain-damaged child. A
member of the congregation, the parish family, of course. Not
wanting domestic help, but who had heard of a programme
which might be able to help cure the child, but it needed commitment, regular commitment. It was the sort of thing that a
Christian family ought to be glad to help with. All that the
mother needed were people who could give a few hours a week to
help with this programme. More details could be given to anyone
who was interested after Mass. Ask one of the Fathers.

She was guilty about her own lack of concern. She was quite
shocked. She who had more time at her disposal than almost
anyone; she who was living a sinfully private life. She sought out
the priest who had heard her confession and asked him for the
details. Not by so much as a glance did he indicate his approval of
her obedience.

She rang the number that she had been given that very afternoon. A young man's voice answered, cool but pleased. But she
would have to talk to Fiona, his wife, the child's mother. Fiona
was in charge of this programme. Incidently was she, Sr. Anna,
reasonably fit, because actually it was quite strenuous. Muttered
voices off while Sr. Anna held the phone and wondered what she
was doing. She quelled her doubts fiercely. Fiona, the voice
informed her, was delighted, would she like to come round and
discuss it. Would she like to come round that evening.

They needed her. Sr. Anna could tell. Behind the cool there
was eagerness. She was needed by someone. A welcome calm
descended. Yes, she would come round later; they'd give her a
drink, then a pause while the voice remembered that she had said
'Sister'. They'd give her a coffee or something. And really he had
not yet said thank you, he was sorry, they really were grateful and
hoped it would work out. They would look forward to seeing her.

The child cannot remember how it was before; before there

was breathing and light. It is lost forever, the underwater paradise, the deep dance without effort, without gravity, without consciousness. The child- is born crying for the dreamland, and must be welcomed into wakefulness. What Caro can remember, what she can feel, is more lost than for other children. She gave up her safe place too easily, too soon, in a driving enthusiasm to be born, to go travelling down the long dark tunnel to the New World. The ocean and the lands beyond the ocean called her. Rocked between the promontories of her mother's hip bones, she was not contented. Or perhaps not that for no one exactly knows. Was it the mother who expelled her, who exiled her and did not want her harboured there; who could not accept the monster, the baby, and drove her forth to the alien country? Together, though, they laboured towards deliverance. The baby plunging recklessly, the mother's muscles pushing down, down, down. And then not down. The child does not know about the midnight ambulance that comes to snatch the mother away from home. The child does not know about legs hung up like beef on meat hooks. The child knows that what should be down and easy becomes up and hard. And there is no space. And it is dark and there is not enough space.

The child knows that the mother, the body of the mother, is a treacherous rat. She gnaws through the umbilical cord too soon. Wait, the child screams, wait. The cord is thick and strong and pulsing. It joins the baby to the placenta, to the source of nourishment and peace, to the primal paradise. It is the movement between the two places, the cord, it holds them together. The cord joins the baby to the mother. There should be time, but they snap the baby off and there is a dreadful gap between blood-breathing and air-breathing.

For Caro, struggling and stuck, the gap is too long. She is jammed, wedged tight, and the journey upwards is too hard for someone so small. She is panicked, convulsed with fear, and trapped in the darkness. Her bowels open, her body is covered with her own black shit, more darkness, more fear and an emptiness in her belly which ought to be full. They snatch her out, and the brightness is blinding. She is swung against the nothingness of air where there should be the weight of water. She is beaten and yelled at. Where is the mother? Why has she let the child be snatched away too soon and too late? The baby is snatched up to heaven to the bright courts of the fathers. The mother, defeated, rushes off to hide in the desert. The mother sells the child to the Fathers, over and over again. The child is scrubbed clean of the black muck and the white cloud that keeps it warm; it is cast out on to a deserted shore with its bowels open and exposed to the scavenging gulls. The child craves not sucking and warmth only, but to be held. Held and rocked to the sound of breathing and heartbeat; the child needs to be held close and warm, for company, for consolation, for memory of the warm dark place, for a time to say farewell; and for greeting and welcome, too, for mutual delight and recognition.

But Caro is not held, she is put away. It is too bright and too quiet where they put her. It is very alone and they stuff hard things into her nose and her veins; her flesh and her self are penetrated, interfered with though she does not yet know who she is or where her boundaries are. The sides of the new place are not soft and noisy with the music of the waters; they are bright and cold and silent. She would be angry but her needs are too great. She would be furious but she needs all her strength to survive.

'Caro is a brain-damaged three-year-old,' Fiona told Sr. Anna. Her voice was clipped and careful, out of keeping with her abundant body, her long hair, her colourful clothes. She had rehearsed this story many times; gone over and over these details too many times before. Her openness was deliberately constructed, and it closed up more than it revealed.

'She was born nine weeks premature, after a really difficult labour. They couldn't get her to breathe for ages. I didn't know then, I was knocked out and no one told me or Stephen for ages. Then she was in an incubator for weeks. She only weighed just over three pounds. At first everyone loved her, she was such a little fighter, she fought to breathe, fought to keep her heart going, she fought with convulsions a bit later on. They kept telling us how brave she was, and everyone fought for her; they were so proud of her. I think if they'd known they might not have bothered. I don't know. But she was a source of pride. When I first knew there was something wrong, nobody would listen. They said things like, "It's bound to take her some time to catch up", and "Of course you must judge her as being a couple of months younger than she is", and "You must try not to worry, would you like some tranquillisers?" and "Isn't she a little doll?" I was depressed after the birth, and of course I really wanted to believe them. It wasn't until about a year ago that we really found out.

'I don't know if you know anything about brain damage. It's not mentally retarded — a child who just happens to have a genetically inferior brain — and it's not like mongolism — a malformation, a mutancy — and it's not psychological either, like autism. It's a child who's conceived with a perfectly normal brain and it grows in the womb with a normal brain and then something damages it. It doesn't matter when. If the mother gets very high fevers during pregnancy, or the child is deprived of oxygen at birth, or has certain illnesses in infancy or even has an accident, say it's dropped on its head, later on. It had a good brain which has been damaged.

'I have to tell you this because the treatment is based on it. Without understanding I think it's hard to be motivated. We've had to learn so much stuff. Inside that damage is an intelligent, well child. For years no one really had any treatment for brain damage; they tried to tackle symptoms, say exercises to improve eye co-ordination or whatever, but it didn't really work very well.'

She and Anna and Stephen, the now enfleshed voice from the telephone, were sitting with mugs of coffee in their hands. Anna could detect the zeal of the convert. Upstairs somewhere, invisible and unheard, was the person they were talking about. Anna could not imagine her, had no sense of her, only a strong sense of Fiona and her determination. She thought Caro was lucky; or perhaps not so lucky. In Santa Virgine those children died. Just died because there was no room for them, no time, no commitment. Nobody fought for them. Nobody could afford the determination. Mid-night baptisms and children's requiems, with their white vestments, were too common.

Stephen went out to the kitchen to make more coffee and Fiona continued with her lecture.

'Then some people in the States, in Philadelphia, started looking at the brain itself, and how one might bypass damaged cells, make new connections, synapses, electrical triggers, pathways between new cells — if one pathway is damaged make a new one, using less pre-programmed but perfectly adequate cells. They discovered that normal children develop these synapses after birth progressively, by using them, by stimuli, especially by movement. They reckoned that if you have a brain-damaged child it can't do that process for itself, can't so to speak initiate it, but you can do it for them. You put a child through the movements it ought to have made itself. So we have to put Caro through this series of exercises and other sensory stimulation stuff. For instance, we put her on a table and make her limbs, force them really, to go through crawling motions. Over and over; over and over. Of course, normal children are doing it by themselves all the time, so to help ours catch up we have to do it pretty intensively. And that's where outside help comes in. You really need five people to do the exercises properly and they have to be done at least four times a day. You see we have to be able to rely on you. I don't mean four times a day, seven days a week, but whatever you say you can do, even if it's just one Thursday afternoon a fortnight or something. We have to know that you'll come — look, that's the schedule.' She pointed to the kitchen door on which hung a massive chart divided into little boxes and marked in various colours. Sr. Anna smiled because it reminded her quite abruptly of their duty rota in Santa Virgine.

'That's why I always try to explain it in detail. We're not taking about forever of course, but for some regular while. We've been going about six months and we think, we believe that it does make a difference, that it is good for her. But six months just about exhausts the immediate people you know; we've hit a desperate bit, for people I mean. One of the women who came from the start has had to move house, and another friend of Stephen's who's been wonderful has decided that he just can't keep up the commitment, that six months is enough for now. And another woman had been coming but her baby is getting bigger and it makes it too difficult. When she started the baby slept in its carry-cot all through but now it's crawling about and she just can't manage. I'd not thought of asking the Church before — we're not such very good Catholics you know. Father David suggested it. We've had a number of calls actually, I'm really grateful. Also you know it can be quite fun. The people who team together get quite fond of each other. Our coffee bills have escalated. I don't know how you're fixed, what you're thinking about. I haven't even asked. How rude of me, I am sorry.'

She ran out of steam, suddenly tired. She was nervous in front of this nun. On the one hand nuns ought, they jolly well ought to be doing things like this; on the other, they seemed to her so distant, so unbodily. Caro was all physical, all body.

Sr. Anna said, 'I'm around until the end of the year. I work in a missionary order, mainly in Latin America, and I've come over, to do some research about the history of the conversion of South America, particularly the Spanish bits. I'm living with some other nuns, just down the road, but as a sort of paying guest; I don't have any involvement with them and their work. I have a lot of time on my hands which is a newish experience for an active order sister, and I know practically no one in London. So I should think I'm pretty nearly ideal for your purposes.'

Fiona smiled. She liked Anna's businesslike approach, without sentimentality or enthusiasm. 'You'd better come and see a session then, and decide how much you want to do.' She paused. 'Also you'll have to see how you react to Caro. Some people can't cope with it. She hates it, you see. I'd better warn you. She hates it and she fights. Some people can't cope with her handicap and some can't deal with her resistance. There has to be a middle ground, between disgust and too much compassion. Can you understand that?'

'Yes,' Anna delayed a little; she could hear the tone of the conversation changing. She knew that she did not want to know about Fiona's own confusions, not now; she did not want to have to be a nun for her. She was willing to work with the child, but that was all, afterwards she would go away. 'Yes, I do see. But remember it's how we're trained, professional loving. There are harsh things about it. But I think it's what you need from me. For mission nuns it's a peculiar problem, how far you can identify with the pain, enough to be there with people, not so much that you fall apart. I've survived it for over twelve years. When I was in Santa Virgine . . .'

47

'Were you there?' Stephen interrupted.

'Yes, do you know it?'

'I've been there. I was on a student programme thing. I was based in Licuna really, but I've been to Santa Virgine. Ten years ago. I supposed it's changed since the coup.'

He was eager to hear about the political developments, but more to have her remind him of the smell and taste of the place. His memories brought out hers. She had forgotten to remember how it was: the rotting sweet smell after heavy rain, the almost livid energy of the slums, where you knew that poverty had gone beyond bearing and the fruit of it was vibrant and deranged. Impossible to describe, to remember alone. From the distance of London she had remade Santa Virgine as a more serious high-minded thing altogether. Now tracking the landmarks with Stephen she suffered a wringing homesickness.

They danced in a whirl under the shadow of the crazy crumbling cathedral. That was her home, they were her sisters, dancing in the giddy green light of evening, while the jungle sucked at them from below and the mountains above boomed with the immensity of God and the cathedral of Our Lady, the dream of a radiant and young Spain, held the two together tenuously, determinedly. That was her home, her place. How could she ever have thought that she would not go back again?

Soon Fiona brought a bottle of wine from the kitchen. She pulled the curtains and a few moments later went out again and returned with bread and cheese and a large earthenware bowl of fruit. She did not ask if Anna would stay and eat, she did not interrupt the easy flow between her husband and this nun. Anna was soothed by the ease of it, the warm offhand hospitality, and the comfort of the home.

She told them, as the evening went on, about her research and some of the dilemmas that it threw up. She told them stories of the mad conflicts of the conquistadors and their crazy visions of a paradise from which they could extract undreamed of treasures. She told them how hard she was finding it to settle back to academic work after so long. Stephen told them funny stories about being a volunteer in South America and about the useless idealism he had shared with his colleagues, which was of course part of the same story that Anna was telling. His own sweet well-intentioned Europeanness and his greed for the richness of the New World. She matched his stories with others about innocent eager missionaries who simply could not begin to cope — including her when she had first gone out there. Their laughter was superior, they had learned, they had understood. But at least it was shared; they indulged each other as Fiona pointed out to them, gently not fiercely. They relaxed, contented with each other's company. Fiona felt pleased, Stephen felt interested and Anna felt blessedly sane, normal. The voices were silent, benign.

Upstairs Caro slept invisible, and in her dreams she danced again and plotted gleefully.

When, later than she had expected, but not so late as to disturb the sisters, Anna walked home under the street lights, she thought that it had been too long since she had had such a happy time. An ordinary nice happy time. Even when she turned the corner and had to pass under the high blank wall of the disused factory she did not fear the shadow of the night, she did not sniff the scent of rapists, she did not hear the voices of the Fathers. She felt that things were better.

Stephen said to Fiona, 'She's really nice.'

'Let's wait and see what she makes of Caro.'

After a pause he said, 'We can't choose all our friends, all the time, by whether they can cope with Caro or not. She's nice anyway.' Then, before she could tell him that he had choices that she did not have, that he was more free to choose his friends by any criteria he wanted than she was, he burst out, 'For God's sake Fiona, let's risk it, let's have another one, another baby. It can't hurt Caro. It can help us. There's no reason. It will be all right. You'll see, I'll make it all right this time.'

'You can't.' Flatly.

'I know I can't. But . . .'

'Stephen.' A deep breath now; because she has kept it from him, kept it secret from him, hugged it to herself, wanted it to belong to her; she was nervous. She leaned towards him and he put his arm round her shoulder; suddenly she flopped against him, heavy but perfectly relaxed. Her head lolled against the upper part of his chest and under the shadow of his wing she dwelt briefly but securely. Her hair got into his mouth when he nuzzled the top of her head. There was a moment of immense

49

warmth and safety for both of them. 'Stephen, as a matter of fact I am pregnant.'

And now there are two children, snugly wrapped in love and darkness in the house. The tiny joyful one and the dark brooding one. Fiona loved being pregnant; her full body was made for this, she felt. She had given her secret away to Stephen though. She had wanted to keep it safe inside her for a while longer, though she had not thought why. But she had told him and that was good. He was delighted. It was a breakthrough back into the world of normalcy. He could not tell even Fiona how passionate his feelings for Caro were; how he felt his tenderness sucked out of him, making always more until he was a melted pool for her. He could not stand so much softness inside him, sometimes he hated Caro for making him so soft. And he knew that this was unworthy, not permissible; a good New Left man should be proud to be so unmanned. There was no one to tell: he had to protect Fiona from his full feelings about Caro, because he knew and understood hers, her mixture of guilt and compassion and endless hard work. He wanted a new baby, an ordinary, unspecial baby who would set him free from his enchantment. Caro was a witch, he thought, who had enchanted him, but she was also the princess who had to be rescued from her enchantment. Caro sucked at their life and he could refuse her nothing. Now he said, 'This birth then, I shall be there; I'll get to see it.'

'You'd like to do it yourself, wouldn't you?' said Fiona. It is mine, she wanted to say, it's mine. You will do exactly what I tell you, you cannot have it, it belongs to me. But at the very same moment she was excited. This one, this time, they would get right; they would go there together and get themselves a child who would come sliding into the world squalling and pinkening, and everything would be all right again.

'Poor Sr. Anna,' she said quite suddenly. 'Poor old nuns.'

He shifts her head gently so that he can kiss her properly, first on the side of her mouth where she has a little rough corner of dry skin and then more fully on the lips, wiggling his tongue teasingly. 'There are doubtless compensations', he said, 'that we know nothing about. Married to Jesus there are bound to be.' He did not want to have to think seriously about nuns just now. 'They get it from God, you know, who's probably better at it than I am.'

50

'You're so sexist,' she said, annoyed with him for breaking into her tenderness, but at the same time knowing that she desired him and not wanting to put him off. 'How do you know God is male?'

'Oh Fiona, please. If not, then they get perfect lesbian sex all the time. Surely?'

She laughed defeated. Neither of them just then was in the least interested in the metaphysical sex life of women religious. She pulled his earlobes, stretching them gently and carefully. He liked that.

On their way up to bed they looked in on Caro, the two of them entwined with each other now, hastening off to be somewhere else. Caro was curled in a tight ball and breathing noisily as she always did. It was a strangely heavy sound and one they had become used to. But they knew that other children did not make noises like that in their sleep; neither of them could help thinking of the new baby who would breathe silently and grow sweetly. But neither of them could tell the other what seemed like a dangerous act of treachery. They made love with each other instead.

III

Initially she gave them three sessions a week. A moderate and appropriate gift. Caro's treatment, as Fiona had said, consisted mainly of forcing her through a series of physical exercises. Force was the only word for it; Caro was never willing to co-operate, or even to consent. Her hatred of it all was painful and obvious. They had to kill something in themselves, the something called tenderness which is dragged out of even the most reluctant at the sight of a small child suffering. Some days it was almost unbearable and Anna would look up from the physical and mental struggle and see Fiona standing there, a face clamped down into stubbornness. The two of them, Caro and Fiona, were pitting their wills against each other.

Caro touched Anna. She had not been prepared for that; she had believed that she had seen enough human wreckage in Southern America to blunt the edge of pain and disgust. But Caro was not, to her, disgusting. She found her beautiful, and was moved again and again by the ferocity and power of the child.

Caro was under a spell. She had been turned by some wicked fairy or ancient witch into a fish. Her body flopped and flapped like a fish out of water, limp, heavy and twitching. If they could only find some way to return her to the dark pool she had come from, she would become graceful again, graceful and powerful and swift. She used her arms like flippers, even while her head sagged from side to side.

They had to put her on a table and work her limbs, trying to convert them from tail to legs, trying to make their movements conform to the movements of human beings. They were trying to pattern her, Anna felt, as she had been patterned into a good nun. Caro fought back. And Anna began to believe that she could hear the deep voice that was the centre of the child, that uttered and mumbled and growled. Not like the Fathers, a clarion from above, but something different altogether, a black quiet muttering that Anna had to listen to attentively to catch the individual words.

They don't love me, said this voice, they don't love me. Me. ME. They want me to be something different. They want a dear good little girl; they don't want this angry one, this fierce dark one. They don't want it. If I come out of the dark cellar they will not leave me alone. They will get to me. I like the dark. I have chosen the dark. Why should I come out and be made over by them. We are the same, Sister Anna, you and I, Sister Anna. Bluebeard's wives, preferring the dark. But I am braver. We are both locked up. We are both locked up. But you don't dare come down here into the dark and set us both free. We go together, you and I, Sister Anna, we are very alike.
  Come down here into the dark with me and I will make it ablaze with light. Come into the dark with me and I will show you things you have never dared to dream of. I am the dreamer, but you will have to come down here and get me. Forget your rules, your order, your commitment to the light. Here you can embrace the dark and escape from them all. Come down here where things are foul but free. Dirty nappies and filth in hair and playfulness. They all go together. Yes they do.

There was a little child in Caro, a little girl in a sulk, a little girl throwing tantrums but who wanted to know that she was loved just as she was. Shit and all. Anna wanted that, in Caro she recognised her own longing. It was too true that they had something in common, but something that Anna had destroyed in herself early in its life. An abortionist, a back-street abortionist, she had aborted the child inside herself. The child who would allow her to play, to be cuddled and be loved. The Fathers did not care for that child.
  'You are wasting your time on that one,' they told Anna. 'You

53

are wasting precious time which we will demand of you. Time is ours, we made it, you owe it to us. We do not love and protect the children of darkness; we will only take care of grown-ups, self-disciplined sane grown-ups. She can only offer chaos. She is the name of insanity, of disintegration. If you join her, if you go that way you will find the monsters, more monsters than you know of. Let her go. She is the price we demand for our protection.'

But Caro said other things. She said,

Remember I am also Sophia, the joyful wisdom, the child at play, who dances in the small open space on the hard bright sand before the eternal throne. I am the everlaughing baby, who sings the creation into life; I am the voice of the voiceless moments, I am the space for dancing, I am the dancer and I am the dance. Don't be afraid, Anna, come to me and live outside the rules. Chaos is not dark, as opposed to light, chaos is before all light and dark, and after it. In chaos you cannot walk but you can dance.

Anna looked down at her hands which were holding Caro's lower leg. Her skin was tanned and dry, years of honest toil, working hands to be proud of. But the rest of her body was white and soft. Caro was not soft, she was tough and hard. The exercises made her immensely strong for her age, but she could not use that strength for anything except resistance. She had to resist, to refuse, because it was the only thing that she could do.

Sometimes that resistance made Fiona furious. She confessed as much to Anna one day. They had finished the session and the others had gone. But Fiona offered Anna coffee, and Anna thinking of the bleak emptiness of her work rather guiltily accepted. It had been a comparatively good session and at the end of it one of the team had, unsolicited, pointed out to Fiona how much Caro's head control seemed to have improved. Anna looked at Caro, now flopped on the floor sucking all four of her fingers and drooling; she wondered. But Fiona was cheered, and later she brought in two mugs of coffee and sank herself into the sofa. Anna sat where she could see Caro.

'It is true, you know, she really is making headway. You don't see it, but you haven't been doing it long enough. You don't know how she was before.'

'She's certainly very strong, isn't she?'

'Oddly enough, in Philadelphia they told us that that was a spin-off; even when they're back to being so-called normal, Doman's children, they have real advantages, like strength and fitness. I just wish she didn't seem to hate it so. I want to explain that it is for her own good. Some days I really want her somehow to show a little bloody gratitude.'

'Perhaps she isn't grateful. Perhaps she doesn't *want* to be normal.'

Anna distinctly heard Caro's deep belly-chuckle, maliciously amused, as though she wanted the two women to disagree; she stared at the inert exhausted pile of Caro on the carpet.

'Oh no. No I'm sure that's not right. You should see her tantrums sometimes. Not the sort of fighting back she gives us on the table, but real tantrums, self-destructive violence, against herself. She's caged, caged not protected by her injuries.'

Anna was following a thought in her own head, not fully sensitive to Fiona because something too important had come up, something very near to herself. It was not like her not to agree with something that someone else proposed, but this time she pushed on.

'The difference is subjective though. Once I, my sisters and I, I mean when I was a child, we were at that sentimental age and we set a canary free. It lived in a cage in the kitchen, it belonged to the cook we had then. We stole it and took it outside and set it free. It was mobbed, immediately almost, before our eyes; it was mobbed by the other birds, they killed it.' They had killed it very bloodily. The dreadfulness of what they had done had smote all the little girls together; they had stood huddled together in real horror. The few little yellow feathers blowing away from the mauling had not been able to move them to tears, it was too awful. 'I don't know clearly what the difference between caged and protected is. But freedom, freedom is dangerous, full of responsibility. We had this poster at the Mother House which said, 'And freedom consists of voices that have been broken and blood that has been spilled. Freedom tastes of pain.' Do you think that Caro somewhere, somewhere very deep, just refuses that; she pays a price of course, but she doesn't have to take it on, all that load.'

She sipped her coffee, unguarded because she thought she was talking about Caro. 'There comes a point you know, it isn't necessarily cowardice or evasion, it is damage, when someone becomes literally unable to live free. During the Chinese revolution they tried to free women's feet, the ones that had been bound. They ripped the bandages off them but it was worse: they died of the pain. The binding may have been caging to start with, but it had become protection for them. Like that canary.'

Fiona put her cup of coffee down on the floor and leaned towards Anna.

'Are you talking about Caro or about yourself?'

Anna started, 'What do you mean? I was talking pretty abstractly I think. I was trying to say that there might be something in Caro that resists the treatment, that really does not want to be cured; both a sense of herself, who she is, and a sense that it might be too dangerous. Though of course how one can speculate about what she might think or want or understand is a bit tricky.'

Fiona let Anna off. Probably because Anna was a nun. She liked Anna, increasingly thought of her as a friend, but there was an ancient custom of respect, respect for the habit, which was an effective inhibition. But she was curious. There had been passion and pain in what Anna had said. And Fiona could not afford even to hear the idea that what she was doing with Caro was not the best thing. As Anna had shifted her own doubts on to Caro, so Fiona preferred to shift them away from Caro, back to Anna.

She said quietly, fondling her coffee mug and not looking up from it, 'Do you know what happens inside a chrysalis, a butterfly chrysalis? It's weird. First the caterpillar grows and all that stuff and then it makes a chrysalis for itself, spins it out of its own flesh, and then that hardens. I suppose I'd always thought that there was a fairly straightforward growing process inside, that the caterpillar grew wings and so on and so forth and then popped out. But it isn't like that at all. There's a total disintegration inside, complete, all the cells break down, break right down into primal slime, into complete yuck. They break down into nothing and then they reform into a butterfly. Isn't that amazing? It seems like a tiny proof of resurrection. That it can happen at all. I mean it's all right being a caterpillar if that's what you are, but you have to aim to be a butterfly and to do that you have to consent. To breaking down I mean.'

'Yes,' said Anna, also staring at her coffee. 'Yes. But how does the caterpillar learn to consent?'

'Faith? Seeing other caterpillars doing it? Having a safe enough place inside the chrysalis? I don't know. I don't even know what we're talking about really, about you or about Caro. Even about me, about letting go, not keeping control. From the caterpillar's point of view it must seem like a one-way street to nowhere. No money-back guarantee, no contract with agreed terms and conditions. It has to be vulnerable, I suppose, vulnerable to truth and love.'

They sat for a moment of possibility. But it was not the time to take it any further, not then. They were still poised on the edge of friendship, not ready to take the leap and neither of them motivated enough to force the issue.

Love, ha ha, said Caro from her heaped self on the carpet. Truth, pah, forget it. There are no promises. This is the place where there are no promises. Resurrection, blah. There are no ministering angels down here, only the roaring wind of forsakenness and bitter vinegar against the raging thirst. I don't make terms; the sides of the chrysalis are not stable. Who says it is a safe place, the rocking belly. The walls of the cellar may well collapse and crush and bury you forever. You have to risk it. You have to come into the dark unprotected, without a thread to lead you back again. You have to leave your protection and come down where there are no words; where words don't work and all sense is broken down into guttural noises. Syllables like the Sybil spoke, which had to be interpreted. There is no interpreter. You are alone. You are stretched out between the Fathers and me. We will get you.

But at least she could leave Caro's presence. Away from her the voice faded, only echoed in the darkness of unremembered dreams. She could not so flee from the Fathers. Caro invited her consent, the Fathers required it. They caught her, hounded her, pounded her on unexpected corners of the street and launched arguments with her even on the underground. Though oddly she noticed that they seemed almost in awe of the buses and so long as she rode right up on the top at the front like a child she was for a while safe from them.

They did not like Caro. They thought that Caro was not a good influence. They did indeed like Anna working with handicapped children and being kind and gracious and patient and always on time, but they did not approve of Caro talking to Anna. When she left Caro's physical presence they would be waiting for her. Caro was right and she was torn between them.

With Fiona and Caro Anna was for the first time in contact with a mother and child. She noticed her elitism even as she noticed the thought. She had of course spent a lot of time in Santa Virgine with mothers and children, so what was different? Not just the poverty and hopelessness and cultural differences. Though partly. The women in Santa Virgine, and still more in Panama where she had been before and had been directly involved with a mother and child programme, they had been like Fiona. By and large, they were as devoted, as determined and directed towards their children as Fiona was. Their love and struggle, though taking different forms, had been as grounded in their lives, as confining, as motivating, as joyful. The difference of course, she realised, was twofold; partly it was the singleness — seeing one mother with one child was very different from seeing twenty at once and trying to generalise, trying to work out the best use of resources, to meet all the needs of mothers and babies and older children in one programme, under-staffed and under-funded. Whereas here it was just Fiona, trying to fit herself around the needs, the very special needs of just Caro. The isolation of the couple intensified the emotion, intensified the maternity. The singleness was, Anna suddenly realised, not what she would want for herself, both too much and not enough at the same time, and Fiona was strained by it; but it made the icon of mother and child very forcefully present.

The other reason that it was different, and this came to her painfully, was that the women in Latin America had been her work; she had never seen them as people who were her friends; they were there for her to serve *en bloc* as it were, from whom she could seek nothing for herself. But Fiona did not want that, did not want Anna's generalised charity; she wanted companionship, pleasure, relationship. Anna found this alarming and realised how well she had been trained in detachment, in distance, in depersonalisation. They had been trained to love, but also to protect themselves against the demands of love, against loss and vulnerability at the personal level. Their training had cut them off. But it did not work any more. Caro had crashed that barrier, had demanded when Anna least wanted to give, had demanded that Anna love her individually and solely, and had demanded that Anna let her, let Caro, on her belly in the slime of monstrosity, love her and serve her.

Overwhelmingly, as she recognised this she envied Caro. She wanted for herself the constant nourishing nurturing that Caro could demand as a right from Fiona. Anna felt herself orphaned, although she was furious with herself for so feeling. God was not enough, she wanted something more physical, a place where she would be held, be held even when she vomited and convulsed and retched, as Fiona held Caro.

Her father had sent her mother, her Mother Superior, his regards. He had handed Anna over to her with pleasure and relief; he respected her and knew she would keep his baby safe. Safe for what? Mother was in the pay of the Fathers.

'Not "in the pay of",' they corrected her. 'Oh no, Mother Clare is in receipt of our favour. She brings up the daughters and then hands them over to us and we are grateful, we comfort her for her loss which is our gain. She is our chosen, the handmaiden, the faithful one. Fiona too. All the mothers. All the mothers know where their interests lie, because the children must be protected. Their interest lies with us and with safety, not with the daughters in the pit, in darkness, in the desert. Look, look and see. Sarah chose Abraham not Hagar. She could have chosen Hagar, Hagar was her daughter, her slave, Hagar belonged to her. But she handed Hagar over, not once but twice. Once for Abraham to impregnate, and once for him to send away. The wise mother runs no risk for the daughters. The daughters have to learn where the power is. The mothers will teach them. You have to learn that too.'

'No,' cried Anna. 'No, no, no. Fiona cherishes her child. Fiona feeds Caro with her flesh, her time and her love. The mother loves the child. The mother loves the child best of all.'

'Oh, come on. You know better than that. You are not that stupid. Fiona tortures her child in order to make her acceptable to the Fathers. She will force her from darkness into enlightenment.

She wants an acceptable child to offer us. She knows our terms and she consents. Why don't you? Why must you hold out against us? We are getting tired of it. We will withdraw our support. You are sustained by our power. We can withdraw it. We can drop you back into the dark pit, into the primal slime, into the chaos where Caro lives, smeared in her own excrement. Don't be deceived by her power. It is only anti-power. There is no power but the power of the Fathers. There is no other power.'

Anna did not know whether to believe them or not. If it was true she would have to obey. Christ had obeyed the command of the Fathers, to go through, to go in, to submit. He had annihilated himself, broken his own desires, he had obeyed, had obeyed in agony. And he had been rewarded, carried triumphant up to the heavens, enthroned on the right hand of God and given dominion over all things. He had been made the heir of the promise, the first born of all creation.

But he was the son.

Not a daughter.

The power of the Fathers was everywhere manifest. There seemed, except in the muttered rumblings of Caro, little or no defence against it. The psalms that Anna read with the other nuns each morning and evening made clear the muscle that God made available to those who kept the harsh laws and were born to the chosen races. The sons of Israel rejoiced in their Lord and he rewarded them with the fat flesh of Canaan. The Egyptians were drowned, the wall of Jericho tumbled and the mighty Lord of Armies favoured and punished his people with an arbitrary casualness and they praised him for it. The Holy Father, the Pope, had in the name of that God divided the whole New World between his two most favoured sons, Spain and Portugal. The foolish, the witty, third son Francis of France had teased them, demanding to see 'that clause in Adam's will which allowed the Kings of Castile and Portugal to divide the earth between them . . . ' The Holy Father was infallible, he had power over the distant seas and oceans, with his words he authorised the killings of people, the rape of women, the armed robbery of the Indian cultures. That was the power of the Fathers. And they had used it. The ship that brought the largest cargo of bullion in the whole history of the world, that brought the ransom of the Incas to the court of the King Emperor was named the *Santa Maria del Campo*; the Fathers honoured the mother because her belly was pregnant with stolen gold. Anna could not face the meaning; that so much power, dominating so much of history, drew its authority from the belly of a peasant woman, a curious inspired child bride who had believed that her pregnancy would set the captives free. The Mayans were enslaved, technically for refusing the gospel: exalt the humble — the Indians sat in their blankets and drank themselves into dangerous furies — and feed the hungry. She had been right though in one of her predictions. God sided with his own and remembered the promises he had made to the sons forever.

The structures by which she had lived were frail: the Mayan cities built of solid rock had seemed to the Spanish so deep-rooted and stable that they could never be destroyed; as a building material alone the store was inexhaustible. And so she had believed of the spiritual resources of Christianity. The conquerors had been wrong, perhaps she was too. It was unfaceable. Her self-discipline demanded that she continue with her work, that she read more and more details of violence and conquest and treachery and vice, but emotionally she tried to withdraw from it into the warm privacy of Fiona and Caro's life.

Gradually she added to the number of sessions that she worked on Caro's programme. She was fascinated, frightened, filled with guilt, but she sensed that Caro was on her side; or at least not on the Fathers' side. Caro comforted her. She did not mind the voices so much when they contrasted with each other. She hugged Caro's low growl to her and though the voices of the Fathers were louder and stronger, at least she knew they were not the only ones.

She particularly liked to do the early morning session. Getting up was no problem to her, trained for years to rise at dawn and unable to sleep. The sense of purpose which the sessions gave her enabled her more easily to throw aside the half-dreams and depression of the early hours. She liked seeing Stephen and Fiona together; married couples were a strange territory, a land of sweetness, but reassuring also because she knew that there was nothing that she wanted there for herself.

61

The other members of the early morning team filled part of the social gap in her life; working through their programmme while knowing that other people were still immersed in breakfast and domestic privacy gave them an odd congratulatory bonding that was almost community. Fiona and Stephen always worked this session together, but the rest of the team was made up from a small pool, all of whom were obviously delighted to have the addition of Anna. She felt wanted but not pressingly needed. There was a stunningly beautiful young man, a health freak who jogged over to the sessions. He claimed to be interested in the physical dimensions of the programme; but often, in some little word or gesture, Anna saw that Caro touched a hidden core of compassion in him, perhaps the contrast between his own self and hers. His main assets though were his implacable calm and his real physical strength. He could lift Caro about with an ease and a grace which transformed the sessions, and he was strong enough not to hurt her as often as the others.

Then there was a slightly punky unemployed teenager who lived round the corner. She denied any desire to do anyone a favour and hated to be thanked, but Fiona told Anna that she had come four or five times every week since the beginning of the programme and never complained, never missed a session and never stayed to socialise afterwards. A young nurse who came as and when she could fit the sessions in around her shifts. A middle-aged housewife who said she came because she missed her own children and did not have anything better to do, and who rather obviously and very reassuringly managed under all circumstances to find Caro sweet.

But Anna's favourite person was a middle-aged woman who had once been in a women's group with Fiona. She ran a book shop and was small and extremely businesslike. She acknowledged simply that she came because Fiona needed her and she thought it was her duty to help out. She was usually in a hurry to leave but would occasionally stay and drink coffee with Anna and Fiona afterwards. She was straightforward and amusing and had an abiding and informed interest in alternative community politics. Her present concern was over the threatened closure of the smaller local hospitals and she was continually trying to involve the others in her campaigning. She told Anna quite candidly that she did not trust nuns nor like them, but Anna recognised a companionship in the lean dedication and practical strength she could sense in her. She did not burn and flash like Kate, but both of them shared that commitment to justice as the only meaningful form of love, and Anna was warmed both by the realisation of this and, more secretly, by the thought that there were other ways of pursuing ethical conduct than becoming a religious.

In the end it was she, Audrey, who solved a simple practical problem that had been besetting Anna. Her habit got tiresomely in the way when they were doing the exercises. It had seemed a functional and suitable garment even in the slums, but that made Anna realise how cerebral, how unphysical her contact with people had been. Fiona had been right, Caro was physical, all body, a strenuous task, and they often ended the sessions puffed out and sweating. Ann's sleeves flapped or slipped down, and the corner of her veil was always lashing someone's face. One day Audrey handed her a carrier bag and said abruptly, 'I don't know what you are allowed but I presumed money might be a problem, so even if you can't wear it elsewhere this might help.' This was a tracksuit, loose, black with white piping. It was completely new. Anna was touched. She wore it from then on for all the sessions even though it made her feel naked, her head cold and her body self-conscious. This in itself was odd; it was not as though she had never worn lay clothes: her order had a general dispensation for holidays and other similar occasions. But the habit had become something to cling to, a sign that she was a nun, a bride of Christ. Without it she was lost, nothing clear or defined any more. And, not wearing it forced her nearer to the fact that she was not a good nun doing a good deed, ministering piously to a disabled child, but that Caro ministered to her, a very secret private ministry, a gift that she resisted receiving. Caro held out to her, in a generosity that had no bounds, a bountiful gift, always offered, out of the dark place, offered freely and without obligation to the child in Anna.

The first time she wore the tracksuit Audrey laughed and said, 'Damn, it looks terribly clerical' and Tony, the athletic beauty, assessed her for the first time and Caro seemed muddled and confused. But thereafter Anna felt less impeded during the sessions.

She even began to walk from the convent to Fiona's house in the tracksuit. And despite the niggling embarrassment she also felt that she had made some breakthrough somewhere, without having the least idea where from or where to.

And by increasing the number of people she knew she had a different sense of belonging, of being located in the city. She also inevitably saw a lot more of Fiona and that was good. After the early session most of the others had to hasten off, but neither Fiona nor Anna had to hurry anywhere; they shared a knowledge that the whole world was moving into business while they, locked in Caro's rhythm, were still. They drank coffee, chatted and moved slow-paced towards the real day time. A warm hour or so, safe because curtailed and lacking the intensity of late-night conversation. A good time for swapping stories and bargaining against the loneliness they both lived with.

Their histories were so different. The year that Anna had joined her order was the year that Fiona had became a student. They were from different sides of the Atlantic too, and from such different families. Fiona was the only child of an academic household. Her father had been a philologist: Fiona loved the word, it expressed for her his remoteness, his failure to connect with the changes all around her as she grew up. He had been liberal, gentle, progressive and detached. Her mother had been a teacher; a strong believer in women's rights and amazed and delighted at herself for having produced a child at all. Fiona was deeply loved, but nonetheless treated as a slightly eccentric hobby.

She found the lack of stability in Ann's childhood exotic. Five little girls, barely six years apart in age, trekking round the world with their colourful father.

'He sounds amazing.'

'He is, I suppose,' Anna acknowledged, knowing that there was something missing from her description of him. 'Perhaps next time he's in London you'd like to meet him. My friends always manage him rather well.' They smiled at each other because of the move forward, the explicit recognition that they were now friends.

Fiona remained baffled by Anna's casualness about her mother.

'You can't just lose your mother, she must be somewhere.'

'But look, I hardly even knew her. It must have been much worse for Lorraine and Helen. And for my father. He's deeply devout, you see, in his own style. But legalistic. I don't know what went on between them. But in his eyes she had left — she was a Bad Mother, a Bad Wife. He saw himself as guiltless, I'm sure, because whatever had happened before, by running off she had sinned, sinned against the sacraments. Claudia tried to find her once actually, soon after she was married, but not very hard because it hurt him so much. It made him sad, so it didn't seem worth it. And after all we do seem to have survived pretty well. Something Dad did was good, because here we all are, apparently sane and well, all of them except me married. And all of us faithful daughters of the Church, which given the way things are is pretty impressive actually. Dad delights in that, he's quite smug about it. I suppose you can't blame him.'

'Smug!' Fiona was appalled. 'Was his criterion of success really to have you all grow up good Catholics?'

'I don't think so, no, well yes. I think he wanted us to be happy, but for him that would be impossible outside the Church. And also, well you know how many Roman Catholic men have that feeling about women working their salvation out for them, so I expect there was that. Bless him.' A reflex, that 'bless him', it had replaced the feeling of fear she had experienced when she had realised that about him at their last meeting. It was the least that she owed him though, he had given her so much. 'What about you though, surely your family wanted you to stay in the Church?'

'Good God no. It was my final act of adolescent rebellion, I think. Before I settled down to be a good intelligent liberal-minded person like themselves. I'm a convert. Stephen isn't, he's Irish Catholic which probably has a lot to do with it. I met him in the early seventies when he was a member of the intellectual Catholic Left and I was just a good student free floating lefty. You know. Or perhaps you don't of course. These was a time just for a while when, well certainly in England, when we thought we were going to change the world, the New Left stuff. I mean I still am, still a socialist in theory, a Labour voter. But so tolerant, and tolerant of myself. I could not have imagined that then, staying at home and caring for the kid with a mortgage, and Stephen going out every morning to earn his salary — however tastefully in his law centre. Anyway, Catholicism: everyone knows that Marx calls Christianity the opiate of the masses.'

'Even me,' said Anna a little dryly

'Sorry. But he also says about religion that it's the heart of a heartless world. I suppose I found that. And it had glamour too. It drove my father up the wall. And it made Stephen love me. So . . . now I don't know. I couldn't stop but I hang quite loose to it. Take what I want I suppose. Not very credit worthy. I love it, but so many things piss me off; the contraceptive thing and women not being ordained, you know. Or again, perhaps you don't.' Fiona was embarrassed suddenly at mentioning contraception in front of a nun, 'Well you know, all the sexism.'

'Yes, I know.' Anna told her about the way her order and nuns more generally had taken up some of those issues and how she felt inadequate. 'I was never really involved with much of that. It never seemed for me the pressing issue.'

But Sr. Kitty had been raped. The weapon held over women's heads always and everywhere. She had been pressed by the issue. She was being pressed, ironed out by the issue, and she did not know how to say so.

But they were good for her these sane morning conversations. They balanced the dark insane conversations she had with the voices of the Fathers and the non-conversations she had with Caro. But even though they were friendly, even friends, Anna kept her shadows to herself.

She did not know how to admit weakness; she had learned only how to be strong for others — love is patient, does not insist on itself, love is not irritable or resentful. Love bears all things, believes all things, hopes all things, endures all things. It is her duty and her joy at all times to stand witness to the security of the living Christ, the big brother. It is more blessed to give than to receive. She has no right to receive.

She did not know how to admit unhappiness; and the Fathers did not permit her to speak about them, ever, at all. If she told anyone about them they would destroy her, they would pounce down open-fanged, all restraint gone. She had known this from the beginning, and was scarcely even tempted.

Fiona knew there was something hidden in Anna, that often they moved close to subjects and there was a sudden feint, a deft passing, and they would be discussing something else. Fiona believed that she was a person who respected the privacy of others. This was because she desperately wanted her own respected: she did not want to have to look too closely at the web of need, escape, anger and passion which constricted her daily, which bound her to Caro. She did not want to have to examine the gap between the way she thought women should be living and the way she now felt she had to live herself. She was not likely to push Anna towards self-revelation because she knew the mutuality of that task. Anna's secrecy was valuable to her and her company invaluable. Gradually, as Caro's handicaps had become more and more evident, she had seen less and less of her old friends. Their lives and hers no longer meshed. When she had turned to the Church for support with Caro's programme it had been at the same time a turning away from her old social networks of friendship-with-demands-and-responsibilities. That had been hard, too hard to maintain. The Church had an obligation to supply her with the loving support her child needed; it welcomed failure, failure to cope, failure to have perfect children, failure to live a charmed life. Her old friends might have supplied the support but they would have asked for more in return, more of herself. She was not without bitterness at this defeat, and at her own inability to admit to her weakness, guilt, confusion. But she had no time for such confusion. No time, no energy and no courage. Life had become a scrambly thing to be got through day by day; she did not want to have to look at herself too closely. With Anna she got the best of both worlds; the conviction that women were still central in her life, and the knowledge that she would never be pushed towards examining the conflicts of that life. The effort of each day, the continual struggle with Caro and now with Caro's gruelling treatment allowed her to be exhausted, to be taken care of, to flop down in the evening and have her hair stroked by Stephen without ever having to admit to her weakness. She was, if she chose her friends carefully, secure in her virtue.

So their friendship broke through the isolation and loneliness with which both of them were wrestling, but it also protected them. They had a contract of silence.

A silence that was broken in varied, particular ways by Caro. Day after day they would put her on that table and fight with her. The strength of her hatred seemed to grow. Was that a positive sign, something they could be pleased about, that she was stronger, that her memory was developing, that she knew what was happening? Some days it seemed unbearable; it could take the whole team an immense and exhausting physical effort just to work through the minimum cycle of exercise. And the effort was not only physical. Caro existed at these times somewhere in a dark land between being a person whom they acknowledged and recognised even when love was hardest, and being an object they had to manipulate. Was her resistance grief or anger or just a dumb sullen refusal to be moved, like a mountain, an ancient rock. Caro bound them back to their closeness with all that was inert, unmoving, unhuman. And she screamed; sometimes it seemed that her screaming was unceasing, part of a vicious knowing plan to wear them all out, to defeat them.

One day her fury seemed especially brutal. There was no articulacy in her head. Or at least they did not know if there was. Sometimes she screamed and sometimes she did not. Sometimes she burbled, drooling but happy, and sometimes she did not. And between these different noises were silences, and in these silences Anna heard her voice, her words. Today she said:

I am who I am. I am not coming out of this place. It is a bad place, but my place. They have decided I am not good enough as I am. I am not the sort of child they want. They are having another child and they will love him better. You think this time he will be the acceptable kind. You give money and time and sweat and labour but it is not for me, it is for her the little girl you would like me to be. I will fight you. I will fight the good little girl. I am the bad little girl. The tantrums and the dark. I am monster and freak. I sit here in the cellar and I scare you all, because you don't want to know you are me. You are me and I am you and we hate each other. But I won't cheat. I won't come into the light and make it sweet for you. Love the new child. I don't care. I am powerful in my foulness. You cannot escape me. I will fight you all.

But also:

Come and get me. Love me enough. Love me who I am. Come and get me, come and love me. Let me make the terms. I will show you my dark castle and you will never want to go away again. But don't cheat me. Love me or I will fight you and kill you. Kill joy. Kill hope. Kill love.

The new secret baby inside Fiona sang a different song. The new baby inside Fiona tried the steps of the dance; fluttering it attempted the steps of the dance and weightless it danced in joy. Fiona took great care of the new baby; she watched and treasured it, so that nothing could go wrong. She kept all the darkness from it so that it would grow in wisdom and knowledge. She stilled her fears and the baby leapt with delight. It furled and unfurled its flower like tendrils deep inside her.

But Caro fights and fights. The grown-ups who are bigger and stronger than she and know what they are doing and why, spread her out and bend her, they invade her space and push her body about. She screams with the anger and resistance; and then she weeps with the grief and the pain. She fouls the cover on the table, and Fiona is weary with it all. When they lift her down from the table and everyone has rushed off into the real safe world, Caro crumples collapsed and inert on the rug by the fireside.

Suddenly Fiona was exhausted and it was all unbearable. Anna, looking at her, went quietly and made coffee. She brought it to Fiona who lacked the energy even to look up. Caro had been dreadful since hours before dawn. Usually she slept well but some nights the storms inside her could not be contained and last night had been one of these. Fiona felt as though she had been cast up by the storms and laid out like driftwood bleached in the sun. When Anna brought her coffee from the kitchen, Fiona with her eyes half shut saw the tracksuit and did not see the nun. She said, 'Oh God, I don't know how I'm going to cope when the new baby comes.' Her feelings were suddenly stormy again. Perhaps she could not have this new baby, perhaps it would all finally shift from being very very difficult to being completely impossible, and she would not survive it. Perhaps the new child would finally kill dead that remnant of love, tattered and battered, that she had kept for Caro through everything.

Anna was privately delighted that Fiona had acknowledged she was pregnant. Anna had known for a while, and had wanted Fiona to tell her. She was pleased and happy. 'When is it due? This new one?' She had thought she knew the shape of pregnant women, but Fiona was quite different, better fed and better dressed than the women whose pregnancies she had encountered before. And Fiona who was over thirty had only been pregnant once before.

'Oh, not till November.'

While I'm still here, thought Anna with a pleasure that surprised her. Fiona was moved by Anna's pleasure. Now that she had spoken of her weariness and doubt, it seemed utterly right that she should have spoken it to Anna, to the nun and to the person. And having spoken she could not stop. The desperation poured out like a river.

'I don't know any more, I don't know how we'll survive. How can I give both of them what they're going to need. People say, you know people say we shouldn't have another one. That it isn't fair on Caro and it won't be fair on the new one either, having to grow up with her, a freak in the home; and needing needing needing. You know what she's like. But I wanted it so much. And now I'm frightened. I'm frightened that it won't be normal; that nothing good can come out of my insides. I remember and remember how it was and I can't go back to that place. And I can't love her, I don't know how to love her anymore; I want to have a baby who will be lovable and loving. Normal, that's all, just normal. Not a bloody freak who makes people sorry for you on the street. And of course I love her, of course I do. I have to. There is no one else. And I'm so weary and sick of it all. You just don't know.'

She was crying. Anna hesitated, unwilling to expose herself, yet knowing that she had to. 'No, I probably don't know. But you do love her, because you act lovingly towards her. That's all it is. I do know something about holding on to a conviction of love even when you can't find the feelings. Doing the love against the heart. Just staying with it. I do know because that is how God is sometimes with me, and with everyone I think.' She paused, the top of her head feeling naked and cold; this was nun talk and she was not a nun because she was not wearing a veil. 'And I certainly know about being tired. We were all too tired a lot of the time in Santa Virgine.' But that was not what she wanted to say, even though she could see that her words, whatever they were, were soothing Fiona; just having someone there and not having to be alone with her fear. She had to go further. 'Look, I don't want to say that you feel these things only because you are tired, that's the worst.' That is what they had said to her those months at the Mother House: poor you, you're worn out, have a good rest and you won't even think these things. Have a good sleep, have a little nap and you won't bother us with your sadness and your anger and your doubts any more. And it was both true and totally not true. When you weren't tired you could cover the feelings up better. 'But Fiona, tired is tired.' She wanted to touch Fiona, she thought that Fiona would like her to hug her or something but she did not know how to do it, she did not know which bits of herself she could bring into contact with which bits of Fiona. But she had to make a physical gift, she wanted that. 'Why don't I take Caro out for a walk for an hour or so?'

'But you have to go and work,' said Fiona plaintively.

'I doubt if the Dominicans will suffer waiting for me for a day, you know. It's all right.'

It was nearly impossible for Fiona to admit that she had got beyond coping. She knew if Anna had not been there she would have coped because there would have been no choice. Coping and coping and being good at coping was so much a part of what she had become. If she once said 'I can't cope anymore' there was no knowing what might come pouring through the gap. But against that was the sudden unexpected glorious idea of a whole hour without Caro. And a walk might tire her out and she would sleep in the afternoon and then everything might seem better.

Fiona hauled herself up from her tears and the sofa. She bent down to pick Caro up.

'I don't think you should do that,' said Anna sounding unusually maternal and bossy.

'Don't be stupid, what choices are there?' Fiona needed to recover some of her lost ground; even as she spoke she felt both ashamed and toughened.

Together they got Caro dressed and strapped her into her

oversized baby buggy. She was heavy and passive. Fiona said, 'She likes going for walks you know.' And after a pause added, 'Please don't let her get too cold. Or yourself too bored,' she added as an afterthought.

'It won't bore me.' Anna felt quite excited at the thought of having Caro on her own.

They went out, Caro and Anna. Anna quickly noticed something: because she was not wearing her habit the natural assumption was that she was Caro's mother and there was no mistaking the looks of both compassion and thinly veiled disgust. How did Fiona live through that? She looked down at Caro whose expression was suddenly absent. How did Caro live through that? Her head lolled over. She was who she was.

Damaged. Damaged. Damaged. Inside all of you is me. The screaming. The no words.   Incontinence. I made different choices, not towards the light and bright. Gold flames and singing. I carry your darkness too. I am the dark hole under your careful houses. In the cellar there is rottenness. I am where you might be and I cannot be moved. You left me behind. You make me carry the darkness of not-made. I am creation's joke.

What is human? you ask and you answer it is words you say and reason. It is conscience and thinking about others. It is speech and responsiveness and social. So I am not human I am animal. I am freak. I am in you.

Anna was frightened of Caro now; but Caro sat inert in her chair and did not care. She was like the great weight of poverty and brokenness. She was like the great hidden place inside Anna; the child who was given no space and so took it, swallowing in love and energy and woman-hours and effort and commitment, swallowing it in, gulping it down and giving nothing back.

'Caro,' said Anna, in a voice of schooled tenderness. 'Shall we go to the sand-pit? Shall we go to the park and play?'

Shall I be good-with-children? and earn a reward for holiness and good deeds?

No, snarls Caro, although her head is still limp against the handle of her chair.

No, there is no cheating me with those things. There is no cheating yourself. If you loved yourself, all of yourself, in the dark corners and the tortured dreams and the dirty bits which are without words, without names, which were forgotten when the sweet brooding dove called all things out of chaos, if you loved yourself down into the darkness, you could love me too, because that is where I am and who I am.

They went to the playground in the park and Anna poured sand into Caro's hands, trickled it through her fingers. Stimulation, sensory experience is very important for Caro, she remembered Fiona saying; but Anna felt torn apart by the fierce silent voice with which Caro mocked the accepted reality of the city.

IV

As working became harder and harder, the excuses easier and easier, her guilt level rose. She would sit staring at books, her will flexing its trained muscles and defeated by something new, some blankness, some inner withdrawal. Her sense of duty did not give up easily. She would sit there, books open in front of her and struggle with her inability to read them.

Discipline. Discipline. Taking the discipline. Her order had never practised that: it was more for contemplatives. When as a scrupulous teenager, she had tentatively asked if it might be good for her, her confessor had teased her gently, told her if she could not find enough mortification in the social world then she couldn't be looking very hard. She had longed though, an adolescent longing, for the drama of it she supposed. Some Benedictines still did: once a week, the long knotted cords, a self-inflicted whipping. A little stinging to remind one of the flesh.

Later, though, she had not wanted to be reminded of the body that she carried about with her. She would have laughed at the idea of the discipline, as the sort of old-fashioned rubbish that had gone out with the reforms, along with walking with lowered eyes and curtseying to Mother Superior, as though to Christ. But now. Now she needed discipline. Her mind wandered and she could not hold it prisoner and slave. The Jesuits in Brazil had penned the native Indians in corrals and treated them like slaves, to 'protect them'; to protect them, they said, from being made into slaves. Like women, like women now. Men offered to protect women from other men, but also the Jesuits had wanted to protect the Indians from themselves, from their own undisciplined passions which would threaten their immortal souls. Like women

74

pinned in kitchen or convent — to protect whom from what? Were the rules of enclosure, applying to women religious only, to keep the nuns in or the evil out? Whose evil? And still she was not concentrating.

Confined in the huge circular room full of their own learning the Fathers' voices boomed, bouncing off the walls and echoing in her head; sometimes she was quite alarmed, scared that they might disturb the other readers.

'We will not tolerate idleness,' they shouted at her. 'Work. Work harder, *ad majorem gloriam dei*. The Devil finds work for idle hands, idle brains, idle hearts. Idle. Idol, idolatory. Discipline, order, industry. Let the idle thoughts find nesting places and they will break you. Keep them out. It does not matter what you feel, only what you do. Break your evil will or we will break you.'

And in sweeter moods, seductive, inviting, 'Come home, Sister Anna, come home. In your Fathers' house there are many mansions, lots of room. Submit to us and we will raise you up. We will say, when you are obedient and broken to our bridle, we will say, "This is our beloved child in whom we are well pleased." We will protect you from everything and especially from yourself. It is so easy. "Come to us all you who are heavy laden and we will make you rest." ' That was not quite right somehow. The quotations that were supposed to sustain her kept going wrong and there was no certainty.

The only certainty was that she could not do her work, and that every time she let her mind go wandering off the Fathers were rightly very angry. This was time that did not belong to her, she had no right to waste it. If she let go of the discipline they would be furious.

The Fathers did protect but they demanded a very high price for doing so. The Fathers ran a protection racket — the Godfathers. If she stopped paying, stopped playing, stopped praying, they would withdraw that protection.

It was the Fathers who could keep her monsters and nightmares in chains. If the price of protection was the dreams of morning, then that would have to be paid. She could not risk it. If she paid the God-fathers what they demanded then they would protect her, from themselves and from herself and from the mockery of the outside world too. The Fathers saw her in her tidy habit, doing mighty works in the hot sweaty city of Santa Virgine, working night and day, tired, devoted, asking nothing for herself except the right to keep the rules and be useful, and the Fathers looked on the thing that they had made and found it good. The rest of the world was pushed back, not allowed to jostle or mock or threaten. The rewards for a fully paid up Fathers' daughter were probably greater than those of a son. The sons come cheaper and without the sweet flavour of victory. The well-behaved Fathers' daughter can be used as a fifth column in the world of women. A drag queen with non-detachable falsies. The sons moreover might well grow up and become Fathers themselves, but never the daughter. She would never become a Father, would never be a god or a power of her own.

'But the rewards have to be paid for. And your price is too high. It will kill me,' Anna tried to bargain with them. 'You are blackmailing me,' she tried to challenge them.

'Be careful,' they said. 'Be very careful. Or you will try our patience too far. Our wrath is very dreadful. Just remember, in the beginning there was not; and we were when there was not. Our goodwill created all things, and we hold it in being. If we are angry it will all go, fall, explode, implode, there will be no more light, no more matter, no anything, nothing real, no ground, no time. Just grey wind and falling, falling, falling. The centre will not hold. We can blow the nucleus out of the atom. This is called Hiroshima and fall-out and megadeath. It is called void, and we own and control it. We hold it on a slip leash and can loose it at our whim. It is ours not yours. You need us and we don't need you. You need us to stay alive. If we are angry we can let you go. It is well known: it is named annihilation, and Armageddon and Doomsday and apocalypse and The End. This is the anger of the Fathers, who hold all things in being. Our anger makes all things unloved, unlovely, unlovable.'

'Stop it. Stop it. What about Christ and reconciliation and sacrifice and love?'

'What about repentance and obedience and work and faithfulness?'

'Leave me alone,' she begged them. 'Just leave me alone.'

'No. Never. We will never ever leave you alone. That you can count on. We will reward you or punish you, but we will never leave you alone. You had better be good; you had better do your work. You had better go back to your convent where the good women are; there alone you may be safe. Shall we tell you some more names for our anger. It is called desecration and violence and Holocaust and rape.'

She had to be rescued, she was too near the edge. Where everything would fall over. And she was: an absolutely material voice broke the silent shouts of the Fathers with a whisper.

'Excuse me, they say, I mean the people at the desk say, that your South American Spanish is excellent. Can I ask you something?'

Anna turned to the voice with a smile of pure relief; a warm and sweet smile of welcome. Perhaps that was the only thing, that smile, that could have made friendship between them possible. Because Karen had not been totally innocent in her seeking out of Anna. She did genuinely need some help with her text, but she was also not above a little nun-baiting. She was wearing a button on her jacket which said, 'Beneath every woman's curve lies a muscle', and it had a picture of Superwoman on it. She certainly could not convince herself that this applied to a neat nun who sat so prissily still over her books in the reading room of the British Library.

Anna's smile warmed her without her even being conscious of it. Suddenly this was not a nun to be teased, but another woman offering her help.

'I can't get this unscrambled,' she said, laying a book in front of Anna. 'I don't have the skills and I can't find a translation.'

Anna looked at the book and knew immediately what it was. She was rather surprised. 'There'll be a Latin translation,' she whispered back, 'but I don't know how you'd look it up.'

Karen looked a bit sheepish. 'I don't read Latin,' she said, 'and how do you know?'

'It's a deposition; there's sure to be a Latin text. But it doesn't matter. Do you want it written out or just read?'

'Have you got time?'

'Better to write it than risk disturbing this place.'

'You're American.'

'Yes.'

'My name's Karen, Karen Lewis. If you translate it for me, from here, just down the page, I'll buy you lunch.'

Anna was as surprised by the text as Karen had been by the smile. She had taken in the jeans and button and physical style quite quickly. Rose of Lima. It did seem improbable. They had, back at home, been bothered by Rose of Lima; on the one hand a saint was a saint, and she the patronness of the Americas. And indigenous and with a real popular cult. But their northern liberal psychologically trained understandings and attitudes had made it hard — well, she had taken the discipline all right. Karen's problem was a grammatical one. Anna had not read this whole text before but she knew it was a report on the ecclesiastical investigations into whether Rose's self-inflicted penances and mortifications could really have been of God, so extreme and bizarre were they. Beatings and bindings and fastings and flagellations. And without the regulatory disciplines of the conventual life, and often against the instruction of her confessor. She'd been a Dominican tertiary and had lived, Anna thought, in the summer-house of her parent's garden. The church had blessed her endeavours in the end; the people of Lima had wanted their own saint. The passage was a bit unclear. Anna ran down the page, sorting it out and writing it all down for Karen. The Fathers retreated, foiled by a genuine act of charity, and thwarted by Anna's competence.

The Beata, very pleased at getting her mother's permission, made herself a chestlike bed out of rough wood. She put a number of small stones — all different sizes — in it, so that her body would suffer more and would not enjoy too much rest, as it might have done on a smoother bed. This bed still seemed too soft, so she put in three pieces of twisted bumpy wood, then seven more, and finally filled up any gaps with about three hundred bits of broken tiles, positioned so they would wound her body. This then was the luxurious couch in which this greedy (unsatisfiable??) lover of the cross took the sleep she needed to revitalise her worn out strength. She always kept a bottle of gall under her pillow, and rubbed her eyes in the evening and her mouth in the morning, in memory of the gall they gave Jesus Christ, her beloved husband on the cross.

She slept for fifteen years on this cruel bed, unless it would be more accurate to call it her cross: she suffered such dreadful pain, that although she was very sweet-natured and courageous about all sorts of pain, she still couldn't lie down on it without trembling and shuddering, and the blood seemed to ice up in her veins, so violent was the feeling of her lower nature at the sight of the pain it was going to have to suffer. When this happened Jesus Christ sometimes appeared to her with a sweet and loving expression and said, to cheer her up, 'Remember, sweet heart, that the bed of the cross on which I died for love of you was harder, narrower and more painful than yours. Think about that and you will feel comforted in the terrible pain you are enduring on your bed.'

In all her frightful disciplines she was not short of resolution; but this spiritual strength did not fortify her body. She grew so weak that her confessors commanded her to use more moderation, at least to get rid of the broken tiles which inflicted the most pain; but she begged them so hard that she was allowed to put them back again, and to sleep on them for the last two Lents of her life. The rigid and intense hatred that she had for her body meant that she always denied it any sort of comfort.

Just reading this tiny excerpt reminded Anna of the other austerities practised by Rose of Lima. The spiked belt she had worn so tight that it had cut into her waist and could not be removed without pulling away chunks of flesh. She had also worn, hidden under her veil, a pewter crown with ninety-nine thorns which she had moved round each day to prevent the skin callousing and tightened on Fridays with strings under her chin; some of the thorns had been over an inch long and when her mother had complained to her confessor he had just bent in a few of the longer ones.

Anna glanced again at Karen sitting a few desks away and wondered why on earth she would be interested in so strange and alarming a phenomenon. She could not help but smile a little wryly; perhaps she did not need to be worrying about her own mental health after all. She stood up and carried the book and papers back to Karen.

'I hope you can read my writing.'

Karen skimmed down the translation. 'Oh yuck! Sorry, I mean

79

that's lovely, thank you so much.' As Anna turned to go back to her seat, Karen whispered, 'What about that lunch then?'

Anna darted a look at the clock and saw it was twenty minutes before her usual lunch break. She wavered. But Karen had already stood up and scooped her things into her bag. Anna consented, good manners ruling and, of course, she had not had lunch with a colleague for a long time. It was a good memory, from college, from work. She was lonely.

They walked out of the library, across the hall of the museum and down the steps side by side. Karen slouched and Anna clipped. They looked odd together. Karen wore apple green boots; they made Anna smile. Karen was suddenly nervous, she had never taken a nun out to lunch. 'Can we go to a pub?' she asked.

Anna had never been in a pub in her life. 'Why not?' she said a bit aggressively, feeling herself at a loss. Karen decided to admit ignorance, 'I didn't know if nuns went to pubs.'

'Neither do I,' said Anna, 'Not many opportunities.'

They smiled at each other.

'Why Rose of Lima?' Anna asked, genuinely curious.

Karen was embarrassed. The whole thing had started because she had wanted to see a nunnish expression when she answered this very question, had wanted to shock and upset. But Anna had left the question too late; she was supposed to have asked it right at the beginning. It had only been half a plan, a moment of mischief, now regretted. 'I'm trying to do some work on women and masochism, sex and violence. I thought God and guilt would be a good place to start.'

And the tears which had dried up since Anna had been in London poured out again. And again she did not know why. She had to stop walking so that they could flow freely.

Karen knew at once that these were not tears of shocked outrage. She did not know what to do. There on the street, beside the overpowering wrought-iron palisade designed to protect the scholarly from the tears of the real world, she was stuck with a weeping nun, a nun whom she had made weep. A woman who was weeping; a woman who had lightened her morning with a smile and helped her with her work without a question. She was ashamed, and also terribly curious. She did what she would have done to any other of her friends who had burst into tears quite suddenly and publicly. She put her arms around her. She was taller than Anna and Anna's head rested for a moment quite neatly on her shoulder. The touch consoled her. She had a tiny fleeting realisation that no one had ever held her while she cried in Santa Virgine or in the Mother House, and the tears stopped.

'I'm sorry,' she said.

'It's all right.'

'No, it isn't.' She would have to explain a bit. She was embarrassed in her turn and heavy with the disgrace of undisguised, undisciplined feeling. 'It's not your fault, it's mine. It wasn't anything you said. It's why I'm here, because I couldn't stop crying.'

She had not expected to tell anyone. She had certainly not expected to tell a fierce young woman who was studying the life of Rose of Lima in order to understand more about guilt and masochism and violence; to a stranger who was buying her lunch. So she found herself telling far more than she had meant, about Santa Virgine, and about the white house on the hillside.

Santa Virgine had been founded in 1574, by a hard case conquistador trained in the Nicaraguan campaigns. Gaspar de Capello had come from Castile as a young man in the wake of the Mexican conquest; he had earned his spurs and his cash in the hot thin waist of America, and had invested every cent of it in the Pizarros' Peruvian venture. He had become rich beyond the dreams of childhood. He had married an Inca, by the rites of the Church, but he had not settled in Peru. The gold fever had eaten into his heart, the dream of El Dorado. History then lost him in the Caribbean for over ten years, whence he emerged with yet another licence for the interior, to find the golden city, the golden prince. In the higher jungle north of the Amazon he went mad hunting his fabulous wealth, until one night he saw the great white unicorn and followed it. He hunted his unicorn across the mountains and plunging valleys east of Equador, eaten with fever, consumed with madness. Gold forgotten, his proud Inca princess forgotten, Spain and the Empire forgotten. Breaking upwards into the sunlight one day, high and cold under a swooping wind he caught up with his dream. The Holy Virgin, Mary herself, was seated on a throne of gold and jewels and the unicorn was at her feet. So he built a city there, starting with the cathedral, enormous, baroque and flamboyant. The local Indians had understood the worship of a God who was mother, son and horned beast all together. Later it had turned out also that the rocks around Santa Virgine were rich, not with gold but with copper, and the city had grown. But the unicorn had vanished. The slums came instead. The nuns had come to the slums.

'Our Mother Foundress, in the nineteenth century,' Anna now told Karen, 'was an obsessive, which of course is how she made things happen. She had eldorado fever too, though she called it a thirst for souls. She wrote once that El Dorado was the dream that brought Catholics to the New World, and that it was a God-given dream, because El Dorado was obviously just the longing for heaven. Santa Virgine was not actually our first mission, but once she heard the story she wanted to have a house there; she wanted, she claimed, to bring back purity, virginity, Christ and the unicorn. Our mission was established in 1912. We've been there ever since.'

'You really loved it, didn't you?' Karen smiled.

'Yes, I guess I did. I loved the work, it was important, and we were developing some interesting things. Shifting over to a more indigenous model, that was good, and working out ways of moving the church hierarchy, the big boys, further towards the side of the people, the poor. And they did need and want us.'

She heard herself telling Karen about Sr. Kitty and the rape. 'I think we all felt terribly powerless, impotent.' Anna did not know that Sr. Kitty had lain in the mud and wept and watched the unicorn vanish across the night sky. She did know other things. 'We had an unresolvable problem. We couldn't report the rape, we all knew that, and there was nothing else we could do.'

'I don't understand. Why not?'

'Oh God. Political reasons. If we had, the authorities — it's a military state you know — they would have moved in and punished someone, or they might well have, with great expressions of outrage. They might have picked on anyone, some organiser, some radical from the community. Kate, Sr. Kate, one of the nuns there, was absolutely convinced that the rape was actually done by the Security Forces. They wanted us out you see; I don't mean just our house but all the orders like us. The Maryknolls and others. The CIA, too, they might have thrown us out "for our protection", not safe for nuns, not safe for women on their own, not safe for US citizens. Or it might actually have been someone from the community, it might have been, we didn't know, but even if we had known how could we have turned them over, how could we, we were meant to be on their side. We couldn't go running to the enemy just because we needed them to dish out some punishment. But it hurt. It was difficult.'

And it ate them up. The anger and the impotence.

Sr. Kate had burned, burned with anger, and her anger had cut her off from the rest of the community, especially now Anna had left. She was blazing and there was no place for her anger to go. Nowhere except down, down inside her and into the valley. In her dreams she had guns in her hand, bayonets and bullets. Nuns, even Sr. Kate, had difficulties with dreams so violent and so phallic; had difficulties with so much futile anger. And Sr. Kate had to carry the anger for all of them. Sr. Anna had wriggled out, run away, and was now trying to explain it all to a stranger on the other side of the world.

'Sr. Kate was my friend, more than just a colleague. And I could not get in touch with what she was feeling. I couldn't feel anything. I disappeared somewhere and I couldn't find my way back. I couldn't feel anything; I'd sit and watch the others and wonder what was wrong with me. We'd go to Mass or the Office or whatever and I'd feel that the others were praying this problem, and I could not pray. Which,' said Anna, trying to lighten what she was saying, for herself as well as for Karen, 'is very disturbing for a nun. I thought God had cheated, he had smashed something up. But I thought it in my head. Like a child I just thought, "It's not fair", and 'Why poor Sr. Kitty, why her?' But I couldn't feel anything. It was as though something in me had gone dead, and there was Sr. Kitty really handling it very well. I did not exactly feel guilty, but I did feel I didn't have the right to make any fuss.

'Then I started weeping. I just wept. It was foolishness, because I didn't feel sad. Just tears. Finally they got really annoyed with me. It was such a bore for them all. I thought I had been trained to control whatever I was feeling. We're trained not to repress but to construct, construct on the emotion. And I couldn't. And then I couldn't eat, and that was the last straw. So they'd had enough and they sent me home. Packed me off to Mother. I was disgusted at myself.'

'To your mother?' Karen asked.

'No sorry, I don't have one, to the Mother House, to Mother Superior, the head of the order.' She started to cry again. 'Oh dear, I am sorry, this is so boring, so stupid.' And why was she telling it all to this woman? She did not understand.

'As a matter of fact it is totally riveting,' and Karen meant it, 'but I still don't see why you felt so bad. I mean rape is a pretty major experience.'

'But it wasn't my rape. Sr. Kitty didn't need to be sent home.' She'd asked to go home, that was the truth, because she had wanted a hot bath. She could not bring herself to say that.

'That still doesn't get you into the British Museum,' Karen prodded gently, she was expert at this.

'No. Oh dear, are you really interested in all this?'

'Would I be here if I wasn't?' Karen grinned. 'There's only so much due for a couple of pages of translating, you know. I'm no nun, not into your good works. Just go on.'

'Well. Well, I went back to the Mother House, in up-state New York — do you know the Hudson Valley? And then everything was unspeakable, just dreadful for a couple of months. God was very angry with me.'

'What?'

'God was very angry with me. I felt that. I felt that all the time.' How could she speak about the voices of the Fathers without sounding completely mad; how could she tell about the anger of God without telling about the voices of the Fathers? The voices in the desert and the crashing of thunder against the walls of the house and the knowledge that the thunder and the blizzards had come because she was there. The house was not safe while she was in it. She was the focus for the anger of God and the Fathers would descend upon the house and wreak their ancient havoc. The night of the storm, Hagar was driven out into the wilderness with the child in her arms, unsustained, seeing the nakedness of God and having to survive it alone. Hagar had stolen the son-right from the real mother, from she who was princess and queen and mother of Israel. She had to go into the storm not because she loved the child or the father, but because she loved the mother, because she loved Sarah and knew there was not room for two boy children.

'I could not locate, get in touch with, any feelings of forgiveness. I could not repent because I did not know what my sin was. I only knew that God was furious with me, and I had nightmares all the time, they were dreadful. And I could never remember what they were in the morning. I was frightened of God and frightened that my fear would separate me from God.'

Even talking about it brought the Fathers closer; they hovered, they waited. They said, 'You cannot tell our secrets to a stranger. You know that is against the rules. You may not tell our secrets to a stranger. If you do we will kill you. Kill you. Kill. Kill.'

She felt suddenly the weight of their hands at her throat. The tightening grip; she would choke, they would choke her. It was too near now. And here, in front of a stranger. Someone who probably did not even believe in God, in the Incarnation. Karen had no existence, she was outside the circle. Only the Fathers were real. Anna must not speak to Karen about the anger of the Fathers.

'Are you all right?' Karen's voice broke those of the Fathers, dispelled them for a moment. Looking concerned, she leaned across the table and touched Anna's hand. She broke into the circle, physically, and the Fathers had to retreat a little. Anna would not tell, but she was saved, just as she had been saved that morning. Karen had become her saviour. But if a woman can be a saviour from the Fathers; if a single hand on Anna's wrist can drive back the power of the Fathers; can silence the voices of the Fathers; what then?

'I'm sorry,' said Anna. 'It was a very dark time, impossible. I don't really like to think about it. I thought I shouldn't be a nun any more, that I wasn't worthy of it somehow. That my vocation had gone and that God did not want me any longer. In the end I told Mother. Of course they wanted me to stay. They wanted what I had been. I'm a credit to them actually, I'm good at it. I had always been a good sister. Mother didn't understand. But she thought she did, because she had been my novice mistress when I was training. We elected her Mother Superior of the whole order

85

the year I went out to Santa Virgine. She could not know what was going on. I couldn't tell her but she did not want me to leave.'

'That must have been nice.'

Karen had some indefinable quality that dragged confessions out of people; she recognised this and was glad of it; she was the recipient of many secrets and she admired herself for it. Anna was surprised however at her own openness, but she felt it as a relief. She need never see this woman again, after all, and she was more than willing to listen.

'Yes. No. I felt that I'd deceived her somehow, that she no longer knew who I really was. But she was pretty sensible. She came up with the idea that I should take some time off to think about it, so she dreamed up this research project. I was trained in Latin American history you see. I didn't want to go to NYC or to Washington. And I think Mother liked the idea of London because American nuns are all in a state of upheaval and lots of people leave and things, not as bad as it was, but still. I think Mother thought I might get mixed up with all kinds of radical stuff, that England would be more peaceful.'

'But I got the impression that your people are quite into the radical thing anyway.'

'There's two sorts of radical in the Church you know. There's good radical, which is rather strong at the moment among progressive Catholics in the States, especially if it has to do with Hispanic America: it's about justice and poverty and anti-American imperialism and all those things. Then there's bad radical which means criticising the Church itself. And they don't like it if the religious get into that, or not in my order anyway. We're quite good radical and not much bad radical.'

'Sounds like the British left to me.'

'I don't really know much about British politics.'

'Well, same old story, but I'm interrupting, go on.'

'Thats about the end of it I think. I came here and I'm supposed to be here until I work out what I'm going to do. Or until I recover, I think they mean.'

'And what are you going to do?'

'Frankly I don't know. I think whatever I do I shall feel bad about it. So perhaps it doesn't really matter, does it?'

'I imagine it does.' Karen got up at last and went to buy them both another drink. By the time she returned Anna had done some construction work and was ready to behave herself. She could sense the exhalation of pleasure from the Fathers.

'I'm afraid I've been terribly tedious. I am sorry.'

'Look, stop apologising. At the crudest level it can't be boring. When do you think I last had a conversation with a nun? I'll tell you, never. Oh yes, two little ancient ones once asked me the way to the tube station. That's it. So it's bound to be interesting. Why did you go in, or whatever you call it?'

'Well, I had a vocation as they say. I really did. It seemed quite obvious.'

'Obvious to you. How old were you?'

'After college. The fall after I graduated. I did my graduate degree from there. My Masters. I never did a Doctorate, there didn't seem much point by then.'

'What in? Your degree I mean.'

'Spanish American history. I was going to do a thesis on the lost cathedrals.'

'Lost cathedrals?'

'South America is littered with them; the colonialists built them all over the place, often with the stones from the temples of the people they were conquering. Santa Virgine is just one example; huge baroque Counter-Reformation statements, and now the jungle has returned and eaten them up. But you know that.'

'Why ever should I?'

'I thought . . . I'm sorry. Just Rose of Lima and things.'

'No. Wrong end. I'm an unemployed teacher really. Well, not quite unemployed. I teach a bit at the North London Poly — a women and psychology course at the moment. And I'm wanting to write this book, about masochism. The whole porn debate has thrown up so many questions, about women and violence and its representation. And the S and M stuff from the States. So I want to look at it, think about desire and violence. I wanted something from Christianity, what the Church does to women and how that's culturally manifested at different historical points. Someone told me about Rose and I thought my Spanish might be up to it but it isn't and here we are.'

Much of what she said was a foreign language to Anna, but she

87

said helpfully, 'I don't quite know what you're after, but there's a much better example than St Rose if you want something Latin American. There's another saint, Mariana, about a century later, and what she put herself through is extraordinary. Much more extreme. Saint Mariana Paredes y Flores.'

'How do you know?'

'I guess I had a sort of adolescent fascination with them.'

'I'm specially interested in Rose because she was Indian and I wondered if that affected anything, and because she got so much praise from the Church, being made patron of America and that. I mean they really got off on her didn't they?'

'It's not that simple . . . well not altogether. Because of the inquiry. Obviously they were a bit dubious. And not always obeying her director. They were a bit dodgy then, you know, those extreme things, you might get canonised and you might get the Inquisition. There were quite a lot of doubts about her. I can't really remember all the details now.'

Not the ecclesiastical details. But she could remember the physical ones. The summer they had been in Quito she must have been thirteen. She could remember all right. She had been full of the idea of suffering for Christ herself. One day she had wound a length of barbed wire round her waist, under her shirt all day. When her father found out he had spanked her soundly and sent her off to confession with the sin of spiritual pride spiking her soul as sharply as the wire had hurt her flesh. He had been angry. Quite right too, and she had never tried it again. Once, shortly before she had entered the convent, he had mentioned it, rather carefully, a tentative embarrassment. 'Do you remember that summer in Quito? About the wire. Was it, do you think now, was it love of God or something else, something to do with your mother?' He practically never mentioned their mother. It was hard for him to have to do it now. 'Oh Dad,' she had said, loving him desperately, knowing how he was prepared to suffer for her, 'Oh Dad, come on. It was showing off. Simple swank stuff, I was just a kid.' And he had smiled because she had comforted him. There had been a dangerous hole and she had covered it gracefully for him. She had made it all right, but now she had to ask herself how or if it fitted in with the terrors and the things that haunted her dreams. But she was not going to think about that.

She was still frail, not well. It would all go away.

'What sort of adolescent fascination?' Karen wanted to know.

'Well, you know how kids are. We were living in Quito then, which is where she came from, not St Rose, this Mariana. I was a nauseatingly pious child. And full of enthusiasm. Do you have any children?'

'No.' Very emphatic.

'I'm sorry. Would you like to?'

Anna's composure, in the face of her clear inner distress, irritated Karen. Her earlier attempt to shock had failed, but she prickled into another try. People usually gave into Karen very quickly, her own apparent candour opening them out. She had prodded at Anna, and Anna had responded but also dodged. The conversation was interesting enough at one level, but suddenly Karen wanted to understand something about Anna, about being a nun, about the strain she could feel in her. But Anna had thrown the ball deftly back into her court, had called her power as a listener into doubt. The question about children had been innocent, asked with a genuine interest, even if the attempt to bring an end to her own disclosures had been apparent. But it flicked at an old wound, a painful set of assumptions. Whatever Karen's principles might be, they were thought out and worked on and practised diligently. She was not oblivious to Anna's very obvious shift of gears and it made her feel cross.

'It's irrelevant,' she said. 'I'm gay.'

There was a pause in which Karen wondered if nuns even knew what the word meant. Then she realised that Anna was not shocked, not threatened. What had been meant as a weapon had become what it really was, a statement of fact.

Karen was disarmed. Quite suddenly, quite simply. The undermining that had been started with Anna's welcoming smile earlier in the day, with her simple willingness and authoritative competence to help her, was surprisingly completed. She was disarmed at a new level.

She could not know then that part of Anna's calm came from her rigorous training and another part from her total inability to read the social signs: Karen's cropped hair was the same as her own, although hers was mostly hidden under her veil. Karen's single silver earring with the double axe-blade meant nothing, a pretty ornament. Karen's sharp proclamation 'I'm gay' meant to Anna a personal communication, not an aggressive verbalisation of what should have been self-apparent. Anna could no more read the language of Karen's appearance than Karen could read the subtleties of Anna's — the information imparted by length of skirt, style of shoe and type of veil. Two women of nearly the same age and with many shared areas of knowledge and interest, perceiving each other as anthropologists visiting a new tribe. Karen at least was aware of her own social curiosity; Anna was not. 'I'm gay' had no political or social meaning for Anna, though of course she knew what the words meant. It was a place where she had never been or thought to go. It was a strange land, a country as alien as the chapel in Santa Virgine would have been to Karen. Her response was accepting, open, relaxed only because she had no information that could make it otherwise. But that response moved Karen.

Karen was nearly thirty. She had been unduly modest in describing herself as an unemployed teacher. She was a freelance socialist feminist intellectual. Perhaps, profoundly, she wanted to be a writer, but her own theoretical bent made her hyper-conscious of the inadequacies of her work; and she had torn into too many of her friends' productions to be able to count on supportive mercy. Self-deprecating, undercutting her own ideas long before they could surface, instead she wove webs of mean-ing around other people's work. She had written helpful intro-ductions to reissues of books for women by feminist publishing houses, and articles of elaborated theory for avant-garde media magazines; she taught courses at her Poly, did research for Chan-nel 4 documentaries, and a good deal of journalism; and she argued through the nights with her friends about semiotics and the collapse of the Labour Left, about how to recover the social in so-called private life and whether Freud was irredeemably sexist. She lived in a communal women's house, had many friends of both sexes and was part of a real circle of like-thinking people; but she was not like anyone that Anna had ever met before.

Karen was completely honest when she said she was gay: beyond sexual activity and deep in her self-identity. A political, social, final choice. She had grown up slowly, an innocent and beloved child, intelligent, bright, articulate. In her early teens she had been slightly petted by her teachers as well as her parents, because she did not move away from success in their world into the new arena where her girlfriends had gone. Adolescence, puberty, menstruation had come to her late, and long after her peer group had started impugning weird things to the games mistress she had been secretly happy on the hockey pitch. Then at fifteen, with no warning, no planning on her part, she had fallen passionately in love with her history teacher, a young married woman with a small child. Their affair had been embellished with secrecy, scandal and passionate moments snatched at greedily in forbidden places. Karen had lit up not just with lustful desire, which exploded on her with delight and agony, but with heroism, with the need to protect her beloved from the eyes of the world, personified by the headmaster, her lover's husband and her own parents; all of whom took on for her ogreish characteristics. She dreamed that the woman would leave her husband and come roam around the world with her, of waking in the morning with that beautiful face beside her on the pillow, of being free to brush her hair with her lover's hairbrush, and of reaching a triumphant old age in some glamorous fantastic Paris. Her favourite novel became not *The Well of Loneliness* but *Orlando*, which she would read lying on her lover's bed while she babysat for her and her husband when they went out to dinner with his clients. Karen wanted to serve her, help her, and protect her from boredom and the world. Despite the difficulties they had being together and the strains that the secrecy imposed on all her other relationships, she was extraordinarily happy.

After eleven months of this exotic excitement the woman told her one evening that she felt she was too old for Karen and wanted to set her free to find her way among her own age group. When Karen protested that this nobility of soul was quite uncalled for, her lover told her that she and her husband were moving to a new town and that in any case she was pregnant. She begged Karen for the sake of what they'd had together, not to do anything foolish, not to tell the husband, and to cheer up because she was only sixteen and her whole life was ahead of her. Karen never saw her again. She entered a dark hole, a time of infinite pain, when she did no work at school, put on over a stone in weight and roamed the streets at night howling like a cat and plotting elaborate revenges against the woman, her husband and the whole bloody world. Fifteen years later she could describe it like this, even in her own mind; at the time she had wanted not to die, but to suffer and inflict suffering. After four months, wretched, spotty, despairing and in desperate need of consolation she confessed the whole affair to her mother.

'Karen, whatever's the matter with you recently? Have you fallen in love, you can tell me you know. I know what it's like.'

'Karen dear, please trust me.'

'Karen darling, you haven't done something stupid have you? Are you pregnant? Even if you've done something like have an abortion you can tell me, please darling.'

She had told her. Her mother had thrown her out of the house.

On to her feet, retrospectively. She had fled to London and lived with her oldest brother who had taken her side in the inevitable family wrangle. He was a left-over hippy, a pleasant if somewhat inane libertarian who lived with a rather glamorous fringe actress in a shambolic flat full of chatter, every sort of chatter. Karen had surprisingly stayed at school, gone to university and recovered. Two years later she had cobbled together some sort of reconciliation with her mother, her father had benignly restored her allowance and everything had settled down again. In her early twenties she had wondered vaguely if her sexual commitment to other women had simply been a case of taking up the first available option, which although it had flung her into a society where lesbianism was not only acceptable but actually rather trendy, did not seem to motivate her towards any sort of separatism. She had conscientiously tried sleeping with men, both with friends which was snuggly and giggly though not very erotic, and with strangers which was more sexy but fundamentally pointless. She did not question her gayness, but she knew that she had never again experienced the passionate intensity of that first relationship. She liked sex and did it often; she had a series of reasonably stable enduring relationships with women who were now her closest friends, but there was something missing, some wholeness and integration. She struggled with this, wondering if it was something to do with the illicit, the secrecy and inevitability of pain which had made her first affair so definitively different from everything since, but that did not seem a complete answer. She was only half aware, if that, that the missing element was the heroism, the passionate tenderness, the need to take care of the beloved other, the need to cherish, protect, serve. These were not qualities with much social credence in the places she inhabited.

Frightened of and fleeing from her fear and fascination with the illicit, the shadowed, she developed in flight the stance of the huntress — demanding openness, inviting women to bring up everything from the darkness and expose it to her light. She believed in the clean fight of choices. She could not let other women rest in their inner night; they had to emerge, bringing with them all the dwarfs and ogres and monsters. Her self-appointed job in personal relationships, though she would not have said so, was to harrow hell.

So they were total strangers, Karen and Anna, but eager strangers. Karen disarmed and Anna articulate.

When the closing of the pub drove them both back to the library Anna ordered up two more books. One on St Mariana and the other, on a sudden impulse, a book by a contemporary Jesuit on sixteenth-century spiritual phenomena. It was a book she had found interesting years before and half forgotten. His thesis was that there were parallels to be drawn between the discovery and opening up of the New World, by men, and the discovery and opening up of a new range of spiritual experience, by women. His argument collapsed slightly with the male mystics like St John of the Cross, but he redeemed it by arguing a feminine anima model for him, which thinking about it now seemed a bit tenuous to Anna; but indeed the more extreme physical manifestations of ecstatic states — stigmatae, survival without food — did tend to be experienced by women. Were these curious distasteful connections between body and mind a demonstration of a holistic dynamic or were they symptoms of repression, self-hatred and a profound penis envy. Or the reverse, thought Anna suddenly: did men have to realise their dreams physically in the new continent, steal its treasures and bring them back to Spain because they were envious of the New World of the world of spiritual experience into which their women had disappeared.

She ordered the books in Karen's name and hoped that Karen would find them in the morning. She felt oddly secretive and shy. But also freed: for over two hours she worked smoothly and for the first time in weeks with a real sense of interest in her holy conquistadors — the burning fanatics of faith who had followed the burning fanatics of imperialism across the bright and dangerous sea.

And she dreamed of the sea that night, not drowning but buoyant and swimming now, a clear dream, though she could remember little of it in the morning; but she woke at last with a sense of lightness, not struggling up through great weights of blackness and depression into gloom and guilt. She tried not to know that she felt so much better because she had spoken, because she had wept and Karen had received her tears as a gift. There was a great power in naming, calling things by name was the act of creation; the eternal Word naming the darkness and chaining it to light and form. She did not know why she had done so unlikely a thing, and she did not want to understand it. But the lightness continued. She was hungry and ate her breakfast; she smiled at the sisters and walked through the morning streets to Caro with a sense of joy.

After the session she found she did not want to linger in the warm arms of Caro and Fiona's domesticity. As soon as the exercises were finished she wanted to be off; to get back to work, she told herself, I want to get back to work. Caro said,

> Don't leave me, don't leave me for the sunlight. Stay. That is too easy. Stay with me and go the whole way. We have something to do together and I won't let you escape. I am jealous said the growling voice. I'll be jealous and sad if you choose the light. That's too easy. Stay in the dark places with me, we belong to the dark, we freaks. I won't play with you. I will sulk and roar. You will never learn my secrets. I won't come out and play. You will be the loser, not me. And I won't care.

Anna told her as silently that she was sorry but today she had other things to do. Not forever, just for today. She fled before the softness of Fiona and the dark voice of Caro could ensnare her, although she did not know what her haste was. She plunged down into the tube and packed herself in with all the others. Densely packed, damp and steamy together, she had a moment of pure nostalgia for Santa Virgine. She did not want to be in this foreign place, doing this foreign task of digging over the bones of dead priests, but back in that bright and squalid intensity.

And with that nostalgia another, unexpected and sweet. She wanted Kate. Even in the cramped tube she could not suppress a smile of delight at the way that Kate was absolutely present to her, exasperated, determined, irritable and her sister. How are you? she asked the image, what are you doing? Is it fun? And Kate smiled too, equally suddenly. Her anger still there, but momentarily radiant, golden, the bright and shining anger of the warrior woman, of St Joan riding out on her horse in her armour, wrapped around with her inviolable virginity and her piercing clarity. Kate was on the move again, no longer trapped, stuck, shadowed. Anna saw Kate with her machete cutting through the swampy jungle of wrath. High above her the green canopy was broken here and there by soaring hard-woods, and in the columns of sun that filtered down, great butterflies danced in the green sweating air. Kate was cutting her way free and she turned to smile for Anna, to urge her too to cut her way out. Across the great salty ocean they smiled and touched each other very briefly, while Anna felt claustrophobic against the too many bodies of the London underground and Kate sweated against the restrictions of the jungle undergrowth. Then refreshed by the contact they both returned to their hard tasks.

But when Anna emerged from the tube it had started to rain. The cold rawness of it when she felt that it should be summer made her feel not miserable but suddenly splendidly angry. Unlike herself, she barged with a tense ferocity through the people cowering under the canopy of the Dominion theatre. She was privately amused by their looks of shock.

She turned into Great Russell Street and as always the crowds were left magically behind, though the rain was not. But her temper refused to be soothed. One hundred yards up the street, completely unexpectedly she had a revelation. It was so abrupt that she walked another five or six steps down the street before jerking round as though to run back and catch it.

She knew absolutely that she minded passionately about the rape; and she knew why. In the brilliance of the knowing she even knew why she had not been able understand before. If God was not going to protect his holy virgins, what the hell was the point of becoming one?

The purpose of the Fathers is to protect the daughters. Of the man to protect his woman. That was their justification for everything. That was what the whole deal was. If they weren't going to do it, if they could not do it, then who needed them? She had sold out to the highest bidder; the One more powerful and loving than her own father. The price had been astronomical, and she had paid it, and it had been a con. Had she failed to read the small print, like the foolish virgins? No. She had been conned.

She spread her macintosh to meet the rain. She would be witch and wild thing. She owed them nothing. They owed her.

Damn you, she yelled silently.

'Sorry,' they said, 'that's our privilege.'

'Shut up' . . . but she faltered, afraid. 'You betrayed your own son. You taught all the Fathers how to betray us.'

But in the face of her challenge the Fathers beat a strategic retreat. They were no longer present. Don't play those tricks with me, she shouted. Standing in the fierce wind that whistled through Bloomsbury, unleashing the power of the Fathers . . .: of all the Fathers she had thought to serve by becoming a holy nun. On the wings of the wind they returned, choosing their own time, their own moment. She could not control them, she could neither summon nor dismiss them. Their sudden retreat unsteadied her, and their swooping return terrified her, on the instant.

'Don't you dare,' they said, 'don't you dare. We can take everything away. We can take it all. Love. Work. Words. Sanity. Order. We made it all. We made it all.'

'Before there was creation there was chaos,' but her words seemed frail, without conviction. While theirs were uproarious and strong: 'We will punish you.'

'It's not fair,' she cried, standing there, her mac flapping, looking like a mad woman on those streets populated with mad women; middle-class mad women, she lashed at herself with the insult.

'Fairness is neither here nor there. Justice however we invented. If you do your bit we will reward you. But we won't tolerate tantrums. We don't allow loss of control. We will withhold the words and you will drown in the void.'

She groped for the anger and the strong sense of herself that she had found in her moment of revelation. She knew that there was some way to contest them, but she had lost all sense of what it was. She wanted to tell them that they had only the power she had given them, only the power that a social structure and years of experience had given them. But she was paralysed, she had lost the words. But she also knew that she had changed direction, she had forced them to withdraw, she would hunt them now, she was greedy to taste their flesh, even in the depths of her fear she was greedy for the hunt. 'I shall hunt them,' she told herself, though in a whisper so they could not hear her. 'I shall hunt them down, I shall find the power of the holy virgins, Mary and Artemis, and I shall hunt them down.'

She was foolish to think they would not hear. She should have run away; there was a difference between courage and boldness. They heard all right and changed their tune, not angry now but mocking and disdainful. 'The holy virgins', they told her, 'defend only virgins. Only the pure. Your dreams are not pure. Your mind is not pure. Blessed are the pure in heart for they shall see God. You are filthy. You are muck. You are bad.'

It was only afterwards, after she had staggered into the library and hidden herself between the covers of some dreary apologist that she remembered that both Mary and Artemis had also taken women in labour under their protection. But the Fathers had vanished, fattened on their victory. She must study the spells of summoning, she told herself; she always let them pick the ground, have the advantage of surprise, and they always attacked when she was defenceless.

She had given up her witch power, like all women. She had sold her birthright for a mess of potage. Moreover she had drunk the potage so that it was hard to ask to swap back again. There were spells of summoning and spells of exorcising. The latter were easier to use. Anna did not yet know that. Virgins did in fact have enormous power; they could summon and tame unicorns. But she wore a gold wedding band on her left hand; was she still a virgin? Karen on the other hand had sex with people ('I'm gay,' she had said, 'I fuck with other women.') but had given nothing away to the Fathers. Was she a virgin? Or, more simply, were virgins, in a place the unicorns have deserted, now redundant to need?

What is this idiocy, she asked herself severely. What is the matter with you? Where do all these bizarre ideas come from?

But before she could think about it too much Karen came crashing through the swing doors and Anna grinned and ducked her head back into her books, and knew that she was pleased to see her.

Karen too was pleased. And especially when she realised that Anna had ordered the books for her. She was curious; and she loved her own social curiosity, it amused her. Her streak of irony was not very deep but it was strong: she liked the oddness of herself knowing and liking a nun; she knew it would bemuse her friends and that in itself amused her. Like a big game huntress with a new trophy she wanted to be seen with Anna and be friends with Anna. And beneath that there was something more; she was attuned to, sensitive of something in Anna — not just the tears, evasions and pain, but especially Anna's distance from her own body. As though inside the habit there was nothing there. She was aware of that and it made her curious. More than curious, it was something she wanted to explore, to open out. For Anna's own good she would have said, but not only.

She found the second book that Anna had ordered for her both interesting and infuriating. She was eager to criticise it to Anna, to expose its fallacies, and phallocentricities. She prepared an argument about it in her mind even as she skimmed through it at great speed. She would lure Anna out of such delusions. The writer assumed, for instance, on no argued basis, a profound and innate and eternal difference between women's and men's 'natures', especially in the area of imagination. But at the same time he also argued that there was a *Zeitgeist*, a cosmic mood of the moment, and men and women were eternally bound to be engaged simultaneously in the same adventure.

She was riveted by the spiritual phenomena too; delighted by so concrete a demonstration that different societies could from the same set of facts, construct interpretations so radically opposed that what would in one culture make you a saint would in another land you in a lunatic asylum diagnosed as suffering from a great range of psychoses from anorexia to schizophrenia.

Guilt and joy seemed from this argument to induce the same clinical symptoms. The man could not really be listening to what he was writing. But the imagery was not trapped by his flimsy theorising: the voices from the dark new continent and the voices from the convent cells were strong and real and full of power. The passion for Christ was passion, and so was the passion for gold; simple lust and often lust fulfilled, satiated, smug, even as she often felt after good sex and musical orgasm. The same tone. Had Anna given her this book because she agreed with it? The huntress in Karen was manifest now. She would not, she decided, go and speak to Anna until she had read enough of the book to form the basis of a whole conversation, an excuse for another lunch, a reason to engage.

She was prowling, predatory for Anna. Predatory but not destructive, because there was a careful tenderness in the memory of Anna yesterday; but greedy for knowing, for getting inside. And for shaping, teaching, redeeming, bringing back again.

So tentatively, during the day, they became friends.

'Stuff work today,' Karen would say, extracting Anna from the library and laughing. She laughed because it always took Anna exactly half an hour to overcome her guilt. 'I can't,' she would begin. 'I really can't, not today. I have to do some work.' And she would sit dutifully at her place and start to read, taking careful notes in her tiny handwriting. Karen would wait, sitting a few places away, her smile nudging at Anna. And after about twenty minutes it would occur to Anna that the books she needed would have to be ordered and were bound to take hours if not days to arrive; or a quick break would clear her head; or that poor Karen was obviously stuck with her own research and might need some help, or at least companionship. She could find an infinite variety of excuses and all of them overlaid the truth which was that she wanted to be with Karen. Karen could silence the voices of the Fathers. She could also silence Anna's sense of herself, of her uncertainties and confusions. She could, also, blot out Anna's integrity: confusion did not seem to exist in her, and it was terribly easy to accept her definitions of reality because they were so forceful and clear. Anna could find no way to contest them, to allow her own ideas to compete with Karen's. Sometimes she felt wildly freed in Karen's space, but at other times wiped out, defeated. But Karen did sweep away her pain. She could make Anna change, she could make change possible. She could give Anna a new framework. Anna had never in her whole life been close to someone who believed, not just as a personal observation, but as a framework, a solid clarity, that being a nun was a bad idea. Karen did not question Anna's vocation: she questioned the whole concept of vocation, of God, of faith.

But she was fun and she took Anna to places she had never been before.

'Let's go to Kew Gardens today.'

'Why Kew?'

'Because we can sit in the tropical house and understand more of what it means to live in Equatorial America. It's research, very valuable. You have to enter into the physical dimension as well as the cerebral one.'

'But Karen, I did that for years. I mean I lived it for real.'

'Reality is subjective, and you need reminding. Anyway, an artificial construct concentrates the mind more than a real one. The Purpose of Art.'

'Like the Mass.'

'Trust you. What does that mean anyway?'

'I'm not sure — it was a sudden thought. You see the sacrifice of Christ is constant, timeless, continual, eternal. But in the Mass we concentrate the moment, recreate it in the present tense. It is an art form in that sense.'

'Oh hell,' said Karen irritated. 'I can't cope with words like "Eternal"; I just can't cope with that concept.'

Anna was baffled by this; they did not even seem to have a vocabulary in common. But she was also challenged. 'What does that mean anyway?' she asked, mimicking Karen.

'Well it means what it says. Especially at the level of imagery which is I suppose what you're talking about. I think images, and values, whatever, are socially constructed. I mean that we actually create reality, or what appears to be objective reality, as we live it out in our historical context. We make it, it doesn't make us. It's socially constructed within culture. And that means incidently that it can be socially deconstructed too, by a process commonly known as *revolution* if you've heard of that.'

She could hear her own voice sounding snide and disagreeable, and she was cross. But Anna took her quite seriously and commented. 'You may be surprised to know that quite a lot of theologians now would agree with you; that their concept of God is open to what is called passibility, change, and even that we do so to speak create the God we deserve within a historical process.' Why she wanted to say, why are you so determined that I'm stupid? She felt challenged to sharpen up what she did think so that Karen would not think her stupid. But she found it hard to argue with Karen, hard not to accept her terms and terminology.

And Karen did not like being lured back into theological discourse; she wanted to bring Anna out of there, not go in herself. Increasingly they found it easier to avoid theoretical conversation altogether. So instead they rode the Piccadilly line to Kew Gardens. It was a bright sunny day and there were not many people on the tube beyond Earl's Court. Karen prodded at Anna, but gently. Tell me about your life in Santa Virgine? Tell me what you did, daily? Tell me about what you thought when you were sent home? Would you call that a nervous breakdown? How can you be a well woman if you don't involve your body, eat, exercise, love it? Tell me more about Latin America? Tell me funny and charming stories about your sisters. Make being a nun into an amusing hobby, a hilarious thing to have done in the past, something you are distanced from now. And Anna responded gleefully, punishing the sisters, punishing Mother Superior for letting her go, for their failure to understand her and keep her safe, for their failure to let her have as much fun as she was having with this unapprovable woman.

They played all day in the beautiful gardens. In the hot house with its high glass roof which cut it off from the outside weather Anna tried to explain that the jungle was not like this, not neat and tidy and warm, but a chaos of dreams broken and lives smashed and greed and gluttony and sweat and hope and muddle. And violence. She wanted to describe that, the daily political social and meteorological violence, but she found it too hard to express, too dangerous and suddenly too near. She shied away from the closeness between violence and joy, and instead delightedly she encouraged Karen to teach her how to play. Karen ran up on to a filigree balcony and, loudly unashamed before the other visitors, demanded that Anna imagine she was a

101

dangerous prowling blow-pipe bearing Indian. And Anna entered into that and acted out, with considerable brilliance, the part of a charming but zealous nun, frightened of the Indian but determined to be brave for the Church's sake, well trained in liberal respect for 'other more primitive cultures' but who nonetheless felt a deep duty to convert the 'downtrodden natives'. Again she had been seduced into mocking her own reality, into remaking it, but she also saw in the response to her own very subtle satire a waking of admiration and respect in Karen. And that was pleasing. But there was something healthier as well: a child in her was released whom she had not even known existed. Not the dark child that is Caro, but a happy new little girl who wants to play and play and have someone to play with.

V

Even before she was clear about what she was working towards Karen was both careful and crafty. Tender towards both Anna and herself. She could feel the power of Anna's strangeness, and she knew she had to hold on to the wholeness of her own life and not get sucked into Anna's dark and isolated places. She wrestled with the tug of her own romanticism, her desire to take Anna away to some beautiful island and keep her there until the emerging child was grown up and they could delight in each other. She knew that it was crucial both to preserve her own social existence and to open it up for Anna.

'I'm off to a meeting tonight.'

'What about?' Anna would ask, at first politely, and then with increasing interest. To Anna's surprise Karen did not go to meetings about how to get more women into parliament or even how to prevent the closures of hospitals like Audrey did. Anna had supposed that that was what active feminists did. But Karen had told the truth that first lunch they had had together: she was not into good works. Nor, it seemed to Anna, was she into personal ambition. That was something they did share, closely, the sense that the right way to live was as part of a group, a unit in a social system. And Karen often seemed to have a better sense of how to do this than Anna felt she had herself, despite the long training in community life. Better indeed than most of the self-declared feminist nuns she knew in the States who talked a lot about 'liberating communities' but who seemed to be working towards autonomy, singleness, more space for individualism. She increasingly liked to hear about Karen's interests and increasingly felt herself cut off from real truths and possibilities by some limitation in her vocabulary, her methodology, herself.

But at other times she would feel infuriated by Karen's theory, abstractions. She wanted to tell Karen that abstraction meant only 'sucking out' and that was what Karen did; she sucked out the interest, content, but left the real form, the material reality aside. She wanted to cry and shout at her, 'You sit spinning theory, spinning words like a demented spider, but they're just games, your clever structures. They don't support anything. They don't create anything. You don't know, you don't taste what reality is. You talk about socialism and it is nothing but a word game; you don't know about poverty and oppression, you don't know and you don't want to know. Your skin doesn't stink of it. You don't know about commitment, about holding on.' She envied Karen her apparent freedom from liberal guilt, but she also hated her for using words that no one outside her charmed circle could understand, for confusing and bewitching and endangering those values which at least were actively involved in the struggle to change things. She did not know how to say those things, how to be angry with a friend, how to risk revelation. She let Karen get away with too much and then blamed herself. Sometimes she would find she had agreed with things that she did not believe, had agreed with Karen because she wanted to agree with her and her own thoughts had been wiped away. But the new ideas were rooted and interesting and needed grafting on, needed to be acknowledged. She was confused and out of touch with what was happening. But excited, expanding, delighting.

And during the nights they were not such good friends. Anna invaded Karen's dreams and that frightened her. Anna was at some level untouchable; in need of protection and tenderness. But in the night Karen's dreams violated her. She sought in her dreams to learn and know what Anna's skin was like under the habit. She hovered, wanting to break in, break down, crack Anna's shell, burst her open. There was violence there and she knew it. In her dreams a dark and dangerous shadow would argue, persuade, impel the idea that Anna wanted, needed to be broken into, that it would be good for her. In the dark morning spaces Karen tasted her own power and knew that she could bore a great hole in Anna, and out of the hole would come disintegration and collapse and passivity. Her dreams made her know that she did want some of that; to smash Anna up and out of the heap of rubble, make something new, something of her own. She hated Anna's God and Anna's commitment. She wanted to destroy, she wanted to recreate. And she was scared of the potency of those dreams; not the sexuality exactly which she thought she could cope with, but the power, the power to hurt, to break, to remake. When she tried to talk to her friends about it she knew they did not understand and did not really want to. It was Karen's new freak; her new hobby. They teased her about it. Was she in love with a nun? How did she plan to represent the cultural symbolism of that? 'Just a friend,' she'd mumble, 'we're just good friends.' And then she would have to laugh at herself, and she did not like that either. Inside her head she knew she was becoming obsessed. Just getting Anna to leave her Jesuits and come and play each day felt like a major victory. But the tenderness was there too. Karen knew for the first time that she was going to have to discipline her loving, and she did not like that either.

During the nights Anna dreamed as well, but in the morning she could not recall the places where she had been. She would wake sensing the dreams vanishing, disappearing into a fog. Then she would lie in the dark trying to think, trying to find a way back to the clarity which less than a year ago had been her own possession; the sense of direction, of certainty and of approval. She would struggle to discipline her mind, to think clearly about her work, or towards making some decisions about what she wanted for her life. Some mornings the very idea of life without the order was unspeakably painful and she would plan to fly back that day; and other mornings, apparently the same with the same grey light sneaking in through the thin curtains, she would feel nauseated at the thought of ever returning. She endeavoured to construct tidy pros and cons columns in her mind, to organise her thoughts about vocation, about the value of perseverance, about covenant relationships. The trouble with the idea of covenant was that its very terms meant that you could not assess whether it had been worth it or not until it was too late, until death and judgement. If you did not work it through to beyond the end you would never know what would have happened if you had. Her mind would skid away from so intolerably rigid and hard an idea. She could not focus, her thoughts slipping sideways and in and out of her mind like worms, and burying themselves where she could not find them. Often in the chilly hours she would perceive Kate quite clearly and reach out for her, wanting her to come and help.

But Kate had chosen a different way. The two of them had split the images between them. There was a deep horror in the virgin too. There was the moment when Artemis turned her head, splashed her fingers in the water and let the man who was watching her be devoured by his own dogs. There was Kore, the bloody one; she left nothing to the hounds, she did her own killing. Her altar was virginal, but decked with rotting bodies, with destruction, and she howled her laughter.

Anna and Kate had been sold a serene virginity; a pure and spacious freedom. They had broken the backs of their own desires on the flaming wheel of St Catherine. They held a world of pain in their hands and smiled on it as on a child. But it was not an innocent child; it was a source of anger, ocean deep, which had to be acknowledged. No one had thought to warn them of the turning point, of the moon's waxing and waning. They fell away from that serene Virgin Mother into dark places. There was Anna's place of passivity, of denial, the place where Persephone was raped by the God of Hell and then desired to stay with him in the darkness for a very long time. And there was Kate's place of fury, where the young bitch wolves not yet come to their first heat descended on the sheep pens yowling in the manic blood greed and there was neither sense nor purpose in their killings.

Anna and Kate did not know that they should have paid their homage to the dark side of the moon: that they needed to face its power. Fury or stupor would dominate them because serving a God whom they were taught demanded abnegation, they went out stripped of all possessions and had no gifts left to lay on the shrine of the shadows. Kate and Anna had fallen apart, toppled from the sturdy safety of sisterhood and succour. They had balanced too long on the frail tight-rope, trusting too much in the laws of causality laid down for them, trusting in the counterweight of the other, never seeking or finding their own.

Now Anna, as the summer dawn inched into her cell, could

not clear her head long enough to find Kate in the jungle. She fretted over her loss. She must write, she must write to Kate, she thought. But she did not. She forced herself out of bed instead and put on the good habits of a nun. She said her prayers dutifully, clinging to a perfect recitation of the psalms. Each morning she climbed away from her own darkness by a conscious effort of the will. The will can conquer infantile feelings, she told herself sternly, if you would just discipline yourself, work harder. The Fathers patted her on the head. Today at least it would be all right, she could keep it all together. She had to keep it together. The alternative was not acceptable.

But she did not attempt to stop seeing Karen. Indeed it never ocurred to her to do so. Friendship was good not bad. Being with Karen made her happy. She refused to listen to the warning voices; she tried to insist to herself that they were only the voices of her sickness, the voices of her unwellness — both the Fathers and Caro — and that Karen, and her bright playfulness, was the shape of sanity and health. A simple friendship; and she hid the rest, denied the nervous excitement and the sadness she felt if Karen was not in the library when she went. She denied too the annoyance that she felt with Karen's friends, the sudden stabbing pang she had experienced when she had been introduced to Karen's 'best friend' Sybil, and even the relief that had flooded her when she had later met Sybil's lover Judy. She did sense somewhere though that these women did not like her, could not see her, did not understand why Karen wanted to spend time with her.

Karen knew though that at least one reason why it was difficult for the two of them to find a social context for their relationship was because of Anna's habit. It was that simple. Her appearance made it practically impossible for the sort of women she knew to see through it, or round it, to see Anna at all. They found it easier to allow a constraint to fall on them, a loss of the sense of what was appropriate, and then to tease Karen, than it was to wrestle with it. And why should they have to, why should they have to wrestle with it, she asked herself angrily. She did not like the way their relationship was forced, by its own inherent difficulties, into so much privacy, so cut off from the rest of her life. She wanted to welcome Anna in, she thought they both needed Anna to be welcomed into her whole life; it would offer both protection and strength. She did not want them to be driven out on to a lonely road with stark confrontational dependent choices; she did not desire to be either Naomi or Ruth. But there was something else too, something she had to acknowledge in herself and which she did not like at all: she liked Anna's isolation, she liked the power that she had over Anna because Anna had no one to balance against her. She particularly liked her role as teacher: Anna, she knew now was clever enough, but she did not know about the things that Karen knew about, and she wanted to. Karen was more arrogant, she did not perceive the things that Anna could have taught her and Anna was not able to assert them. But she was receptive and eager to learn and Karen found that this was one of the most endearing things about her, one of the sweetest parts of their friendship. Of course Anna had told her about Fiona and Caro, but because she could not tell Karen about the voices of the Fathers she could not explain about Caro, and so she presented her relationship with them almost dishonestly, entirely in terms of charitable work, helping Fiona with Caro's programme, the sort of thing that nuns had to do.

Anna could stifle the sense of being struck dumb which she sometimes experienced with Karen mainly because she felt increasingly excited by the intellectual tools that Karen was offering her as a gift. Endeavouring originally out of good manners and loneliness to enter into Karen's passions, she now felt as though her brain was waking up afresh from a spell laid upon it long ago. She was eager to learn, to absorb and to wrestle with ideas. They were useful too in her private struggle to find answers to the problems of Church history. Karen loved her eagerness, loved finding ways for Anna to enter into new areas, new subjects, loved protecting her from ideas that were too threatening. She always loved teaching, a born pedagogue, but with Anna it was relaxed, unprepared, warmly personal.

One day she decided on an impulse that she wanted to give Anna a present, buy her a book, partly to illuminate something she was trying to explain, about how she believed that mythology was born out of quite specific ideology and social and historical need. Anna was trying to cling to a more universal symbolism, a psychic patterning that was transhistorical, a Thomistic model.

'You'll end up as a bloody Jungian,' Karen teased. 'I'm sure that Catholic teaching doesn't permit that either. Look, come on, we'll go find you something. Not in the library, something of your own. It will make a change from the library anyway.' And she dragged Anna off to her favourite book shop. Anna felt humbled and stupid, like a panting puppy trying valiantly to follow where its owner led, but when they entered the bookshop it turned out to be the one managed by Audrey.

'Hello Anna,' said Audrey, 'did Fiona send you?'

'Hello, no I didn't know this was your shop. What a coincidence. Here's an advertisement for you — I've just been brought half-way across the city by someone who says it's their favourite shop in London. Karen, this is Audrey.' Karen was scowling and Anna did not understand why.

'I need a copy of *Tearing the Veil*,' said Karen abruptly and Audrey went to get it for her. She stood by the till easy, ready to chat, and Anna was suddenly pleased with herself; it was nice, it was very good that she knew these two women and could introduce them to each other, could bring two separate parts of her fragmented life together.

But Karen was furious. She stormed out of the shop dragging Anna with her. 'Why didn't you tell me you knew her?' She felt like a fool and she hated it. She felt as though Anna had deceived her, tricked her, conned her. Her anger swelled.

'Knew Audrey?' asked Anna surprised.

'Knew Audrey Poole.' Karen was already realising that her anger was inappropriate, silly, unhelpful, and she was unable to control herself. 'Just happened to know one of the most respected, the most influential feminist writers in London.' She did not know Audrey Poole, not on those relaxed terms that Anna did. If Anna knew Audrey she might know all sorts of people and Karen had spent over a month imagining her so sweet and innocent and lonely in London; and herself, damn it, as Anna's only access to the brave new world of feminism, as Anna's only way out of her sanctity trap. She found too that her respect for Anna had been increased by Audrey's obvious friendliness, that they were more equal than she had thought, and that ought to please her and it did not. She knew quite suddenly that she was bitterly, painfully jealous, and that she had no right to be, that this was pathetic, that Anna was a grown-up and her friend not her child, and that somehow the whole thing ought to be easier now, that she ought to be joyful and she could find no joy. All the complicated messed-up suppressed feelings erupted and she knew exactly what it was she wanted from Anna and she wanted it now and she was not going to get it.

Anna said, 'Is she? I never knew that. She's just someone who works on that brain-damage programme I told you about. She's very nice.' She was aware of Karen's anger and fought to ignore it, to pretend it was not there. She did not want to have to deal with that. Karen liked to have her rages met head on; when people were frightened of her explosive temper something in her shrivelled, she could not contain her own power. She wanted her friends to stand up to her and balance her alarming loss of control with their own strength. She was scared when they could not. Her fear drove her into ever wilder expressions of rage. Now, as she turned towards Anna, frustrated, furious, unhappy, scared, she was looking for a weapon, any weapon. Anna, struggling against the dark power of Karen's wrath had moved inside the structured control of her training; she seemed so far away, so contained and inaccessible, and also so frightened; and that did nothing to soothe Karen's flames.

'Do you always have to wear that stupid uniform?'

Anna was completely taken aback by the unexpectedness of the attack.

'That idiotic costume. You hide behind that preposterous garb and it's impossible for anyone to find you. It's bloody cowardly. You talk about being unhappy in your pinched little life but you daren't try out one little thing to change it, do you? Just try being an ordinary unprotected unspecial mortal woman for once. You don't even know who Audrey Poole is because she wouldn't like to mention anything as interesting as feminism while you're lurking about looking as through butter wouldn't melt in your sweet little mouth. Can't you see the problems my friends all have with it? Can't you see that their good manners put a restraint on every damn conversation we might have with them? It's selfish; it just lets you out. Wrapped in the robes of a pretty bogus bloody purity you can get away with bloody murder. It makes me sick.'

110

Karen did not know that Anna had heard all those accusations over and over again; from other nuns, rather than the outside world. Kate had argued almost identically, though abstractly. It was the veiled passion of this attack that assaulted her. She knew too well that there was some truth in what Karen was saying, and the knowledge of the truth was a chink in her armour. She felt unable to defend herself against Karen's attack; she was exposed, endangered. All she could do was try and stay calm, to be nun-like, unmoved, disciplined:

'Perhaps the problem is not just mine, but something broader, more social. Perhaps everyone wants to see nuns in a particular way because that's easier for them than having to try and find the person.' She wanted to say that Karen was in just as much of a uniform, the lesbian feminist uniform, as she was in her habit. She wanted to say that Karen and her friends hid behind their jeans and jackets no differently, and used them both as defence and weapon against the rest of the world. Karen's outfit declared her sexual identity just as clearly as her own did. She also wanted to cry out, 'What is all this? What am I supposed to have done? You know it isn't the habit that you're angry about, but something else, something deeper, something quite other and I don't know what and I'm not sure that I want to.' And she wanted to plead too, 'Please don't be angry with me, please like me, please don't go away. I need you.' She was not able to say any of these things, she was not able to catch Karen's anger and give it back to her as a present.

Karen yelled, 'For God's sake what is all this purity, this bloody virginity stuff meant to be? What is it for? If you want to stay in your frigid world, don't bloody sleep with anyone if you don't want to. Escape from your bodies and life in your tight little heads if that makes you feel better, but why go round ramming it down everyone else's throats? Why bother?'

Anna, seeking a refuge, found a pedestal; she climbed up on to it and waved a practised flag: 'It's a sign, a mark of witness. A sign of commitment. Like a married woman wearing a wedding ring.' It was what they learned and even as she said it she knew it would be like a red rag to Karen's anger.

'A wedding ring is a bloody bondage symbol. It's just meant to say "Keep off, private property" to other men. "Trespassers will be prosecuted.'' And yours does that too. You' — and even there locked into her own fury there is still a sensible place which says that if they are ever going to be friends again she must be a little careful, must generalise, must keep it to nuns not specifically just Anna — 'All you bloody nuns, you're not virgins, you're just married to the Top Man. And he keeps a bloody harem.'

Anna wanted to touch her, to hold Karen safe against the waves of anger that she could not understand. But she did not know how. The storm clouds gathered at the top of the valley; the shadows of the Fathers waited, waited to remind her that they had said no good would come of this friendship. They waited for her to defend them against the blasphemous charges of this obscene woman. They waited, threatening her with what they would do if she gave in and became involved with the crazy woman's evil anger. They swooped, warning her to be calm, demanding that she be on their side, that she did not involve herself, insisting that she did not notice Karen's pain, that she respond only on the level of reason and history.

'Come on Karen,' she said, as serenely as though it were one more of their debates about feminist theory, 'you know better than that. You know that over a long historical period the religious life has offered women a lot of autonomy, both individually — all those medieval women having access to learning and self-determination, and as a role model for other women, an abiding sign that marriage and childbirth aren't the only options. Nuns have defended the idea of freedom for women for over a thousand years. To be effective a symbol has to be visible. We need to see the symbols, the archetype of virginity, just like we need all the other roles.'

'Sod archetypes,' Karen screeched. 'I don't believe in archetypes. Sod the historical bit too. Of course I know there's bound to be some point when any and every choice may be a radical confrontation, but that's within its own context. It's not now. Can't you see that? Don't offer me some damn medieval saint as a model for today, for what you choose to do with your life. You're overlooking what matters, what feminism is supposed to be about. It's not about understanding the past, it's about bloody changing the present. It's meant to be a revolutionary movement. Did you know that? Did you know that when you were

112

dishing out pious colonialist goodies to the deserving poor? It's about change, Anna. We're trying to talk about changing the present and creating the future. So some sodding mitred abbess in the thirteenth century doesn't move me and it doesn't excuse you. Mythic heroines of the past don't do a lot for us now you know. And the so-called archetypes are even worse. Mythological wanking doesn't change a damn thing, they just transcend bloody oppression, eliminate it, they just let us off the hook, they're indulgent consolations that's what. Don't come at me with archetypes as though there were some immutable transhistorical psychic truths.'

Somewhere in her own articulacy the anger was partly absorbed; she and Anna were both impressed by her verbal concentration. Although she was still wild she was also moving into the ideas and the two of them were no longer locked motionless in the street but were able to turn and carry on walking. But Karen did not stop talking and she did not want to.

'I'll tell you something. All those symbols of strong women, all those mythological virgins and Amazons and matriarchs, they're not about us, they're about men and their lousy little fears, and their lusts and their power. Quite possibly virginity had a radical function and radical manifestations too if you want to insist; but negative, negative, defined against male supremacy. They set it up, they set it up like they set up all your damned archetypes of strong women. Look Anna, for God's sake use your atrophied brains. Look at the archetypes; what have you got? You get the wife and mother, and the sex symbol and the friend-and-companion, and you get the virgin, all in this nice tidy balanced square, polarised, orderly, acceptable. But who's standing in the middle of the square? Who's holding it together, keeping it in focus? Men, that's who, they're doing the defining. And the virgin bit is where you see that most clearly if you ask me, because it is a totally negative image: it's the power of not, of not being owned by a man, of not relating sexually to a man. Virginity doesn't go far enough, it's as simple as that. It's an image of resistance not of change. Just to wear that habit and wave your virginity about is a fucking consent to society's bloody rights of ownership, because all it says is 'not-owned'. If we want to talk about change and freedom we have to change the dreams, smash the square, not just bloody analyse it.'

113

So much clarity inside so much anger. The Fathers retreated from the fierce cutting edge of that articulacy. Anna felt them stagger back, aghast at the brightness of Karen's shekinah. Anna was more grateful than she could find words for; she wanted to give Karen a gift, a gift of gratitude and also a peace offering, a thanks offering because the perilous place had been passed through on the wings of Karen's words and Karen was no longer lethally angry with her. She said, 'Look Karen, if it means that much to you, I'm quite prepared not to wear the habit all the time. There's nothing ritual about it.' The last sentence was not true; as soon as she heard herself say it she felt that the whole offer had been a weakness, a mistake, that she had been forced here and that it was therefore not a true gift. She could not take back the gift, but with a sudden bitchy perceptiveness she threw in a little barb without knowing quite what it was: 'As a matter of fact Audrey has just given me a very nice tracksuit. I'll wear it tomorrow.'

But Karen did not even feel a prick; she felt powerful and victorious. She thought that Anna was making some acknowledgement of the true source of her anger. She said, 'If you wear it tomorrow I'll invite you to my house for supper.' She had never done so before; it was a leap forward. They grinned at each other, grins of relief and acknowledgement. But Karen had not really finished her lecture; she wanted to say, 'Anna, I'll tell you what is missing from the square, from the archetypes, from all the myths. The missing ingredient is the lesbian. And that's how we break it. The dyke is the positive image of the negative virgin.' She wanted to say, 'Beloved Anna, the hour of the virgin is over. Come on to my side. Come over and play with us. It is the virgins who have the power to move the square; the lever to shift the world. Virgins can stop being good women and become bad women, that is all it will take. And it will be fun.'

But she had lost her nerve and she did not want to push that hard. Anna had responded with a gift and gratitude was appropriate. The next move could wait.

And the next morning Anna appeared punctually in the library wearing her tracksuit, and facing out the mild surprise of the library staff and readers who recognised her. Karen could not know about the shyness and the hours of rationalisation that

Anna had wrestled with. They all knew she was a nun anyway; there was no deception. It was her duty to be available, open, accessible to any community that needed her. She managed to hide from herself and even from the Fathers that really she wore it to please Karen, and because she could not bear, could not face the threat that Karen would be that angry with her again. The anger had opened the door to some dark things that Anna did not want to have to know about. The anger must be propitiated, because it could overwhelm her, break her. She could not bear it if Karen withdrew her favours and returned Anna to the pit she had been in before. There was a deep unease and she did not want to work out why. She felt oddly compromised, though happy to be so compromised. So she was very collected, very careful not to reveal her own self-consciousness. And after all it was a black tracksuit. She hid from herself the fact that she had washed her hair especially and spent longer in front of the tiny square mirror in her room than she had done since the day she had first put on her habit. She hid from Karen the fact that she had had to go and ask the convent bursar for a late key: she knew that Karen would find it a childish restriction and she wanted to conceal all indications that she was not free and self-determining.

Karen was more simply happy. She was delighted and a little smug. She was also relieved that she could now find it possible to take Karen into her own house. She desperately wanted to establish a social context for their friendship, it was terribly important. She knew that she had in some ways bullied Anna, had somehow cheated, had not been as careful and gentle as she had promised herself she would be. In the night she had been frightened that Anna would not come or would not have kept her side of the bargain, because if she had appeared in her habit then Karen knew she would in slashing rage have ended the friendship. And she did not want to do that. She did not want to do that.

Anna would come now and meet her friends, be in her family. Her friends could meet her properly and she would become someone real and observed and Karen's feelings about her more manageable. The observation of her friends always reduced people to the size of material reality; they were anti-romantics. Then her friendship could become less of a secret obsession. She felt tender towards Anna now, ironically amused by herself and her idiotic sentiments again, and somehow deeply delighted with and protective of both of them.

Despite the emotional build-up it was a surprisingly good evening. Karen lived in a big shabby house in Hackney with five other women. Their social life centred on an enormous kitchen which they had created for themselves in what had once been the front sitting-room; a lovely well-lit space with bow windows, the original elaborate plaster mouldings still on the ceiling and an old carved and tiled fireplace. One wall was covered with cork board on which the complexities of their daily lives were pinned up: rotas and phone numbers and reminders — '*please* change your damn cat's litter', and 'plumber coming Thursday. Can someone be in?' More personal things too; torn-out cartoons, and a newspaper clipping in which Anna could recognise Sybil and Karen with some other women, a signed photograph of Martina Navratilova, a snapshot of two small children, a Victorian photograph of some women's gathering, and a number of odd post-cards with cryptic messages.

In the middle of the room was a large battered table, around which they gathered generally but casually most evenings. Elsewhere they had more private space; it was a house where privacy was respected and where it was perfectly acceptable to take one's food and friends and eat elsewhere. Anna and Karen were both slightly nervous, unsure what to expect. Karen found she very much wanted Anna to like her household, not to find it strange or dangerous; she had worried through the day about the mess and bustle. Anna had no idea how it would be, how they might all live. She had a sense that the mystery of Karen's real life would be revealed to her here. But both of them had overlooked the fact that the plan and style of the household was entirely normal to Anna: it was very like how she had lived for years, in the framework of her order's small community projects. In their mission houses in South America the nuns too had a communal room in which they ate and organised and socialised. And they had other places where privacy was sancrosanct. They, too, busy with their complicated and different schedules, left lists and notes stuck on a board in the common room. Almost immediately and quite unexpectedly Anna relaxed; she felt more at home here, more socially secure in an odd way than she ever did in the cosy domestic privacy of Fiona and Stephen's house.

So Anna was comfortable and Karen warmed. And, as Anna noticed when the others came home, the absence of her habit really did make a difference. When they first arrived no one else was home; Karen felt generous and eager. She did the cooking and would not let Anna help her with the chores; she sat her at the table, gave her a glass of wine, and pleasurably awaited developments. The next person to arrive was someone that Anna had not met before; she tossed her jacket on to a chair and looked at Anna with neutral interest. Karen said merely, 'Paula, you haven't met Anna have you? She's been working in South America and I thought she could give you some political instruction.' She grinned at them both and turned back to her work, and from there on it was easy. Anna really did know a remarkable amount and particularly about the development of socialist movements in the northern half of the continent. Paula was happy to pick her brains. Anna thought Paula surprisingly well informed in some unlikely areas and appallingly ignorant in others, though she refrained from saying so and they found enough common ground for a relaxed discussion. Paula's ready acceptance of the use of violence seemed alarming and Anna tried to explain how she felt that this would not always work to the advantage of the most disadvantaged. However she recognised that in a society with so little respect for the process of law, passive resistance was not likely to be very effective. It was a question, she tried to argue, of modes of resistance. She was still trying to give instances of effective community movements when Sybil and Judy arrived accompanied by another couple. Sybil could not resist commenting on the disappearance of Anna's habit. 'I might not have recognised you,' she said. Karen felt a momentary alarm but Paula was sufficiently engrossed not to be thrown off; 'Oh, are you the nun? I hadn't realised.' 'The nun', Anna noticed, so Karen had talked about her. She felt pleased but did not have time to work out why.

'Yes. I'm sorry, I thought you knew.'

'How does that fit in with what you're saying about resistance? I mean that and turning the other cheek and all that stuff?'

'Oh dear,' said Anna. 'We've put so much time in trying to work that out you know. But I don't think accepting violence done to yourself is the same thing as accepting violence done to others.' She saw Sr. Kitty's torn habit, Sr. Kate's exploding pain. Was it the same thing? Could it possibly be the same thing? How could one find a way through? And suddenly she could hear the warning rumbles of the Fathers whom she had thought excluded from this warm and bright place. They expected her to do her duty and defend the purity of Holy Mother Church against the aggression of these wild women who knew nothing of and could not understand such concepts as love and service and sacrifice. But Paula waited patiently while she collected her thoughts and said, carefully, 'I suppose in the last count that's why I'm not a pacifist. There might come a point where one had to defend the defenceless and not to do so would be an act of violence against them. Though I still think it would be wrong. I mean war and even smaller acts of violence would always be wrong but they might be a necessary evil, at least in theory. There's always Jesus hurling over the money changers' stalls for those who need a biblical example.'

Paula was not very interested in biblical parallels; she was quite curious about nuns, however, and with Anna's ordinary appearance she seemed to find it easier to take the point further. She said, 'Somehow that doesn't sound very nunnish.'

Anna wanted to say, 'Perhaps you don't know very many nuns,' but she did not dare to be so rude. Instead she said, 'There's supposed to be a balancing point between justice and mercy — which I suppose we'd call love. The religious, women religious anyway, have traditionally been cast rather heavily on the mercy side, quite possibly to allow some of the male hierarchy to come on as heavies. But that could change; we might want to function on the other side of the balance, throw our corporate weight on the justice side.'

'But look,' argued Paula, 'then why be a nun?'

Karen standing at the sink with her back to the room grinned happily to herself. Paula was doing a terrific job. She felt suddenly powerful; these were things she wanted to say to Anna. A part of her wanted to see Anna stand at bay, her back against the wall, and Karen was delighted to have someone else so calmly doing her painful work for her.

'What?' Anna asked, thrown by the directness.

'Well if nuns are historically constructed to be on the mercy side, as you call it, and if you want to be on the justice side, or whatever, then why be one?'

'Well, it could be functional. I mean it got me to Latin America which is something you say you've found impossible to do.'

'Not good enough,' said Paula, 'and you know it. Come on.'

'Hey, steady on,' said Sybil, protective not of Anna but of Karen. Karen was irritated though she knew that the response came from Sybil's affection. But tonight Anna did not mind, she felt at home and safe. She felt for the answer. 'Well, I do think people change, don't you? I mean when I entered I probably was on the mercy side anyway. I could hardly be otherwise, given the privileged American middle-class childhood I'd had. Then you learn things; I learned things just by being in Santa Virgine, and before that in Panama; things that would shift one over as far as sides go. So there's that.'

'How far do they shift you though? All the way? Do you ever think of leaving?'

There was an abrupt pause, Anna's silence catching all their attention; even Karen wondered if this was too much. But Anna broke the silence herself, even though she did not answer the question: 'Look, almost everyone I know has to work in an imperfect institution. I don't know how you earn a living, but we all have to. If I think my view of how nuns should be is better than the more commonly held one, then that in itself is a good case for staying and struggling with it.' It was not her own line, it was not even what she really thought; in fact she seldom questioned the structural organisation of the religious life, only whether or not she could fit into it. The words were Kate's and they were a gift, received across the years and the ocean. Only Karen knew her well enough to hear the wobble at the bottom of what she was saying. She was not sure whether to challenge Anna's statement or to admire the dignity of her evasion. Before she could decide Sybil had leapt in, shifting the conversation, bringing them back to London, asking how one could tell when the organisation one worked for, she worked for, was irredeemable and then what one did about that. Karen was both touched and peeved. Anna was grateful.

Anna did not speak a lot, but enough, that evening. It was all smooth from then on; they ate and laughed and gossiped. Anna did not always understand what they were talking about, but she enjoyed it. She did not want to have to defend the Church against these women who had welcomed her in and treated her as though she was a normal person. She was glad that she was not called upon to do so. She realised quite suddenly that it was not just a matter of feeling comfortable in their house, it was more positive. She admired these women, she realised suddenly, she admired them because they were clever and charming and because they were not asking for anything.

She had thought she had known about Women's Liberation, a useful tool of her trade — the trade of being a good missionary nun engaged in proclaiming freedom to the captives. She and her sisters used any and all tools for the good of others and feminism had been one such tool. Women's poverty had been a special issue for them, because their own vocation particularly called them to enter into it. They had struggled to learn more about the poverty of women so that they could identify their chosen poverty with the reality of the unchosen poverty of all women. Kate had taught her the theory; she knew how to say the words: the poverty of women lies in and under all the poverty of the world. They had chosen to be where that poverty was a reality: a painful guilt-inducing wearing reality. A reality that she knew none of these women really understood, and perhaps she did not understand herself, because it was too exhausting to take on unless you had to. And in understanding, relating to and trying to change that poverty feminism was valuable; for instance, the underlying sexism of many of the aid-granting bodies actually reinforced the poverty of women while alleviating the poverty of men. But feminism had remained — she thought for all of them, even the most articulate of the self-styled 'liberated sisters' — a way of describing, a way of working, not a way of living, being. And further away, more pressingly for the sisters who actually worked in the USA, there were other questions, about mysogyny in the church, and finding patterns of living that were not predefined by the hierarchy; and grasping hold of the holiness of power and autonomy and self-respect. But all the time these were no more than interesting ideas, helpful insights into better ways of living out their calling, not immediate and central to daily life as coffee and underclothes.

She had not imagined women like these, who shared the house with her friend Karen. She had not been prepared for women who as well as being articulate and educated simply assumed the centrality of feminist perception, the centrality of women and politics in their lives. They were not begging. They were not whining and they were not apologising. They asked for no special tolerance and space, they took it. They had moved the centre into their own place and it was other people who would have to beg, ask, require their attention.

What surprised Anna she realised was how much she liked it. She found some of the conversation itself difficult, to follow and to accept. But she watched them and thought about them and entered into the conversation enough not to blight it. More and more she realised how stunning, how truly amazing these women were. And Karen, with a deep awareness of Anna, even as she took deliberate pains to take no special care of her, knew that Anna was admiring not just her, but them, their way of life, their style. In the glow of Anna's admiration and in knowing that her friends did not find Anna too cranky or weird or deranged, she became all delight. She glowed. They all laughed, loving her. Anna looked up at one point and found Karen radiant. The carefulness and moderateness she had always tried to maintain in her relationship with Anna was thrown off, not as yesterday swept away by the force of anger, but discarded in the safety of her own home. Anna watched Karen's face even while she tried to follow the wild loops of conversation, the tight webs full of internal references, the easy intimacy of women who had known each other for a very long time and were having a good time together, and she thought only that she was happy and Karen was not just witty and elegant and brilliant but also beautiful, and that this was a new and better place to be. She did not consciously observe that there was so much babble, so much sound of women's voices, so much assertive joy that there was no room for her fears and doubts, no place for the power of the Fathers. She did know that she did not want to go back to her solitary cell.

But eventually Sybil offered her a lift home. Karen in her optimism thought that it would be a good opportunity for Sybil and Anna to get to know each other properly. She did not offer to go too.

'Is that all right with you, Anna?' asked Sybil.

'Yes. Thank you,' Anna said.

Anna, as a nun, was used to accepting favours and gifts; she did not have the habit of protesting. Sybil experienced her simple acceptance differently; she assumed that Anna wanted to talk to her. She wanted to talk to Anna.

They drove off in Sybil's small elderly car. Sybil drove fast and bided her time. But Anna did not speak. Sybil at a red traffic light said suddenly, 'I love her very much, you know, she's my closest friend.'

'Karen?' Anna asked, taken aback. Her first thought was that Sybil was seeking her advice on some personal problem; and she did not want to hear confessional material, she did not want to be nun and helper, it was not fair of Sybil to ask for that. She refused to be constructed as mother, as nun, not here, not by these women. She was irritated.

'Yes Karen,' said Sybil, feeling somewhat irritated herself. 'I've known her a very long time and I don't want to see her hurt.'

The lights turned green and she accelerated into the darkness. There was more silence.

Finally Sybil said, 'She's not as invulnerable as she likes to think.'

Anna was now thoroughly lost and confused. Her head was still spinning, reeling from the wonderful conversation and the unaccustomed lateness of the hour. She said vaguely, not knowing what was required, 'I haven't known her very long.'

Sybil shoved viciously at her gears and Anna cringed as though she thought Sybil was going to hit her. Sybil pulled her car abruptly over to the side of the road, switched off the headlights, put both hands back on the steering wheel and said, 'Are you really not at all aware that she's in love with you?'

It would have been better if Sybil had hit her. Anna was stricken by this body blow. There was nothing to say. Had she known? Does she know? What difference can it make? She could see Karen's face and Karen's hand, suddenly, vividly. She was both excited and appalled. She felt physically shocked. It did not occur to her to question Sybil's perception. 'Selfish. Selfish.' The

Fathers' voices suddenly crash into the car. 'Insensitive. You have endangered another's soul by your insensitivity, by your greed, your greed for companionship. It won't do. We won't tolerate it.' Anna knew that they were not telling the truth, that whatever was involved it was no threat to Karen's immortal soul which was either already damned by her own sexual choices or sexual choices had been wrongly construed by the Fathers' laws. But she could not form the thought. She shrank back against the door of the car, her hands still tidily clasped in her lap. Her face was unmoving but the great terror was very near. Even Sybil, though incomprehending, could sense it. She reached up over Anna's head and turned the interior light on. When she looked at Anna she was scared. But after a long moment she asked, quite neutrally, 'Do you fancy her then?'

'Certainly not,' said Anna and burst into tears.

Sobbing, sobbing, racked with sobs. Painful and humiliating and, oh God, dishonest. Before Sybil had asked the question the answer would have been true. Now it no longer was.

'Yes,' she sobbed. 'Yes I do.'

'Oh shit,' said Sybil.

They sat mutely in the car.

Anna had no feelings. She refused the feelings. She thought only that her head, naked without its veil, was cold. Dreadfully cold.

'Can you take me back please?' she said to Sybil.

'I'm sorry.'

'Karen doesn't let me apologise.' Anna wanted to cast herself on Sybil's mercy and tell her everything. I love her I love her, I think she is beautiful and magical. She is my saviour. I love her hands and her funny face and how strong her shoulders are. How lovely and alight her mind is. How she is beautiful and Sybil has revealed in her stupid question the bones and marrow and sweetness of desire. But this was absolutely not permitted.

Sybil smiled slightly at so typically Karen a regulation, 'No, well she wouldn't. I didn't realise.' The silence is weighted now. Sybil wondered if she should touch Anna, comfort her. She did not want to. On Karen's side, on Karen's behalf she is furiously angry. Angry at the denial, at Anna's evident refusal to face up to what was happening. Cross about Karen's stupidity and at the whole rotten situation. But she could also understand that there was a difficulty here that she could not understand.

'Do you have someone to talk about it with? Is this the first time? What are you going to do about it? Does Karen know?' All the questions went too far. There was no starting place except Anna's defence that very evening of being a nun. Her clarity had seemed to Sybil rock-like, bell true. Chosen committed virginity. I should have known, she told herself. I should have bloody known. I should have bloody well not meddled too. Karen was going to be furious when she found out. I've loosed the demons from a bottle and I can't make them go back in again.

Anna's tears stopped as suddenly as they had started. She sat rigid looking out of the window. Her face was white and closed. Sybil knew there was nothing she could say now. She turned out the light again, taking extraordinary care not to touch Anna as she did so. 'Fasten your seat belt,' she said. Safety seemed suddenly important. Anna did not move. Stillness takes practice but hers was trained. If she moved a muscle bits of her would fly off and she would disintegrate. She did not dare to move. Sybil drove on. The silence remained. Even when she asked Anna for directions and Anna told her with precision the silence was not broken. When she stopped the car in front of the convent, Sybil tried again, 'Look, I'm sorry. I don't think I've been very useful. But . . . but if you want to talk about it . . . if I can help. Oh damn. You know where to find me.'

Anna did not reply. She got out of the car with great care, walking as though she were carrying a very full container of liquid which must not be spilled. She opened the door and went inside the house of chastity.

But the safe walls were shaken by the storm in her gut. These were not the storms that had assaulted the Mother House last winter, from outside, from outside her. These were the storms of her own desires; the ice-cold linoleum lifted and creaked down the passage. Anna struggled along the cold dark corridors, the pathways of the labyrinth; she had no choice, she had to go through, but in the centre was the chamber of the waiting minotaur; the maw of darkness that would consume her. She found her own room, the safety of her own bed. But it was not safe there. She had named her evil desire, and naming it had loosed it from its prison. It was alive and free; it had lived unfed in its dungeon for too long, now it was ravenous and devouring. Flat on her stomach, her face buried in the pillow, half-stifled her hands reached for her genitals, her imagination for the brightness of Karen's face; there was the animation of hands that played with the air, and then not with the air. A still untouched part of her mind thought quite clearly that she had not done this since she was about twelve and probably wouldn't even remember how, but that thought was swallowed up too. What she experienced now was a driving force of desire, a great fierce demanding thing which she did not like and could not control. She tried to keep a hold of Karen in her heart, but the Fathers descended on her and took over her body and her fantasy and were without mercy. It was horrible. They beat her and they buggered her and that excited her and in the end she did not know, she could not tell, she did not care whether it was punishment or pleasure for it was both and she was humiliated. And in the humiliation she found relief, and she felt the needs of her own body taking over and she fought against that and she lost; so that the pounding orgasm at her own hands was not victory but shame and darkness and that shame was thrilling and she did not know what it all meant.

The rituals of masochism were complex, especially when carried on not with a human lover but with invisible demons. There was secrecy and terrible shame, but there was also relief and escape. What was it that she wanted? She lay in the dark sweating and frightened. She turned over, trying desperately to get outside herself, to see what she had done and was doing. The world she had pledged her faith to was broken, but in the midst of the shattered fragments there was still herself. She must still be there, but she did not know what or who that was; but there was something something real, however chewed and fragmented. They all wanted something from her; the powers of darkness, the powers of light.

Caro's dark sulk demanded that she consent to it.

But the Fathers' hard mockery and cruel dealings were demands too. Shape up, come back, do as we tell you, kill the other voices. Silence them. Yes, see, we can punish and humiliate you, but only if you disobey us. The Fathers know how to punish but they also know how to reward. Take up your cross, deny yourself, deny all the shadows and dark places. Repent. Turn back to us and we will reward you with the crown of ever-lasting life. Our rewards are sweet, for the good daughters. We name the price and you have to pay it, but we keep both our sides of the bargain. Reward. Punish. Kiss. Kill.

And now Karen demanded consent. She gave love and demanded sexuality. Karen said, this is normal, sisterly, good. This is body and blood, this is riding on the tube train to the gardens of Kew and riding my body to the gardens of delight. Karen said, come with me to a high place and I will show you all the glories of the world. Come into the woman-place with me. Give your virginity to me and I will return it to you, all new and polished and as bright as the sun. I will enthrone us with the goddesses and we will be true virgins forever; women who hold themselves, and hold themselves free.

The unicorn would only drink milk from the virgin's breast. Virginity tamed the ferocity of that purity. He laid his head on her lap, sniffing the strange woman-smell. Virginity could tame the wild excesses of his lust. (But Artemis is fierce and destructive in her purity too.) Sr. Kitty lay on her back in the dark and saw the white unicorn vanish. The unicorn was unique and was male. In the dark land of the interior the Spanish warriors thought they would find the city of gold, the city of untarnishable purity. For that they had tarnished the pessimistic purity of the Aztecs, and the high mountain fastnesses of the Incas. The conquistadors thought they would find the unicorn in the dark interior; they sold their own purity in search of its purity. The unicorn was male purity, it was the Christ who loved the Virgin. The unicorn who loved virgins had a virgin mother. The unicorn made its demands too.

The conquistadors had thought they would find the unicorn in the dark interior. Instead they found the Amazons. The sisters, women together. The power of virginity is a negative power; it is the power of not submitting. But the power of the sisters is communal power, positive power. The community made demands on Anna too. Come to us, come back to us. Sisterhood was not soft, not an easy way out; it was strong and tough. Kate demanded that she return and that they balance each other again in a positive power.

And she . . . Anna . . . what does she want? Now in the darkness, her tensions and defences broken together she did not know. She wanted it all. She wanted none of it. She wanted to be warm and still and safe. She wanted to be wrapped in a soft blue blanket with a satin edging, wrapped warm and held close. She wanted a mother.

Mother.

Mamma. Mamma. The child cried in the dark, cried without knowing if someone would come. Why did the mother not come? Mamma. Maa. Maa. Mmmmm. Anna did not hear her thoughts now, she had rolled over and curled up tightly and fallen asleep.

And in the morning she had forgotten. Blocked out the storm. Shut it away. She went to confession in the chapel. She confessed to unclean thoughts and to not avoiding the occasions of temptation. She confessed to tiny detailed failures of observance. Somewhere in all the details she managed to lose the reality. The priest took it away. He was young and busy and he failed to hear. But she had failed to tell him too.

She decided that she would not see Karen any more.

She clicked away busily, neatly, to help poor Fiona with her burden: a brain-damaged child poor thing and expecting another baby soon. Anna was rigid. She would not bend. She would be brave and clever and virtuous and good, her father's daughter. The Fathers' daughter, sprung to life fully armed on the emanation of the Father's Word, armed against darkness and chaos. The bright virgin warrior, the beloved daughter.

VI

So in the next days Anna spent a great deal more time with Fiona, and equally with Caro. It was a fortunate time for her to be with them. As she moved further into her pregnancy, Fiona moved further into herself. She was brooding over the child, growing it carefully and tenderly, protecting it fiercely from her own fears, cherishing it against the memories of the last time, weaving around it strong spells and charms. She was guarding it too against Caro, against the gleeful malevolence of the dark child. She was appalled at herself, eaten with guilt at her animosity towards Caro, worried that she could not bear to have those smudgy fingers touching her body which was now the throne of the child of light. Caro's treatment sessions went on inexorably, and Fiona continued to organise and mobilise them with her customary efficiency, but they became strangely easier because she was no longer torn, no longer ravaged and hurt by Caro's anger and refusal. She had withdrawn her passionate commitment.

What would happen, wondered her dream self, living out at night the feelings that her guilt would not allow, what would happen if Demeter lost interest in Persephone, if she just left her in the Kingdoms of Hell? What would happen when the mother no longer searched for the maiden, but handed her over finally to the powers of the underworld? But she could not face the consequences. She tried to tell herself that it was just a side effect, a natural flowing over of pregnancy. That she was tired and stressed and absorbed in the new life, and that later everything would return to normal, Caro would be all right. But she was delighted by Anna's sudden and absolute availability and she could not resist using it. She was too delighted, too needy, to risk asking why Anna had apparently given up her studies and was prepared to spend all day with Caro. It was easy enough and a relief to accept her day-to-day appearances, to think that she was just-taking-a-day-off-today-for-a-change. Anna was there, which counted for a lot; Anna was a safe barrier between her and Caro; and in a different way between her and Stephen whom she could not face in the shadows of her guilt. Anna was, after all, Sister Anna, who had a duty, a place, to help those in need of help; exploiting her, ignoring her real needs, using her time was some-how not quite the same as doing the same thing to other women. This was her job.

And Anna, fleeing her own darkness, fleeing her own reality, was eager to be accepted on these terms. A new and delicate antenna that she had grown in one night sitting in Sybil's car told her that this was not her truth. There had been an acceptance of her in that vast bright kitchen, an uninterest in her role and its expectations, and this had released something in her. But she refused to think about it, she would cauterise the antenna. Surely part of who she was was truly nun, was woman religious, and they, those women, had not been able to incorporate that. She knew that Fiona veiled her daily whether or not she wore the habit, just as Karen's household had undressed her, stripped her. There was a flabby comfort in Fiona's expectations, and in the knowing that she could indeed live up to them. A part of her knew too that Fiona was going into a difficult and private place, and that she Anna was standing between Fiona and her family. She wondered if she ought to leave them, Fiona and Caro and Stephen and the new child, to make this journey unaccompa-nied. She was not only cheating herself; she was cheating them too. But it was blessedly easy not to ask the question at anything except the most superficial level, and to agree that Fiona needed and valued her; that Caro needed and wanted her; that they were both grateful and appreciative. One evening she did ask Stephen, but he too was locked into his own confusion. He had sensed that something was going awry and he did not want to have to find out what. Anna could protect him from the know-ing. He smiled, making a joke out of his words, and said, 'No, no. We need you. There's a crucial role for virgins at the time of birth. You bring the balance. Virgin and mother. Sister and mid-wife. Did you know that all the great myth virgins always have the job of taking care of women in childbirth. So, you see, you're very appropriate.'

She smiled, pleased that he should have noticed this oddness in the pattern, and then quite suddenly was assailed by fury. She did not want to play a bit part in his archetypal constructions; she wasn't some appropriate symbolism she was Anna, she was who she was, a person, a woman. She was shocked at her own anger and the loud roaring of her ego, which leapt out like a tiger in the night and pounced on his innocent good will and gratitude. 'I am the handmaid of the Lord,' she tried to meditate on the words, 'be it unto me according to thy will.' I am needed by them in this important adventure. Of course it is a bit part, and that was suitable. Of course they wanted and deserved the centre of the stage for this important moment in their history. And she stamped on the memory of Karen shouting about archetypes in the street; she crushed the thought, ground it under her heel. For so long as she did her own censoring, the Fathers would leave her in peace. They waited, waited in the wings with their whips and whiplash tongues; she knew they were there all right, constantly and continuously. They would let her discipline herself so long as she would, but they would not let her escape. She must not think about Karen, she must not think about leaving the religious life, she must not think — above all she must never think about or acknowledge what had been torn out of her in the car by Sybil's bullying interference. She should not mix with company like that, she should avoid all occasions of temptation. Flee tempta-tion, it said in the Bible, flee temptations. But Christ himself had gone into the desert and for forty days was tempted by the Devil and stayed there to learn about himself and wait until the angels were ready to minister to him. Who was she though, fouled and sinful and weak, who was she to take those risks; he was the beloved son, he had heard the heavens declare it, whereas she was fit only for punishment and shame. She must avoid all occasions of temptation.

She did not even read the notes that Karen sent her. She threw them away unopened; she tore up the envelopes, ripping up the sloppy brown writing, denying the event.

130

Caro was a danger of course. She fought against hearing that low growling voice. She tried to refuse it. And so long as she pleased the Fathers and did what they told her, they helped her to hold Caro's voice at bay, they were willing to reward her effort. But it exhausted her, it wore her down and it made Caro angry. Anna could sense her anger deeper than her isolation as she lifted her and fed her and changed her: an inert heaviness . One afternoon Caro got herself into a terrible mess, she had dirtied herself and the shit was everywhere, messy and foul. She had an extraordinary talent for this all-embracing filth. Fiona was sleeping and Anna decided that she would have to bathe her herself. She hauled Caro upstairs, ran the bath and firmly lowered her into it. The child was transformed, her floppiness suddenly graceful, her resistance evaporated. Happy within her filth and within its washing away. Caro was enchanted, she smiled delightedly and opened out to Anna like a flower. And Caro's voice came.

Why don't you want to speak to me? You don't want to speak to me because you are a coward. You think the Fathers will look after you but they can't make me go away. So what are they worth? I'll never go away. Never, never. You'd have to stay awake all the time. I can sneak into your dreams. Don't resist, don't resist. Come into the dark and play with me. It doesn't matter if you're frightened; frightened can make good games too, which are fun. You come into the dark places and be with me. You are me. We are us. I am you. There are no promises. Or com-promises. But you have to come into this burning dark place and find me, and find yourself. You can't sit and wait for me to be a good girl. I am never a good girl. If you try and dodge me, try and forget me, try and leave me, I will hate you, I will hate you forever and I will ruin everything for you. Everything you touch will be rotten. You are afraid of the rotten. You are afraid of the dark. Hee hee. You are scared of the dark and the shit and the mess. You want everything neat and tidy, but I don't. I choose to shit and piss and make lovely horrible messes. You want that too, you are as disgusting as me, and perverted and abnormal, but you want to cover it all up by being a nice good little nun. Ha ha. Of course you are afraid of me. You should be. I know. Under your layers of sham there is nothing there, except the dark and putrid stink of you. There's nothing there but me. I can redeem or destroy it. I am strong. I want to dance and prance. And, oh yes, I stink. I love it. I am foul and that is fun. I'm not always a little girl you know, sometimes in the night I creep out and take wing: I am a bad mad incontinent old witch, and so are you, and so are you.

Anna listened in silence to the happy fury of the child and when Caro knew that she was truly listening she sang a different song.

I can be joyful, she sang, I can be joyful and lovely. I told you that. I can play and play eternally. My play is delightful anarchy. Not for learning, for taming, for training, for ordering, not for decorum and deportment. But for joy and kaleidoscopic light shattering and reforming in the depths of the unmade stars. Leap high or fall deep, the void is the same and drifting down or up there is no difference. Floating and swimming and otter-dancing on the unconfined waters that are chaos. Come swim, sing, play, dance, float with me. It is against time and order, it is for joy and lightness.

Anna listened and Caro sang in her stomach and in her ears. Caro sang more wildly now, the tune mounting towards danger but still beautiful and joyful.

The terrain of the great war between the girl child and the great Fathers will be devastation. Fall out will kill millions, will render desolate and uninhabitable the fields of time. Broken, broken things will fall. Anna, the battle field is your flesh, and the Fathers and I will fight over it, and your skin will be burned by the falling stars, deafened with the jarring chords of the now discordant spheres, crippled with the weight of our armies. Red dragons and black dragons, dancing on the smooth plain of your belly. Teeth and flames. Great striped scars from our claws. I want you on my side. If we win, if we daughters win this battle the climax will not be down-pushing and thrusting, but uprising, whirling, oh so graceful flight and consummation and new birth in a darkness ablaze with light. And into that cosmic post-orgasmic hush, a new song and new sweet flowers growing, the desert blooming like a rose. And from your body new birthing; from your virgin flesh a new and joyful birth for the daughter of darkness, gestated in silence and brought to birth on wordless song. And courage rises to the fear.

Anna cried out aloud, on her knees supporting Caro in the bath tub, 'But Caro, how can I know I will survive it?' Caro's hum continued.

You don't. You don't know, you don't know, you cannot know because love has no meaning until after the breaking. But, but I can tell you there is a way of giving birth. When they shout at you to push and struggle you must not obey them. She did, Fiona did, she fought for my birthing, but there is another way. You, Anna, you must breathe me to my rebirth, breathe into that last dark place, just holding still reposed on the breath, in the darkest place that is before the dawn. Breathe me into life by loving me, loving yourself, loving the dark and the waiting. Baptise me. Name me. Birth me again in water and the word. Let me live as I am and love me. Go down into that silence, even quieter. Consent. Consent to me. Come down deeper below
the words.   Let   it   break   down   all   the   way.
E   ven   to   the   bot   tom   of   se   nse.   and
          be   low.
da   na   ga   el.
And when there is silence and the blood red moon setting. the stars dying.   when we stride without fear on the vast vacuity of choas.   then there can be birth and creation. then there will be calm.

Anna experienced a sudden moment of peace and optimism. She believed Caro. In the strength of that moment she raised Caro out of the water and wrapped her in a large soft blue towel. Cradling the child in her lap she petted and stroked her. Caro had gone floppy against her, soft, calm, almost limp; Anna knew that a sensible person would take advantage of the quiet moment

133

and get her dressed again while she was not in the mood to fight, but she did not move. Fiona and her bright determination and effort had gone away somewhere else; far away in another land Fiona and her unborn baby was sleeping. Caro was contained here, not in her mother's shining zeal but in Anna's acceptance. Caro liked this. They rocked together sharing the exhaustion of those who have to travel in the dark. Anna knew that if and when they moved, if and when she left the protection of Caro's magic power all the pain would come back again, the Fathers would be waiting to pounce. The optimism fled, the tiredness remained. She was too tired, too frightened. She was frightened by what Caro was offering her, and frightened by how severely the Fathers would punish her for even considering, for even hearing the offer. She was completely alone. She was convinced suddenly that she would have to go back to the convent; it was the only place of safety for her, the only walls strong enough to protect her. But the knowledge gave her no joy, no pleasure, only weariness and defeat. She rocked Caro, now the little brain-damaged child of her friend Fiona, no longer the strong voice of the wild places. She could feel her thoughts moving off towards Fiona, how she could rescue her, bring her home. She could not value, she could not sustain her determination to value Caro. She was not able to go down into the place where there were no promises.

Very briefly she thought also of Karen, clearly and with a flash of polished desire. She knew she could not risk it, it was too far to jump. Karen stood with her arms out and called leap leap and I'll catch you, but the fall would be too great. She rocked Caro, both of them dozing, the child on her lap gathered into the curves of her adult body, fitted and contained.

Stephen found them there when he came in from work. His heart was tugged by their gentleness, their closeness. 'Oddly enough,' he said, 'you two look very alike.'

'We are,' said Anna, and Stephen looked puzzled but let it pass in the sleepy ease of the steamy bathroom.

He helped her get Caro dressed for bed and then carried her downstairs to feed her. Fiona, had woken up, comforted and fortified by the long sleep, and she made them all supper. 'You'll stay won't you Anna?' Outside it was growing dark, the Fathers were waiting on the peaks of the wind. She knew she

134

would not be able to escape them and her peaceful melancholy turned to fear. 'Are you sure you want me to?' she asked.

'Yes please,' said Fiona, 'I need to ask your advice.'

They put Caro to bed. The three of them ate, chatting comfortably, normal grown-ups at the end of a normal day. Anna accepted with relief their assumption that she was a part of this normal life. They did not ask for too much; not for the transformation and revolution that Karen required, not for the disintegration that Caro pleaded, not for the perfection that the Fathers demanded. Stephen and Fiona respected quietly and left her alone.

Fiona said, 'Anna, do you remember once, ages ago, quite soon after we met, you said you wondered if it was necessarily right to try and cure Caro? You said perhaps she didn't want to come out.'

'Yes, yes I think I remember. I think I said that she might want to duck the responsibility. But now I think I'd also say something else, something about the reality, the positive side of who she is as well. But yes, I do wonder, I still wonder sometimes if it's worth it, if she really . . . but Fiona that isn't my business. I'm sorry if you feel I haven't been committed enough. It was never meant as a criticism of you. It's your choice. I really have tried to work with that.' She felt convicted; this very afternoon she had consented to Caro, had been drawn into Caro's world, and not tried to fight back to lure Caro out into the world of grown-up reason and sense. Was Fiona going to dismiss her from the court.

'Oh God, I didn't mean that. No no, you've been wonderful with her. Just wonderful. That's one of the things. You see the baby will come, and you'll go back to America, and I very much doubt now whether I can cope. Whether I can get it all going again. I'm thinking of stopping the programme, I'm thinking of quitting.'

Stephen gasped. She had not mentioned any of this to him; he was hurt. But he knew too that Fiona needed Anna there, needed her to allay the guilt. He tried to enter into her painful place. He wished she had warned him. He was glad that it was Anna.

Anna asked, 'Are you wanting me to soothe your conscience? Because I can and will do that. It has to be your decision, you have to weigh it up, but personally I don't think you'd be doing

135

something bad if you stopped. I suppose . . . how much difference, honestly, do you think it has made, this treatment? What about you Stephen?'

She tried to be calm, tried to hold herself to the agony that Fiona must be suffering, and to sanity and sensible supportive listening.

Fiona tried to follow Anna's guidance. Part of her wanted Stephen and Anna too to cry out in protest, to force the task upon her, to make her go on; part of her wanted them both just to hold and hug her, to tell her how wonderful she was and right, and make everything nice for her. But the fact that she had even raised the possibility changed something; the world had not collapsed in shock. She sought out an honest answer:

'At first I think it really did make a good deal of difference she certainly got stronger and I think she got a good deal more co-ordinated. Her head control *has* improved and she has some mobility now, a bit anyway which she didn't before. But it's been a year and perhaps that would have happened anyway, I mean with ordinary love and stimulation. It's hard to tell, I'd say it had made a real difference, but not miraculously, not . . . I can no longer imagine that she will ever be normal, whatever that means. Of course they didn't promise, but they did suggest . . . I'm not blaming them, but we have worked damn hard on it, and really I suppose it isn't a lot for the effort, not just our effort but so many people's. Stephen, what do you think?'

'Oh Fiona my love, I don't know. I mean she's certainly healthier, isn't she? And we haven't had any of those nightmare fevers recently and those unbelievable screaming sessions. At one point Anna she seemed to scream all night, scream and scream, almost to the point of convulsions; we'd arrive at the morning feeling that we'd weathered a monsoon of grief. I don't feel that anymore, and that is important. Her breathing is better too. But I also know what you're saying, that our whole life is taken over by this treatment thing, our social life built around it, yours more than mine. And we've done exactly what we were told. Fiona, you know it has to be you; I can support you and try and make it more possible, but it has to be your choice, it has to be because that's the reality of our lives. I would never even have dared suggest it if you hadn't . . . and you know she does hate it so, she really does hate it, fight against it and us. That may just be because she's stronger though.'

'I don't think so. I think she really does hate it.'

'So do I for what it's worth,' said Anna, 'though I don't know whether that should be a reason for giving up; I mean kids hate taking medicine too, but you make them.'

She had to keep a balanced viewpoint. If they stopped, would they be abandoning Caro or setting her free?

'I do love her,' said Fiona, on the edge of tears.

'Of course, of course you do. Of course.' They petted her, comforted her.

'I think we ought to pray about it, of course,' Anna said, 'but I also think, could you consider taking a break, just a holiday? And see if that felt good. You don't have to decide for ever. A break is often a good thing, I mean that's why I'm here.'

'Does it work?' Stephen asked, both anxious to get away from this whole painful subject and oddly pleased to be prodding at Anna; she had heard their intimacies, she ought to offer some of her own.

But Anna was not to be drawn. She was concentrating on Fiona. 'Look,' she said, 'of course you're tired. What you're doing is tiring enough in itself without being pregnant as well. Why do you have to make a final decision now? Just take a little break. Seven days a week of anything is too much. Even contemplatives get holidays nowadays you know. We all did; a day off a week and a proper holiday once a year.' The people of the shanty-towns had never had holidays, but there was no need to tell Fiona that. Mothers never had holidays either. Perhaps, the wicked thought flashed through her mind, perhaps the religious had it pretty easy these days. But, well, she was being calm and sensible and holy; the Fathers would be pleased with her, or at least less angry with her for listening to Caro. And she was good at it: she could see Fiona comforted, relaxing, accepting the idea of an interim period; she could feel Stephen being grateful; she could even feel her own inner turbulence being soothed by her own good sense and competence. She should stick to what she knew. That would be better, safer, simpler.

But she was lonely.

Nonsense, she was called to a lonely life; it was the nature of

137

her vocation. Community did not eliminate loneliness and had never been designed to do so. Intimacy was a perilous road, only to be trod with the greatest care. True intimacy could only come from God and should be kept for God.

But she was lonely.

She had never really known what that meant before. Karen had taught her something that was not going to be useful, something she would have to unlearn. Although of course she had had friends before: her family; her community; Kate.

In the nights when she woke up she realised how much she missed the simple companionship. Perhaps she was being silly. It had been very late at night; she might even have been a bit drunk. Or she had not properly understood Sybil. She had been rather overdramatic about it all. And she could hardly avoid the British Library for ever. She had to do some work too. That primarily was what she was here for, after all. To do her job: and important though it was to help Fiona and Stephen it was perhaps, almost certainly, more important to do what she was meant to do, to be obedient. She ought to go back to the library and work. It would not be her fault if she met Karen there; and anyway now she was forewarned there could be no harm in it. She would be careful, and friendship was itself a virtue. Karen had never said anything that could be understood that way. Perhaps Sybil was jealous or something. Perhaps she had just got it wrong. Or she, Anna, had not really understood her.

After the evening when she had been such a support and succour to Fiona in her distress she knew there would always be something missing from that friendship. She could not use it as a replacement and she did not want to. It was something different. Good in itself, but not a substitute for the fun and joy and nourishing that she got with Karen.

Karen had been surprised by Anna's disappearance. She had thought the dinner party a success. Anna might have felt a bit strange but she had obviously enjoyed it.

Karen leapt into the library the next morning full of delight and anticipation and when Anna was not there she was annoyed at her own disappointment; she commanded herself to imagine unknown religious duties which might be keeping Anna busy. After a couple of days she sent her a note, bicycling down to deliver it by hand in the middle of the night, whooping along the deserted roads and laughing into the dark. It was a long ride and she felt filled with zeal and love, powerful and determined and crafty. It was a ride of pure joy. Outside the convent where she had never been before she stood quietly for a long while looking up at the windows and thought of Anna asleep and was gleeful. The secrecy of her coming pleased her. Behind the neat row of windows were rows of nuns asleep. She knew really that they did not sleep in their habits, but it amused her to imagine a tidy line of them laid out neatly with their chins tucked tidily over the edge of their sheets and their veils spread out on the pillows. Somewhere in that line was Anna, looking like all the others but in fact dreaming sweetly of very un-nunlike things. She smiled tenderly. It was years since she had stood outside the house of the beloved and indulged in tender wit. She was in love. But her note was careful and precise: she hoped Anna was not ill, if so to let her know, otherwise see her soon. She just happened to be passing, but it was rather late and she thought she had better not disturb the peace of the household.

Later she sent other notes too. Increasingly they had a sharp edge to them — Anna was after all being bloody inconsiderate. Friendship carried some obligations, although she restrained herself from actually saying this. Soon, she thought, she would have to. She was not going to let Anna get away with this sort of thing; she couldn't always use her special status to behave so badly. It was not fair.

Over the next weeks she went over the evening with a fine-tooth comb; remembering everything there was to remember, trying at all times to see Anna's face as it had been then. It had been all right. Or rather, everything that she had seen had been all right. She went to find Sybil.

Sybil was already feeling guilty. She knew she had been meddling where she had no business to. She told herself, and it was true, that she had meddled solely out of love for Karen; she told herself that Anna was an adult and had to take some responsibility for what was going on. She had also, she realised, rather liked Anna. She had ended the evening respecting her: she recognised that Anna was trying to tackle something terribly difficult; even if she Sybil did not understand what it was. She had not meant to do any harm, and she knew now that she should have kept her silly mouth shut. Even though, even though the two of them might have gone on for ever, or until Karen exploded violently as they all knew she could well do. They might have gone on for ever in oblivion and missed something that was important for both of them. Better out than in, Sybil told herself, but she saw Karen's stricken face and remembered Anna's unnatural stillness in the car. She had touched something too deep. She felt guilty and confused and was finally quite relieved when Karen came to ask her what, if anything, they had said in the car going home.

'Syb, I haven't seen her since. She has disappeared. And yet I'm sure she was fine when she left here. Do you think we were all a bit much — you know, a bit too heavy for her.'

Sybil was furious that Karen should even consider apologising for them all, should think of them as somehow not suitable for her girlfriend. She replied a bit tersely: 'It wasn't that. She enjoyed it. Karen, I honestly don't think she's quite as frail, as in need of your tender loving care as you seem to want. I think she's quite tough.'

'Well, what did she say in the car?'

'It wasn't what she said, it was what I said.'

'What?'

'Look Karen, I don't think you're going to like this too much . . . I'm not even sure now why I did it. I, oh damn.'

'Come on Sybil, out with it, it can't have been that bad.'

'I told her you fancied her, were in love with her.'

Karen hit her. She did not even know she was going to; there was in her mind no gap between hearing Sybil's words and hearing her own ringing blow against Sybil's mouth. A bit of her stood quite still, as stunned as Sybil was, a moment without control and without self-consciousness. Then her guilt and fury drowned her. She felt lethal, unforgiving, crazy in her belly. She had been so careful, so fucking careful, she had exercised a restraint, a delicacy she didn't even know she possessed. And Sybil, the treacherous bitch, had blown her cover.

But it was Sybil; she had hit Sybil, she had taken advantage of

140

her own extra seven inches and the trust of ancient friendship to hit her. She did not think there was another person in the whole world that she could have hit. She took her in her arms apologising, reassuring, crying herself and guilty, guilty, guilty and hating to feel guilty. Personal guilt towards Sybil and a deep moral guilt which heard all the voices in all the Battered Women's refuges in the world, and all the Peace Women in all the camps, and all her own scathing attacks on masculist violence. As well as feeling blind, out of control and furious, she also felt stupid, childish and bad.

Sybil, though outraged and shocked, knew that she also felt relieved; the burden of guilt shifted from herself to Karen and also she knew it could have been worse. Karen's capacity for sudden and destructive anger was well known. It was unforgivable but it was also Karen and better in a way than Karen's seeringly accurate abuse, her ability to find the psychological jugular, the soft underbelly places, the tender points. Though, Christ, her lip hurt and she could taste the blood.

Karen tried despairingly to explain. 'I'm sorry, I'm sorry. She's driving me fucking crazy. Not she. It. It's driving me crazy. I think there's something in her that is damaged. It's like, it's as though she really doesn't know what she wants. I can't cope with that, with that split, she makes it all so complicated but it's as though she, as though inside her there's an absolute communications breakdown; between her and her body, between her and herself, somehow. And I can't find a way to talk about it. You have to be careful all the time. I have to be careful, I feel it all the time, all the time that there's something that may just snap, as though she's right on the edge and reaching out to her may make her fall over even though it may be the only way of rescuing her. I can't stand it. I can't stand my own feelings about her because they're so bloody stupid.' She tried to laugh at herself, shaky but resolute. 'You know Sybil, I look at myself and I think, "There goes one bloody stupid dyke." God knows, we say it all the time about women who are falling for straight women, for married women; never mind a woman who's living with, married to, bloody God. She's thirty-eight years old, she's a virgin, a Christian, a bloody nun, and I have to go and fall in love with her. I hate the phrase and it's true. I don't simply fancy her, want to go to bed with her and all that, although shit I do want to — I want to take care of her, look after her, make her well, protect her from her own fears and one of her fears is me so I want to protect her from the dangerous woman with the unnatural passions that is me. I haven't felt that about myself since I was a teenager and I hate it, and I hate her for making me feel it. And she's so out of it really, so hopeless and stuck, stuck in her guilts and fears. I don't want it. I don't bloody need it. Life's hard enough as it is. I want a nice healthy gay feminist I can go to bed and have fun with. I don't want this grand passion stuff any more. In theory I don't even believe in it Sybil. I just can't cope with the whole damn thing.'

'Well go hit her, go hit yourself; you don't have to hit me.'

Karen is silenced, a silence broken by Sybil. 'Look I'm really angry with you, because you hit me and because you've kept me outside all this for so long. I'm angry and I can't be sure whether I'm telling you this because I'm angry or for some nicer reason, but I'm going to tell you anyway. I don't think that it was discovering that you fancied her that wound her up. I think it was admitting that she fancied you.'

'What?'

'C'mon dummy. I asked her. Of course I asked her at that point. I asked her and she said yes. She didn't like it and she wept all over the place and she went extremely odd afterwards, but she said yes and she meant it. So now you know. Being you and thinking you're so damn irresistible anyway, I expect you probably knew that already, but she knows too and she told me so.'

Karen had to think fast. She was angry with Sybil still but filled with joy. She knew it would be difficult, but if Anna was able, was prepared to recognise desire, then the whole situation was radically changed. Karen had thought that Anna really did not, could not know. But now. To Karen that was the final immorality: to love, to know you loved and not to act on it. There was nothing, fundamentally, in the way. It would be difficult, she did realise how difficult it would be for Anna, but now nothing was impossible. She had to come up with a new strategy, a new plan. The first thing was to find an easy way for them both to be together again. In her presence, surrounded by her love, Anna would be able to overcome her guilt, defeat her fears. Of course she would. But she Karen would have to be careful, not hurry, not be clumsy. She had to think, and take care. She must not frighten Anna, not scare or pressure her. But first they had to find each other again.

A few mornings later Audrey said to Anna, 'That friend you came into the shop with, remember? Karen. I saw her yesterday and she asked if I'd seen you. She said to mention to you that if you've finished your work in the BL could you give her a ring, she wants some reading list or other.'

'Thanks,' said Anna.

'She's a nice person, isn't she? And clever, I've seen some of her stuff.' Audrey was casual, because Karen had been skilful.

The two of them bent back over Caro.

Audrey's tone of casual approval and Karen's easy message were balm to Anna. She was being terribly silly anyway, she told herself. They could still be friends. Karen was perfectly sensible. She was lonely, she wanted to see Karen. She blotted out the conversation with Sybil. Karen had never said anything. She wanted to see Karen again because she could be useful to her and her work; because she wanted friendship and someone to talk to. She almost managed to forget, almost managed to hide from herself, her own confession to Sybil. It never occurred to her that Sybil would have told Karen. Brought up in the practice of personal reticence and trained in confidentiality and discretion, finding her own words embarrassing, sick, sinful, deranged, it never so much as crossed her mind that Sybil would have repeated them to Karen.

And it never occurred to Karen that it would not have occurred to Anna. Their models of friendship were too different, too far apart; the gap was wider and more real than their imaginations could bridge. Karen thought that now Anna must have openly acknowledged what was between them; she assumed almost that Anna would have told Sybil so that Sybil would tell Karen. She knew she still had to hunt carefully, stalking through the forests and jungles of Anna's fears, but she believed there was an agreement that in some clearing, some opening of her own choosing Anna would turn and come to her. Her reconciliation was based on hope, Anna's on denial.

But they were so happy to be together again. They played and frolicked as never before. Anna even began when she was with Karen to explore the possibilities of leaving the order, leaving her community. They were new words and Karen gave them a safe place to be heard. She did not address the important questions, why she had entered in the first place and why it had gone wrong; but she opened herself to consider the practical implications, what she could do, how she could live. She allowed herself to be critical of conventual life, and to form in her mind new ambitions, although she was still just trying out of the sound of the ideas, putting them delicate and cautious against the voices of the Fathers who were forced into retreat by Anna's new-found boldness. Their voices could be heard now only in the darkness of her sleep where they entangled in her dreams, but Anna never listened to her dreams and when she awoke in the mornings she would throw them off with the bedclothes and wash them away to the chant of the morning psalms.

Fiona had taken Anna's advice and a holiday from Caro's exercises. Anna still spent a good deal of time there but now it was different, it no longer had the edge of duty and necessity. She felt she had entered into a smooth space, a gentler place; she could stay in London. She saw the city anew, not as a tourist attraction or rest home for a battered nun, but as a place where she could live and be alive. Yet she did not write to Mother Superior and tell her this, she did not mention it to Fiona in their long conversational rambles, nor to her own father when she wrote to him. She skirted it even when she went to confession and not liking to do so went less often and barely noticed. She went on happily saying her Office and going to daily Mass and she felt newly comfortable there, no longer eaten with misery and confusion. But she clung to Karen and her company; the new ideas could only exist when Karen heard them, only dare to poke their heads out of their burrows when Karen was there dangling tasty carrots. It was a secret place she shared with Karen, but not an evil secret, a little cell warm and private, she tried to tell herself, a room where no one else could come, a place where she could try on the new clothes. She did not know why she could not mention her newer plans, hopes, aspirations to anyone except for Karen. She refused to ask herself that, floating in the pure pleasure of the days and the times together.

There was a public element in it too. She went often to Karen's house. She was too naïve to realise that they all assumed she was Karen's lover and were waiting for her to leave the convent and come and join them. They thought she had made a choice and was on their side. They did not press, but except for Sybil with whom Anna avoided real conversation, they assumed and that assumption changed something for Karen. But for Anna their friendliness was happy. The heaviness was gone from her life. Little pleasures remained. Walking all the way across London in the dark of the evening and forgetting that being a woman alone at night was dangerous. Flying a kite in the park with Sybil and Judy and Karen. Accepting from Judy who seemed the same size as she was other clothes to wear, now that she never wore the habit any more.

Admiring one slightly tipsy evening Judy's new tattoo; a tiny elegant blue leopard with white spots low down on her back.

'Judy, for God's sake, why?' Karen and Sybil are both amazed, while Anna is totally baffled. They tease her, warning her that she'll turn into a hunky marine before their very eyes. And also slightly repelled and slightly envious.

'When I'm old and grey and right-wing,' said Judy, 'I want to be able to remind myself that once I was otherwise.'

'I don't know that leopards are a sign of radicalism,' Karen said laughing. 'You're just driven by anticipated guilt.'

But Judy caught Sybil's eye and the two of them giggled and blushed and it was clear to both Anna and Karen that there was some sexual implication in the leopard, and that made them feel closer to each other though differently.

'Did you know,' Judy asked,' that there's an Amazonian tribe where they believe that it is the ability to change and affect the body, to ornament oneself, that is the sign of being human. If you're not tattooed then no one can distinguish you from a pig, so they tattoo all the babies to stop the pig ancestors coming for them. Isn't that interesting?'

'No, it's gross,' said Karen.

'No, look.' Judy was obviously pleased with her tattoo but she still wanted their approval. 'If the way we see bodies is socially constructed within society, then I do want to control my own construction. It makes me feel good.'

Karen said, 'I read an article the other day arguing that artificial insemination was more human than conception by coital sex, because it was artificial, a move towards control, away from animal nature.'

'I think that's rubbish, it's denial,' Sybil said. She touched Judy's leopard gently; 'but this is bringing the inward dream outward, socialising it. And it is beautiful.'

'You didn't think that about my habit,' said Anna. She was surprised when the others laughed, she had not meant to make a joke, but was content to be heard that way.

Judy said to Sybil, 'I'd better warn you, my love, he's a lovely man; the best tattooist in London, and a perfectly magical.'

'Where does he hang out? I think I want one too.'

They fantasised about Sybil's tattoo and their jokes became coarse and coarser, and Karen took Anna away but still laughing.

Anna started to worry a bit about money. She accepted without reporting it a cheque from her father. His letter said that he was sorry he would be out of England longer than he had expected but he guessed being a nun in Europe was more expensive than being a nun in Latin America. This was a gift not to her but to the order so that they would not have to subsidise her themselves. Please would she accept it in that light.

She and Karen spent some of it on new jeans and shirts for her. It was not what her father had had in mind but she could not bring herself to care. She also bought a present for Caro, a soft blue blanket with a satin binding. She discovered that she liked buying presents for people, it had been too long since she had enjoyed that privilege of affection. After a great deal of thought she bought a present for Karen too: it was a Käthe Kollwitz print of the Visitation — two strong women leaning on to each other's arms. As soon as she had given to Karen she knew that it was absolutely the right present and she glowed with joy. It brought their two worlds together, close like the women in the lithograph. Karen smiled and hugged her and said, 'Of course you do realise that the Visitation is ultimate Dyke moment, don't you; when two women get together and in love proclaim their freedom, they sing that the personal is the political and from their love will come freedom for all the world.' She was laughing at Anna, but the

146

laughter was a deep pure stream breaking up to the surface and love seemed innocent and easy in the moment.

Paula asked Anna shortly afterwards if she would write an article about the Church and South American politics, based fairly straightforwardly on her own experience in Santa Virgine; and Anna kept the money she earned secret too. Once or twice, when she left Karen and was alone in the convent, she knew that what she was doing was strange and dangerous; she had often heard about nuns who just drifted off, away, who never came to any real moment of decision, but whose vocation died like a dead marriage and the date of its demise was elusive. She did not want it to be like that, she was frightened of that. But also she did not want to stop; she tried to call it exploration, experimentation, she rationalised that she had to try out another sort of life style so that she could discover what she wanted. But what she wanted was to be with them, with Karen and her friends, who shut out the voices and eased her days. She certainly did not want to press herself for decisions, to cope with anything difficult.

She found too that she was working more smoothly. Karen was as well. The library was utterly safe grounds where they both had a right and a duty to be, an unquestioning space that was not about the shape and development of their feelings. They were excited by their lives. She and Karen entered into each other's excitement and were nourished by it, and they worked and played and were for the time being content.

It was a happy valley, the real world of decision and pain cut off, and they dallied there in delight until the mountains came crashing in; a landslide that neither of them could have been prepared for.

One morning Karen was reading the newspaper. She was feeling pleased with herself, and not without self-consciousness. She sat on the top step of the portico of the British Museum, rather to the left of the central entrance; her jeans were tight, her green boots polished and her t-shirt loose and comfortable. This was Bloomsbury, she was writing a fascinating book, she was having an interesting relationship with an ex-nun. She was not stupid either, she noticed how she had smoothed down the sharp edges of all those things even in the privacy of her own head. But her hair was clean and shining and she was sitting in the sunshine

147

feeling pleased with herself and reading *The Times*. There were moments of pleasure so much simpler than joy. That morning she had bought her copy of *The Times* sneakily; not because she did not like the *Guardian*, their household paper, but simply because she had this one all to herself, dodging communal high-mindedness and coffee stains on half the pages. She smiled affectionately at herself.

She did not hear Anna come up behind her. Often she noticed odd skills in Anna, presumably learned in the chilly corridors of her far away convent, and one of them was that she could walk even quite fast without making any noise. Anna touched her on the shoulder and squatted down beside her.

'Here's one for you, Anna,' Karen said, shuffling back the pages of the paper. ''US Ex-Nun Shot with Terrorist Group.'' There's a picture.' She tipped the page round for Anna to see the crazed-looking woman between two men. She laughed. There was a silent moment while Anna, poised to dodge Karen's probable barb about the possible consequences of frustration, looked at the photograph.

'It's Kate,' she said. Karen looked up, hearing unexpected words and not understanding them. She saw that Anna's face was drained, wiped blank. Anna stood up and walked away from her down the steps of the museum. When she got to the bottom she turned round and Karen knew that she had never seen Anna furious before. She, Anna of all unlikely people, there in that very public place, suddenly yelled, 'You stupid bitch, that's Kate. That's my sister.' And ran away.

In the shadow of her anger Kate could no longer run away. She turned and ran towards instead. There was no more space for running away. She did not, like Anna, seek Mother, Mother House, love or home. One evening, after night prayer, she tidily laid down her breviary and walked out. Sr. Jo had not been paying proper attention; for the last several months Kate's anger had been escalating, but Sr. Kate was always unnecessarily irritable and all the more so since Sr. Anna had gone. Really, Sr. Jo tried to tell herself, it was not her job to mother these women who were no younger than she was. There were more important things to do. She did not know who Sr. Kate had been seeing. No one ever knew how she had come into contact with the guerilla group, nor how she had decided to leave the convent and take to the hills. The danger, the fear of death in her mouth was the only thing that lifted the corner of her suffocating anger. People who would go all the way out, not defend themselves passively. People who would take arms against the sea of troubles. Sr. Kitty's rape had only been a symptom. Soon after Sr. Anna had left Sr. Kate had stopped thinking very clearly — it had seemed a waste of effort. Kate had taken all she could take; she had run too far and fast before the hounds of her own anger and now she turned at bay. There were the hard wonderful months during which they slogged across the mountains and carved their way through the jungles, slipping away at night, and no one knew where they were. Half contacts with other groups, half-formed plans, nothing organised, nothing certain in the wild lands of the interior. In the end it reminded her of childhood games with her brothers, in which they had been heroic outlaws fighting against the forces of evil. They were armed and trained. She had finally got outside.

The Times informed its readers that little was known of this particular group which had been caught during a bombing attempt on a conference of the League of South American Bankers. Kate and one other man, wrongly presumed to be her lover, had been short on sight by the security forces; their companion had been arrested. It was an international incident in a small way. A very small way.

Kate who had been burning with light had chosen the darkness. Anna saw her picture in a newspaper eight thousand miles away. Kate had tried to shoot her way out of trouble. Anna had tried to weep her way out. Which was less likely to succeed?

Karen, unclear, ran down the steps after Anna.

She stopped again at the bottom, watching, not knowing what to do or how to do it. She saw that Anna was walking extraordinarily fast and with alarming eccentricity. A senseless bouncy weave in her gait. At the gates she turned left and swayed along Great Russell Street. Her sister?

Karen did not understand.

Sister?

She had never seen Anna angry before; not angry and shouting on the street, that was her not Anna. Karen felt a wave of jealous resentment. Who was this damn dead nun who could release such a tide of feeling in Anna that she would stand in front of the British Museum and swear. US ex-nun. Anna's sister.

Suddenly there was a context, and some comprehension. Karen leapt down the steps of the museum, surprising herself by noticing that there were twelve of them. She began to run. What the hell had been going on in the convent? Anna crazy, this Sister Kate dead. She pounded out of the gates, splashing through a puddle of Japanese tourists.

I love you. Your grief is my grief. Let me have it. Let me have some of it. Share it, you can't carry it alone, share it with me, Anna please. Karen knew that she did not remotely understand Anna's relationship to her convent, and she also knew that for Anna this would not be about Kate alone but about Anna too, and nunnery.

Damn, Damn Damn thought Karen, running towards Bloomsbury Square. What was all this? What the hell was she doing? She was in love with a goddamn nun. Her friends all thought she was a bloody lunatic. And she was, she was. The only people Anna really seemed to care for were one brain-damaged toddler and one dead terrorist. Karen was irritated by herself. She wanted out. But she pursued Anna too.

Anna wanted. She did not know what she wanted as she careened along the street unseeing.

'How dare you,' she yelled at the Fathers. 'How dare you? This is too much.'

'Good nuns don't get shot,' the Fathers retorted smugly.

'I hate you, I hate you, I hate you.'

'Don't be so childish. Don't be silly. You can't blame us for this one. She's the one you ought to angry with. She was very bad.'

'But why? Why did she do it? What are you playing at? Why Kate?' She was so angry, she was exploding with anger, she had found her own anger in her belly, furious, furious. Kate.

'She was too much. Saw too much. Wanted too much. She was getting out of hand. She thought she could ask questions. She thought she could find a shorter way through. And she was violent. Dangerous and angry. But it does seem worth pointing

150

out to you that guns are clean and guns are quick. You wouldn't choose that way would you, not you. You want to wallow in filth. You had better watch out. Incidentally, for your information, they shot her in the lower stomach; her guts were on the street.'

Anna bent forward, falling, clutching her own stomach, feeling the bullets ripping in, penetrating her secret places, feeling the pain and the low dreadful buzz of excitement. Was this why Kate did it, because there was nowhere else she could take her blazing anger and turn it outwards before it chewed up her insides: had she felt that buzz? Or was that Anna's evil secret, her dark sickness. She slumped against an elegant area railing, retching, gasping, wanting to vomit, wanting to be safely held.

And Karen held her.

Anna was inside the vortex of her own need, where all the stars crashed together and endangered the creation; where the centre cannot hold and chaos is come again. The great pit that Caro invited her into was here, here at her feet, the plunge so easy now into not-ness, insanity, collapse.

And Karen held her. First squatting on the street beside her, pulling Anna's head against her chest, wrapping her arms around all the shaking pain, kissing her hair, her forehead. Holding her as a mother ought to hold a child in its nightmares. It was physical contact, it was warm and sweet and unremembered, something she did not know about. It pulled her back from the edge of the place where she had been going, it drew her homewards. She leaned against Karen, giving her all her weight, resting her head on those welcoming breasts, knowing that within this magic circle the Fathers cannot come, the bullets cannot break through. The simple presence of a body so close and so accepted was enough to keep all monsters at bay. She reposed in the arms of another woman — mother, sister, friend. And something missing. But Karen carried the missing word. It was lover. Anna did not know it.

Karen tugged Anna gently to her feet. They could not stay there forever.

'Tell me,' she urged. 'Tell me. Kate.'

But Anna could not answer at that moment. Kate had fallen into disintegration in her mind. Kate. Sister Katherine Mary. She could still feel the bullets ripping their way into her gut and while she felt that so keenly she could not find Kate. All she could find was the anger, Kate's wild anger going out in rays to welcome the bullets in. She could see the bullets homing in on target, a target so illuminated that even in the depths of the jungle the bullets cannot fail but find her.

Karen said, 'I'm going to take you home.'

'We have no home. Kate and I have no home. We are drifting together on the Great River and have no home. Nothing. This is called poverty, detachment. Having no home.' Anna's voice has a dreamy chanting quality to it. Karen was alarmed, aware that wherever Anna was, it was not on the street with her.

'I have a home,' she said firmly. 'I have a home and we are going there now. I have made myself a home and I am taking you in.'

Anna was passive, quiescent. A vast silence took over her head. Kate was dead, the silence said. Kate was dead and she had never known how much Anna had loved her. She had stolen from Kate, taken taken taken; drawing on her reserves of energy and strength and positiveness and wildness. If she had loved Kate better, if she had poured back the energy she had stolen, if she had prayed harder, she could have caught Kate's anger, drawn it off into a bottle and kept it safe. But she had run away from Santa Virgine and the glorious pursuit of the unicorn. She had run away and left Kate on her own; alone Kate had not been strong enough, the horn of the unicorn had gorged into her belly, seeking out her uterus, her womb. She let Karen wave down a taxi and she got into it meekly.

'Kate.' She tried to recall her, tried to summons her back again in all her brightness. 'Kate and I were in the novitiate together. I was a year ahead of her. She liked me. I liked her. We were close then, well balanced, and it was very good. We were posted. Then I didn't see her for years. She came out to Santa Virgine about three years ago. It was lovely. You'd have liked her. I don't know what happened . . . I don't know . . . I don't know.'

There was a long pause and Karen, trying to joke said, 'I know you're about to apologise for being a bore; if you do I'll be really angry. Nobody's friends get shot dead every day of the week. It is a big thing. You're meant to let it be a big thing.' Why in God's name didn't Anna cry or weep or something. Damn, I'm too old for all this drama, this adolescent romantic bullshit. I'm a bright lesbian feminist and I can sleep with anyone I want to — well within certain limits, she conceded — and I don't have to spend any valuable time mothering a nun with a nervous breakdown. But I love her. Damn it, I love her. Karen still kept her arms round Anna, holding her together, stopping the little bits flying off and shooting through the window of the taxi; darting away across London, across the Atlantic and destroying themselves in the jungles and the mountains of the New World.

Karen's house, to Karen's relief, was empty when they arrived. She led Anna into the big happy front room and sat her on a chair; she made some coffee and wondered what she ought to do next.

'Have a bath,' she suggested. 'Have a bath and then I'll give you a backrub. And then if you want you can tell me about it.'

Anna seemed limp, but not protesting. Karen went upstairs to run the bath. The bathroom had been made out of one of the upper bedrooms, a larger than normal, cosy room, carpeted and with a couch in it. They all indulged themselves in the bathroom. The couch was there for sitting on and chatting. Some evenings the room would be filled with warm steam and four or five of them would be gathered there sweating out the day, their work their friends and their thoughts. Sybil often said there was something alarmingly Sloane about all this girls-together-in-the-bathroom stuff, but Karen knew that for herself it was a special place and a favourite time, a victory they had won for themselves from a hard world, and a sign of friendliness and hope. A bottle of wine and steamy chatter. Would she stay and watch Anna in the bath? What, if anything, would Anna feel? She had to be careful and considerate right now, but on the other hand if she took no risks, no chances, then nothing would happen and eventually Anna would drift away on some current, wander off back to America and sink into being a good nun again. What a waste. Well, not without a challenge, Karen thought, not without a challenge. But it had to be the right challenge. Anna knew. Anna had told Sybil that she desired Karen. What did she want, Karen wondered as she splashed the water into the tub. Did she expect Karen to force the issue, was that what she wanted, needed, was she waiting for Karen's directive? I'm in love, thought Karen,

I'm in love and the woman I'm in love with needs me. That was enough. She opened the airing cupboard and removed one of Paula's enormous fluffy and sacrosanct towels. She would explain later, this was an emergency. She chucked the towel on to the couch, sloshed some expensive bath essence under the tap and ran downstairs again. Anna was sitting exactly as she had left her, staring out of the window.

Karen led her upstairs. The bath was nearly full of water and the room of steam. She stood hesitating in the doorway watching Anna who was looking around her blankly. Anna said, 'Do you know I left Santa Virgine because I wanted a really deep hot bath. You have given it to me. But if I'd stayed, Kate would not have done it. So I killed her for a hot bath.' She undid her shirt buttons, looked at Karen and said, 'Please don't go. I can't be alone.' Karen watched bemused as she stripped her clothes off. This was not how she had imagined seeing Anna's body. A nice body, she noticed, very white. She was too thin though. She needed fattening up. Anna showed absolutely no self-consciousness; she climbed into the bath and lowered herself into the water with an exhalation of relief, and smiled at Karen like a child. Dear God, thought Karen despite Sybil, despite what she had told Sybil and Sybil had told her she was completely unaware, no sense of sexuality at all, like a kid. She didn't know what was going on. But Anna was so clearly unhappy, not fulfill-ed, out of contact with her life and herself; on her own admission it was driving her to the edge of endurance. If she ran away from that edge, went back to her convent with nothing changed, with-out any movement, it would finish her off. It would kill her, kill the authenticity of the woman whom Karen really liked. It was an unbearable thought, worse than not having her. Growing space, she needed growing space, and Karen had to give her that; but it had to be physical it had to be. Karen could not believe that anyone could go on that long journey of self-discovery if they refused to do it with and in and through their body; their body's desires.

'Do you want a back rub?'

'A what?'

'Massage; I'll rub your back and smooth you out; don't you do that? It's very sisterly.'

154

Anna lay on the bed. She was perfectly submissive, Karen could do with her whatever she wanted. Was that trust? She had come so far now, so far from Santa Virgine and what she knew how to handle. She lay on the bed wearing only her knickers and Karen knelt beside her. Karen poured soft oil on her back and began to rub. 'Don't let me be too heavy, stop if it hurts. OK?' But it did not hurt, it was a good feeling, Karen's strong fingers finding the muscles in her shoulders, each vertebra in her back. She went into the feeling of it, floating, breathing. She was lost in a pleasant wood and she wandered there. It was not a wood, it was a forest, a jungle. Not frightening though. It was the forest where she and Kate had gone together. The jungle of the Amazons; velvet black at night; garish but lazy all day. Hot and soporific, draining away the energy. The dry cold men who had gone to North America had defeated the land, had fought and wrestled with it, and countered its energy with their own fierce protesting energy; they had been energised by the cold winds and icy blizzards that would otherwise have overpowered them. But the golden Spaniards who had come from a land as harsh and barren had slipped off the mountains into the great jungled valley and their energy and dreams had drained away, leaving little to show for such proud and high hopes, just cathedrals that were swallowed up again by the giant trees and a few decimated broken tribal peoples. They had come there with the bravest dreams; dreams fired by the gold of Peru, the silver of Bolivia, the emeralds of Bogata, and pearls from the island of Cubagna. Visions of glory from the convents of Spain and visions of domination from the greatest King Emperor in the world. And all the dreams had been sucked in and grown heavy rotten sleepy and warm in the great valley of the Amazons. And now she was there again, floating, uncaring, laying down all dreams of perfection, all fears of hell, all hopes of heaven. Nothing was left but she and Kate floating, gentle, at peace.

But Kate was dead.

And now there was only silence inside her where Kate had been and no longer was.

Karen, massaging her back, while Anna drifted on the great rivers of her memories, felt the change; felt the muscles contract. 'What are you thinking?' she asked. 'Tell me what you're thinking about.'

Anna struggled back to the surface and said, 'How could she have done anything so stupid, so totally brainlessly stupid.'

'Kate?'

'Yes Kate,' But Anna knew that stupidity was not the issue when it came to breaking one's way out. There came a time when violence was the only option. But violence against whom? Oneself? The powers of darkness? One's friends?

Kate's choices had been extreme, but at least they were choices. Even if lousy rotten vulgar choices, dying with a gun in her hand and dreadful destructive hatred in her head. Kate would not have sat around being dictated to by mad voices. Kate had not laid down her arms and sat in London weeping. Kate was Perpetua, ready to trample the head of the devil, ready to arm herself like a gladiator and storm the gates of hell. But Perpetua had to become a man to do it; in her dreams she had become a man. She gave her baby son away to her friends and became a man in order to challenge the devil head on. Was that necessary? Perpetua strength is the power of violence. Perpetua had, with her own elegant hand, guided the hand of her executioner. She had longed for the consummation, the power of blood and its sweetness, blasting through the gates of heaven noisy with the clanging power of her faith. Was that the only way, was that the only way?

If Kate was Perpetua, then she would have to be Felicity. Felicity, crying out and making a pathetic fuss in labour, suffering great pain but having no visions, no authority, no power except the power to consent, to consent to the pain and consent to the dying. To consent to what was happening to her and believing that it was good, it was of God and of the order of living. Should she go consenting to the death of her old self as Felicity had gone? Must she learn to consent to the turning of the seasons?

'You know,' she muttered now to Karen, 'I always wanted to understand why she entered and now I never will. Why? It was so unlikely. I mean it's quite usual for it to be unlikely, lots of the best nuns, but in her case . . .'

Karen said, 'But Anna, I wouldn't understand why anyone at all wanted to be a nun. Why did you?'

The question was too weighty. Why indeed? She tried to apply herself to this important question, but she preferred the gentle strength of Karen's hands. She could not concentrate, could not make the effort; she wanted only to lie here drifting, Karen's warm hands on the back of her legs. She did not know, she could not remember.

'It seemed so right at the time,' she said to Karen, and it had been right then, she knew that certainly, not an evasion, not an escape route, but a good strong growing decision. Before she fragmented under the pressure to change. A framework to live with. Order and freedom. Commitment. Now she did not know. Could not tell. Stand by that commitment, trust God, trust her own self? Or admit that it was all changed, she was all changed and could not longer fit into the frame which was not support but emprisonment? Or was it? She had to think, decide, act. But the langour was swallowing her up. All the energy was flowing out of her, she was limp, washed up on the sands of the islands of the lotus eaters. Sleepy. She had to think about it, had to think about what she was doing and what she was going to do. But not now. Now there was the warmth of soft sheet under her belly, there were Karen's hands, there was gentleness and playfulness, and the feeble tug of the tide of the great river. She had lost touch with that. Here she was centred. The shadows were driven away. Centred. Soothed. She fell asleep, not knowing.

Karen looked at her with tenderness, covered her over with the duvet and, leaving her to sleep, went downstairs.

Anna was dissolved in softness. Something hard unbending wilful had rotted away leaving only a soft damp thing deep in her belly. Had Kate been her hardness, so that when Kate had gone it had gone too. Or had hardness proved too dangerous? Waking in the mornings, walking on the streets by day she would feel suddenly the bullets enter her flesh; it was something quite real to her. She would crouch down doubled forward and in pain. She would feel the bullets opening the holes through which her guts would stream out, blood and water.

Karen's tenderness swelled; Anna's need drew out of her a depth of caring that she had not known existed and which she slightly despised. She wanted to hold her safe, make her well, nourish and contain her. She wanted to be the firm wall around Anna's softness, a cuirass, a breast-plate to protect her exposed belly. Late one night she watched a nature documentary on television; there was a scene that showed a doe trying to protect its fawn from the attack of some bird of prey. Karen had to leave the room abruptly. It was an image of herself that she did not like, did not want, and now could not resist.

Externally disciplined Anna went on working, insisting on the daily routine as something that she could trust. But the content of her reading changed. She went further and further back trying to find the places where Kate had been. She read the sad stories of the conquest of Peru, the defeat of the golden Incas, high up in the mountains where Kate had died. Kate was one of the hard golden warriors who had proved incapable of defending themselves from the Catholic soldiers simply because their imaginations failed. They could not conceive of a people who would kill and betray and murder and deceive for the sake of the yellow shiny plaything. They were not guileless, the Incas, they were not primitive innocents, they were a fierce destructive people and the laws by which they lived were merciless. But they were different and could not imagine people who could preach a gentle god of love and then lie and destroy even each other for the sake of the gold.

Somewhere in her reading Anna encountered a man who seemed as baffled by it all as she was. A man who seemed to have turned quite deliberately away from the harsh reality of the high mountains where even the air is thin and bright and had sought the underbelly of the jungle. His name was Francisco da Orellana and he was the accidental discoverer of the Amazon river where she and Kate had drifted together and been joyful. For over a year he and his companions had drifted, powerless and apparently not caring where they were going, down that enormous river. His thoughts of gold and conquest and victory and God had grown vaguer and dreamier, they had faded away. Around food, sleep and daily survival the days revolved and they had drifted down the endless muggy river just as she drifted now. Each bend threatened to reveal horrors and only revealed another bend, while the jungle clung close beside them like a mother holding its child by the hand.

Anna travelled with him as she had travelled with Kate. There was an account written by a pompous Dominican who had been on the expedition, who alternated between his passionate devotion to his Captain and his determined recollection that God must in all things be glorified. Anna ignored his pious platitudes and heard only the strange distant dreams of this man who had been where Kate and she had been, had lost touch with his own hardness and become so soft and flowing and pointless as she was now.

He and his companions had come at last to a new land of which they had been warned by the tribal people higher up the river. Here the native Indians were stirred to a new level of energetic resistance by their officers who were women, very tall and white-skinned and wore their hair coiled around their heads and were naked apart from green hair ornaments. These, the adventurers learned, were the great mothers, the women who ruled the interior and lived entirely without men, rounding them up for insemination and returning all boy children to their care. They lived in white stone houses and traded in green jade jewels. This was the land of the mothers, the warrior women. There they were, for no apparent reason, harried and attacked mercilessly, driven and persecuted and killed. They could not understand it.

Anna could not understand it either. 'Karen,' she said, 'did you know that the man who discovered the Amazon did not experience the warrior women as virgins but as mothers?'

Karen asked, 'Did he really experience them at all?' She looked at what Anna was reading, then said, 'He's just recording the old classical mythology; the women were in his head. Men don't know whether they fear matriarchs or amazons more. Perhaps the guy was just scared for his life and got both at once.'

'Cynic,' said Anna laughing. 'Before the Europeans arrived the tribes of the Amazon were quite sophisticated, you know; they migrated in their canoes all the way up the river network and out into the Caribbean. They had highly developed ritual lives, including cannibalism, and they were expert herbalists.' She looked sideways at Karen, wanting to please her. 'They may really have had female leadership you know, there's a clue. They had effective oral contraceptives made from herbs.'

Karen teased her back, 'I can't see that they had much on offer for either you or me then. Do you really believe in matriarchal, women-led, exclusive men-free cultures in the Amazon?'

'No,' said Anna, 'but it's sad. I'd like to.'

Karen was about to joke about Anna becoming a radical separatist, but she looked up and sensed a great fear and a great longing in her and held her breath. She did not know what it was or where it came from, but she thought that she would have to go out boldly and wrestle with Anna's demons. Go into Anna's labyrinth and kill her minotaur. She was not frightened but excited by that possibility. But Anna would have to give her the end of the thread. Would have to trust her and invite her. Anna seemed consenting, but not actively trusting. Not clear. Karen felt that wrestling matches should take place in bright dry deserts; she knew less about jungles where nothing is clear or hard-edged or defined, but melting, changing, all profusion and confusion. On their different terrains they stood, and neither knew how to leap across into the other's country.

'For Christ's sake,' sighed Sybil, driven beyond bearing. 'For God's sake Karen, find out. Or let it go. Just lay it down, Karen, it's not your problem. It sounds to me like she needs a shrink not a lover. Let her go.'

'She won't let me go,' said Karen sadly, hearing Sybil and wishing it were that easy. She was sitting on Sybil's bed trying to make some sense of her own feelings. And even as she drew comfort from Sybil's presence and genuine if irritated interest, she felt a great compassion for Anna whose only friend was dead and far away.

'It's not her, you know,' Sybil said suddenly, smiling at Karen to take the sting out of her words and feeling full of both love and exasperation. 'It's not her, it's you. It's you and your damned arrogance; you can't let her go because you can't admit that you've failed. You can't believe that you can't be her fucking saviour.' Suddenly she was worried for Karen and even a little worried for Anna. 'Karen, you must do something. It's dangerous. You're reaching a point where you'd rather she was stuck forever than she found a way out that didn't mean you.'

'Yes. Yes that's true,' said Karen. 'I was never interested in good deeds.'

Sybil noticed the little tense muscles of strain around Karen's eyes, but she also knew that she did not really understand what it was about. 'If you can't let it go, at least force the issue. Apart from anything else everyone around here thinks you're sleeping together and I find all this discretion rather a bore.'

'There is no issue. You've got sex on the brain.'

'But surely you're suffering from a great deal of frustration if nothing else. I've never known you do without for so long. For God's sake, girl, get down the bars and get laid.'

Karen barely even smiled. Sybil's concern swelled into a real antagonism. 'What's the matter with you, is all this chastity infectious or something?'

Karen's self-irony rose to that bait. She grinned sheepishly. 'I've become a romantic troubadour,' she said, 'faithful to my cold lady until death ends my pains.'

Sybil hopped out of bed in her flannel nightie and hugged her. She wanted Karen back, back in her club and her life. She wanted her out of this unprofitable chilly relationship. She did not dislike Anna, but finally she did not care, she just wanted Karen happier.

Karen looked at her anxiously. 'Don't meddle, Syb, please don't meddle.'

'Now would I?'

'Yes.' They grinned at each other, old friendship and too much knowledge. Sybil said wearily, 'All right, I promise I won't meddle, but please Karen, please don't be so bloody passive. It's driving me up the wall. Do something. You can't go on forever like this.'

Karen could not help hearing her; it was so close to what she was accustomed to believing. Two days later she said, 'Sybil love, will you lend me your car?'

Sybil hated lending her car, and Karen knew it.

'Please Syb, just for one day. You know I wouldn't ask if it didn't seem important.'

'What for?'

'I'm tired of Anna's gods. I'm going to take her away.'

'Where to?'

'Avebury.'

'Turning back to the goddess, are you?' They both laughed.

'Perhaps, you never know. No, I thought I'd take her to the White Horse at Uffington. I love it there. And it's always windy. We're stuck in a swamp, so I thought some wind might blow things clear. Avebury is the cultural bait — I thought if it seemed

161

respectable, there'd be more space on both sides.'

'It never works you know, planning out-of-doors seductions. Either it rains or there are cowpats and nettles.'

'Oh Sybil.' But Karen grinned slyly.

Sybil said, 'Look I want to make it clear that I think you're round the bend; but yes, all right. What about Thursday?'

'Bless you. And thanks.'

So Karen and Anna left London early on a bright and sunny Thursday morning. Anna realised with relief that for the first time she was actually profiting from the ending of Caro's sessions. She would not have wanted Karen to see Fiona, enormous, rounded and full compared to their two spiky selves like children running away from the grown-ups.

On the motorway there was little conversation, Sybil's car too engine-noisy for comfort, but fat white clouds bounced along beside them and the downs as they approached them seemed clean and curvaceous. Anna thought it innocent country, neither claustrophobic nor threatening. She was at ease suddenly in the brightness and placed a new faith in Karen who would know the way, tell her what to see and instruct her in its meaning. Avebury itself was too full of tourists to be personal but the presence of the monument was undeniable; a strange dark magic from too far away to be imagined. The ancient standing stones and laborious ditchings were baffling and demanded too much thought, too much imaginative effort to make sense of. They were touched and interested, but in their heads alone. Karen felt disappointed, as though her spell had not worked somehow; but then she realised that she was relaxed. Her disproportionate expectations for the day were evaporated and she felt comfortable and pleased.

Silbury Hill was better, rising beside the main road with that abrupt authority. Breast and belly and so much extraordinary work for so apparently little purpose. Karen wanted to climb to the top and was furious with the barbed wire prevention; furious that other people's desires should so match hers that she could not be allowed to fulfil them. But then they drove on and had lunch in a pub, and everything became lovely, happy, carefree, sweet, fun. After lunch they drove on through Swindon and out on to the tiny road to Uffington. There was no hurry, the summer afternoon long long and lazy, forever, endless and easy. They walked from the car park across the timeless hill fort and the wind curling over the distant sunlit fields caught them playfully and they felt free. They broke out of the circle and the valley lay below them, serene and stunning. Tranquil, amazing, a free gift. Karen led them so that they came upon the chalk horse from above, directly over its face, and there was no way to make sense of the stencilled shapes. It took a proper time, walking round, backing off, speculating and calculating; an effort of imagination commensurate with the reward.

And then suddenly the horse was whole and galloping free across the hillside and of course the stencil was the true way to make it move so and so freely. It was a gift but not free like the valley below, a gift from Karen to Anna, a gift they had both worked into fullness. They were moved by the horse and sat above its ears on the crisp grass. Now the valley was changed by their poise over it: the drop foreshortened, the unexpected humped shape of St George's Hill flattened off by the angle, and it was too easy to believe that here he had fought the great white dragon and conquered it. Further below them the steep-sided rough hillface met the upreaching cultivated curves of the field below at the point that was exactly beautiful. They sat in peace and thought their thoughts. Looking down from there Anna entered into a silence that she had not known for a very long time; her head was swept clean. She heard no voices and wrestled with no shadows, except the distant moving ones of the friendly clouds. The roads and the railway line ran neatly horizontal across the landscape and were there for balance not intrusion. Karen noticed that all her impatience was gone; she would wait forever if the waiting was like this; there was no hurry, there was no driving need, just sun and wind and Anna near her, clear and calm. Further away they could hear voices, the area was not empty of people, but they felt not isolated but uninterrupted. And miraculously, without warning or expectation, there was a hang-glider sailing underneath them, wings like a bird but magically below them.

'God, I would like to do that,' Karen said, delighted, as though it were something laid on just for her and Anna, a treat from the heavens. Now there was one there were more than one; in differing patterns four or five garish giant birds moving through the air somehow lazily. Flying, not free but visibly dependent on the invisible winds. They watched for at least an hour, wishing joyful flying and soft landings on each of the strange graceful craft. When they finally stood up to leave they were holding hands and neither of them had noticed when or how it had happened. They were as innocent as children and they ran like children across the steep side of the hill and back to the car, laughing, panting, racing, not competing.

They drove back through the gently folding evening and were at peace, relaxing their bodies in the noisy car. Karen stole a glance at Anna on the motorway and saw a sweetness in her face which reminded her of that first smile which had been the basis of their friendship. Sod it, she thought, what does it matter? We're friends and that is good. Not all she had wanted, not the whole; but so much, so good and so comfortable. She would never be free of her, she thought; Anna had called out a tender passion in her that would never be dissipated, never abandoned. Everything before had been half; and this was the other half. All it needed was patience. Sybil simply had not understood. No one but she could understand what Anna needed: time to find a way back to herself. She could wait for ever and be happy while she waited; she was strong and tough and solid and she could wait out Anna's fears, Anna's doubts, Anna's slowness.

Anna barely thought at all. Her head was soothed and sleepy from the sunshine and the wind. She saw Kate now flying free, floating on the shoulder of the wind. She saw Karen as a friend. She saw the curved movement of the white horse, a muscle from the beginning of history, linked somehow to all those other ancient reminders that people thought in other ways and of other Gods, joined to the lost cathedrals of the jungle and the strange harsh temples of the Andes' Indians. She saw Mary lean into Elizabeth's arms and the two women empowered by each other singing the songs of freedom. Visual images were enough. She was locked inside the car, the outside could not reach her, a lazy easy moment. She would have liked the journey to go on forever, never to have to move from this noisy peaceful silence, the rumbling of the motor simpler than any other rhythm, and Karen, dear Karen, her hands long and eager, fine-boned on the steering wheel. And Karen had given her this day as a joy gift. She owed Karen so much, loved her so much, and the spaces which would be destitute without her were full and running over with sweet oil and delight.

It was dark by the time they got back. Karen drove beyond the convent doors, looking for a parking space, a place to say goodnight, to part without haste, to bring the day to a gentle end. They sat for a moment or two as though waiting for an excuse to present itself, some reason to prolong the pleasure of the day. Then Anna turned to thank Karen for the whole loveliness of it all. Moved by gratitude and by something in Karen's face she leaned forward to give her a kiss, casual, affectionate. When their cheeks touched something exploded, the trumpets sounded and the wall in Anna came tumbling down. Without conspiracy or forethought they were wrapped around each other and Anna knew blindingly what she had been waiting for. She felt no surprise and without consciousness she moved into the embrace; unthinking, unquestioning, her lips sought Karen's greedily. Then they were kissing, tongues both tentative and eager; lips and faces and ears and eyes, eyes especially thought Anna with delight who had never imagined such a thing; and her tongue curled delicately along Karen's eyelids, and how could she not have known the unbelievable excitement and sweetness and need to be nearer, closer, inner. And desire, exploding desire and greed and driving wants. She could not stop now, did not want to stop and did not need to think where this was going. She was perfectly and uniquely in the present, there was no point of reference outside, nor anything but enormous melting and longing and demanding, which had no name or description except Karen, and to kiss and kiss and be closer.

Karen felt more control; she was intensely surprised; but there was no reason, she knew no reason to hesitate or to hold back. She had known always that they would come to this place and it was not necessary to know the times and the seasons. She had a tiny regret, a little hovering sorrow, because she had wanted to take this initiative, she had fantasised that it would be she who would have the power and she would surrender it to make things tender and sweet and easy for Anna. But now she knew that there was little careful tenderness here; she tasted Anna's lust and her own swelled to meet it. Delicately, ready to make more space if Anna seemed to need it she reached for Anna's breast; it was firm and pleased through the shirt and she, with the skill of practice, undid enough buttons and reached for Anna's skin. She found her nipple; she was not gentle now, the time for gentleness and withdrawal had suddenly passed. How had she ever imagined that Anna was not sexually responsive. Her own desire, disciplined and controlled for too long, leapt out of its hiding place and devoured the two of them. (Sybil was right she thought, they could have done this weeks ago, and it would have been more convenient somewhere else though the car was adequate.) And she knew that she was physically stronger than Anna and that delighted some part of her. She was here with Anna and Anna desired her, and desired her desire. She wanted her. Her head was filled with glory and triumph, with joy, with joy, with the joy of being wanted so hungrily. The hunger of twenty years and all given to her now with passion and enthusiasm. And indeed skill. That might have surprised her, and later was to surprise her very much, but then it was just a part of the explosion and the victory.

Anna was lost. She had plunged too far, too fast; it was too like the great fall that she had feared for too long; this was the dreaded falling into the depths of chasm where she would be smashed and destroyed. She was panicked suddenly and pulled her head away. But then the air was too cold and the distance unbearable and she had to go back. The wave of terror subsided, but she knew that it was there. She needed, she had to, she must get nearer, nearer to Karen, to be enclosed there in her, lost within her before the terror could find her out. But that was too near and too much and too much, and between the terror of loss and distance and the terror of need and openness she was battered. Her hands discovered new places and those places in herself cried out for Karen. She tried to find something, something to say, and she attempted to laugh and said, 'It is the jungle, it's the great jungle swamp.' But she ought not to have spoken, because words were the possession of the Fathers, and in using them she was dragged back into their power. They crashed in on the sides of the car. She could not. Too dangerous. She could not. Too wonderful. It was all too much. If she went any further here she would never get back again: they would eat her, destroy her, break her, no she was already broken, but they would smash her bones and grind them between the thighs of the high mountains. The storms that had threatened the Mother House when she was there before had been held at bay by the ghosts of dead virgins. But now there were no virgins and no death, no propitiation to offer them.

They will kill her.

Karen experienced her fear as excitement, and as mounting towards somewhere else. She said, 'For God's sake, dearest, let's go home. Let's go somewhere we can have a bed.'

The fear took over. Anna jolted from her arms as though struck by an electric current. Quite deliberately, although she did not know why, she banged her forehead ferociously, dangerously hard against the windscreen of the car. Karen reached for her, confused, alarmed. The pain devoured all of Anna. She banged her head again. Then she did not need to repeat it; the Fathers took her by the scruff of the neck and pounded her against the glass until her teeth shook. The Fathers took over her physical co-ordination and they took over her voice. She was their victim.

'I have to go in now. Thank you for the day.'

Even Anna knew it was unforgivable. It was not acceptable. But she did not know what else to do; trapped between the two terrors, the terror of the fury of the Fathers and the terror of the delight of her desire.

Karen was pale with shock. 'You can't.'

'I can. I don't have to make love to you. It's not obligatory.'

'No it isn't, you're right, it fucking isn't. But you do have to follow it through. You can't set up something like this, you can't want it as much as you want it, and set up that wanting in me, and then just walk out. You bloody can't.'

She tried to calm down, tried to put a brake on her anger. 'Look Anna please, please just come home. You don't have to do anything. Just don't leave me, don't walk out on me like this. Come home and talk to me, be with me, please.'

Anna said, 'They'll kill me.' She was pleading with Karen, but Karen could not hear her now, it was too late to ask for Karen's tenderness. And she could not understand what Anna was talking about; she assumed that she meant the nuns behind the convent door, so she said, 'Oh don't be silly; they can't hurt you.'

167

But Anna knew that this was not true. There was no escape. If she gave even a tiny inch to Karen now, if she consented to Karen, if she consented to herself, they would kill her, they would carry her off to their dungeons and torture her. She was a witch and she knew what they did to witches, the Fathers. They tortured witches until they were unable to stand, to talk, to think, and then, when all that was left was the reality of pain, they took them out into a public square and burned them alive. Alive she would smell her own cooking flesh and her soul would be damned for all eternity to that burning, burning, burning. For if she gave herself to Karen she would not be able to repent; that she knew.

She could not even speak, locked into her fear, her pain and the physical effort of moving her heavy body away from Karen. It would break her, that effort to move away. She would have cried out from the strain except that the Fathers might think she was asking Karen to help her. The desire and the fear, the sex and the violence were too close, too near each other. She could not have one without the other, it was not permitted. She would have to do without. She might not even look at Karen, she must drag her broken body away from the only waterhole and crawl out into the desert to die like all sick animals. She had no choice.

But she knew that this was not true. She had a choice: she could defy the Fathers and she would be free of them forever, but there would be nothing left. She would always have to live without their rewards and their comforts. She could not live without the power that could control her, could discipline her, make her behave. She did not dare; she did not dare take the risk, make the leap. She held her body so rigid that to Karen it looked hard, uncaring. She must not even let Karen see how painful the choices were; she must not see the confusion and the melting longing. The Fathers would not tolerate even that.

Pleading, begging, needing, Karen said, 'Anna please. Please don't go. I love you.' She had not said that for fifteen years; she had never said it as one adult to another. Anna could not bear it. Karen's needs and submerged angers were yet another threat, another force that would destroy her. If she listened to them she would die. She opened the car door and stood up. The effort made her walk as though with decision. Karen exploded with wrath. She switched on the car engine. For one delightful moment, in colours of scarlet and purple, she thought that she would drive up on to the pavement and run Anna down and kill her. In fear she saw her own fist swinging back to hit Sybil; this bloody nun had broken her, had stolen her fine high courage, and all her self-respect. She had been reduced to violence and pathetic passivity. As Anna moved towards the door of the convent, Karen rolled down the window of the car and shouted, deafening the blank windows of the night-time street, 'Go fuck yourself, you stupid bitch. It's all you want to do anyway.' She gunned the engine and drove off towards Hackney ferociously. At least she would be the one to do the leaving.

Anna collapsed, hanging against the door, weak and battered.

The Fathers found her there, their fangs tore into her. The soft damp place between her legs, marinated and ready for Karen, gave their teeth a sweet meal. Her skin was all open and vulnerable for their whips to scourge. They no longer wasted breath on speech. She stumbled into the still, virginal house where the prim and holy sisters slept undisturbed. She cringed past the chapel which she did not dare to enter and sought the privacy of her burrow. But there, with their lone prisoner kept so long in the isolation cell, weakened by sensory deprivation, she was at their mercy. They were not grateful that she had stopped and left Karen to her own misery; in their opinion she had already gone too far in her desire. They would break her and punish her and she would thank them for the pain and the humiliation. She was to be grateful for the punishment and adore them for the pain. They laughed at her without amusement and without pity as she took Karen's parting advice and hated herself and Karen for it. She submitted herself to their rigours; all alone she learned just how closely the sweetness of orgasm and the violence of self-disgust could entangle themselves, and she fell not so much into sleep as into unconsciousness, her body wracked by pain, electrocuted by lust, whipped and pierced and penetrated by the Fathers, flagellated by her own guilt.

VII

Anna awoke before dawn; the paling of the sky still not casting any light on the world below. She woke, as she had fallen asleep, to pain. And with the pain now were waves of shame, pure shame; the only pure thing left in her. She had stopped, she had stopped and come home, she tried to tell herself, but it was not good enough. The earliest movements of the sisters below heightened her shame and she blushed, sweating. She had presumed to judge them, to find them soft and cushy, to find their lives boring and unshining and complacent. Judge not that ye be not judged. Sweet Christ help me.

The Fathers pounced again before she was fully conscious. She attempted to excuse herself before them:

'Don't I get a day off ever?' she pleaded.

'There are no days off in hell,' they told her. 'You have committed adultery. You are married to our son and you have been unfaithful. Whore. You will be stoned according to the law. Stoning is among the most painful ways to die. Do you think you will like that?'

'No, No. I came home. I came home.'

'You have no home.'

'But I fled.'

'You were not even honest with her. Actually we are not interested in lesbian sex, we do not count it, but we do count adultery. He is bleeding, bleeding on the cross for you, for you, for you. You will eat his beloved body, like a savage, like a cannibal, like a parasitic worm in the belly of the Church, the bride. They are starving in Santa Virgine. Sr. Kitty was filled with barbs and smelly semen, but she did not surrender. Who do you think you

170

are? Do you think we will pardon you? We are only faithful to those who keep the covenant. To those who read and mark the letter of the Law.'

'The new covenant is a covenant of love and forgiveness,' she tried to tell them, but they roared with bleak laughter, full-bodied scorn. 'Oh, come on. You know better than that. Don't you remember what he said? ''Don't kid yourself that I have come to abolish the law; I haven't come to abolish but to confirm it. I'm telling you that till heaven and earth have returned into the waters of chaos not one jot or tittle shall be removed from the law. Whoever relaxes even the least of our Laws shall be damned for all of time.'' ' That was not what it said, she was sure that was not what it said, but she could not confront the voices with accuracy, for they made the laws of logic and of truth. They boomed on. 'You poor liberals. Do you know that one of our favourite amusements is looking at the surprised faces of cheating liberals when they discover that hell hurts. It hurts them especially because they let their skins get white and soft. Is your skin soft, Anna? Won't it hurt?'

It had been soft, soft and damp in Karen's hands.

'Soft skin, hard sin,' mock the Fathers. 'You have heard it said that you must not commit adultery; but the son says that everyone who looks at a woman lustfully has already committed adultery with her. You can't even say it's sexist, can you? We punish you know, we punish you, we punish you for your own good. Don't be taken in by the gentle-Jesus-meek-and-mild school of thought. You know better than that, don't you. We punish. We will punish you.'

'Punish me, punish me, please.'

'All in our own good time.'

'I belong to Jesus,' she tried to say, 'not to you. The husband will protect the wife from her father. I don't belong to the Fathers. I belong to Christ who feeds and loves me.'

Unified Will, they pointed out. One substance. The inseparability of the Trinity. The logos is the word of the Father proceeding forth, but it never leaves the Father's side. Whose side was pierced? Whose back was beaten?

'I'm sorry,' she sobbed. 'I'm sorry.'

'So you should be,' they replied smartly and departed to their own place.

She was left in silence. The silence was bottomless. If they deserted her she would have nothing. If they shut her out she would die in the desert.

She went to Mass. 'She who eats and drinks unworthily, eats and drinks damnation unto her soul.'

'I'm sorry, I'm sorry.' What to do? A good deed, think of others. The cross is 'I' crossed out, ego eliminated. All that catechistical stuff, she could hang there, pinned to the cross by it, bleeding but very secure. She wore her habit again, that was important, she was still a nun, a life given in service, service and penance. All sins truly repented of can be forgiven. Repent. Penance. She needed penance, punishment, humiliation. She needed that.

She stood back a little. No hysteria. That did not help. She had not gone all the way, she would never do it again, never ever again. She had better stop thinking about it and get herself over to Fiona's. That was better. Put it aside, deal with it later, when you're calmer. Run away, run away when the pace gets too hot. Be good, be virtuous. Cover this up. Fiona and Caro need you.

But Caro was strong in her own darkness that day, and not pleased with Anna. Surely this was just a coincidence. But Caro was black and shouting.

I don't want that. I don't want that you. You want to make me a grown-up and make me face those horrible feelings. That evil place is where I crept in, a tiny seed. I crept in and grew and flourished in the dark damp hole. It is wild. I do not want to come out. I will stay here in my own hole, with my shit on me warm and soft. I won't be made clean and good. I want to stay the wild child. I want you to love only me.

Anna wrapped Caro in her blanket; Caro took the satin corner and sucked fiercely, squirming uncomfortably on Anna's lap.

You will leave me behind. You want to be with her, with the grown-ups. I am the little dark girl in you and I will never let you go. You are like me. You don't want that bad stuff, you want shit and poo and mud and slime.

172

Anna sang to her, wordless crooning, but inside them both were the shadows of lust, unwanted, undeniable. I won't go away, Anna tried to reassure Caro. I won't go away again. I don't want to go there either. I won't ask you to grow up and come out until you want to.

  Until you want to is not enough. This is a long-term plan. I refuse, I want to wallow. I want to go back where it was all right and there was gurgling and turning in the bowels. I want you to come in with me. And I want to be left alone.

Neither the Fathers nor the little girl could approve of what she had done last night. Neither would forgive her. Karen did not approve either. Karen had revved up her engine and roared off to Hackney with fury in her face. And who could blame her? Not Anna. Now Anna was completely alone.

She had to go back, back to where she had been before, where she had known her way and her place, orderly, useful, structured. That would have to be enough. They at least wanted her: Mother wanted her back and her sisters would welcome her return. The generous mother who lets her children spread their wings and see the world, but is waiting, ready and eager to welcome them home again. She would be the prodigal daughter. It is the duty of the good daughter to go home and help mother. I will go home, she thought, I have to go home. I chose, I chose and purity of commitment will validate that choosing. Those are the rules.

Sr. Kitty had been raped. That was not in the rules.

Sr. Kate had been mowed down, phallic bullets penetrating her insides. That was not in the rules either.

Kate had not kept the rules.

Kitty had.

Help. Someone help me. Anna rushed through the city trying to escape from herself. She left Caro with Fiona and fled down the highways and byways of London, trying to escape. It was not easy. 'Hail Mary full of Grace, pray for us sinners now and in the hour of our death. Jesus, son of God, have mercy on me a miserable sinner.'

'Come unto me all you who labour and are heavy burdened and I will give you rest. My yoke is easy and my burden is light.'

Submit your will to mine, submit. Belong to me. Don't question, consent, consent, go with the moment. Consent to belong to me. Forever. Now, just come. Come to me. Come. Come now. Come.

Not so different from . . . but no, she was not going to think about that any more. She belonged to Jesus. To Jesus alone. She had promised. She must reaffirm that promise. Remind herself. Bind herself. Accept her penance and turn back to him.

She had not planned it. She was quite sure that she had not planned it, it had not crossed her mind. If asked she would have said that she did not even remember the name, let alone the address of the tattooist who had given Judy her lovely leopard. But here she was.

Comport yourself, she instructed herself. Deportment, whatever you may have learned in grade school, is not about standing up straight and keeping your fingers clean, the novice mistress had told them. It is about a whole bearing and body language which manifests the serenity of the love of God. Now obviously you cannot work from the outside in all the time, but the body is an integral part of us all, one more special gift from God. Deportment is a way in to that, a safety net and a source of strength in times of trial.

So Anna comported herself, cut herself off from the wildness and the pain and the lurking shadow cloud that was waiting for its moment, and she went into the shop. 'The best tattooist in London' was a small man, surprisingly young, Anna thought.

'I want a crucifix,' she told him.

'Really, where?' He did not seem surprised particularly, though Anna even from the inside of her impeccable deportment realised that a nun must be quite unusual for him.

Where? Where? 'I hadn't thought. Somewhere I can see it.'

'Arm? Leg?'

No, she knew that was not right. 'I want it between my breasts.'

'I think that you had better come inside,' he said.

He was magical. He was completely calm. His calmness reached out to her and she was soothed by it. Perhaps he too had good deportment, but if so it said a lot for his novice mistress. His eyes were ancient. He knew the inside of things. He worked on the frontier where myths and history meet. Like Christ. That place was called the body. He worked there and saw the two made one. The social and the secret. The public and the inner. He pulled the two together and united them. She submitted, suddenly and completely.

He took her not by the hand but by the wrist and led her like a child, first across the waiting-room, then through the studio where she had thought he would perform his ritual and into a chamber behind that. This was a work room too, but instead of a chair this one had a couch. There was no window, but a fan hummed gently. 'It's all right,' he said. 'Out there I do public things. Some people like to watch, some people like to be watched. Arms, ankles, men's shoulders, I do those things out there. Here is more private, for breasts and buttocks.' He made breasts sound just like ankles. He gave the two words exactly the same value, a high value but not a charged one. She had never before met anyone who could say the two words exactly the same like that.

'You have to show me,' he explained, 'exactly where you want it. If you don't know, then you probably haven't guessed right about what you want.'

'Does it hurt?' she asked, like a child at the dentist.

'Wait and see,' he answered, not at all like a mother.

She took off her veil. He took it from her and placed it on the plain wooden chair beside the couch. But when she reached up to undo her shoulder buttons her hands started shaking. He said, 'Sit here,' and she climbed into the high couch and sat there with her legs dangling. 'Wait,' he said. And he went back through the outer studio and out of her sight into the waiting-room. Through the two open doors she could see the sheets of designs hanging on the waiting-room wall — everything from Mickey Mouse to dragons, very brightly coloured. She thought of Judy's dark blue leopard and was comforted.

'I've shut the shop door,' he explained returning. 'We needn't be disturbed.'

He undid her buttons for her and she pulled the top half of the dress down so it sagged around her waist. She reached again for her bra strap but he forestalled her, leaning over with his arms to

175

undo the back hooks himself. 'You're too tense,' he said. 'Choosing a tattoo is too important: you have to be open to your dreams.'

'I never have any,' she said. She was exhausted she now knew, beyond self-consciousness, just leaning on him.

'Rubbish,' he said, but very gently. He began to rub her neck and shoulders, quite abstractedly. She hovered towards thinking that the Fathers would not approve of a nun being here, but her forehead dropped into his chest and she could feel his hands, quite different from Karen's, his hands small and strong massaging her spine and high up her neck round her hair-line. Safe. She felt safe.

Without stopping the massage he said, 'I don't think you want a crucifix.'

'I do,' she said. 'I have to have one.'

'No.' He said and his hands went on moving over her back. There was no obligation in them, no demands, a free gift. 'No,' he said, 'I know more about it than you do. Not more about you, but more about tattoos. You don't want a crucifix, you want a Christ. But that one is too painful; too guilt-ridden. You want a Christ, but something that is nearer to nature, to the creation.'

Still his hands went on caressing her. 'I can't tattoo when all these knots are here, you see, it would mess up the design. I need a smooth canvas, well primed. It's professional.' She could feel him smile.

'I'm magical,' he said, very sweetly, 'I do know. With you I know. Not always, but with you. What about a pheonix? I can do a lovely pheonix you know, rising from the flames.'

'No flames,' she said with a flash of fear.

'No flames,' he agreed without a pause. 'Unicorn? No . . .' He interrupted himself before she could even feel the delicate sharp unicorn hooves seeking a path across her breast. 'A unicorn might be good for some nuns, but not this time. Right?'

She was relieved, she did not want a unicorn nuzzling her breast. She did not want to have to capture the Christ, but to have him capture her. This was not the hour of the unicorn.

'Hang on a minute,' he said, taking his hands slowly off her skin, with no sudden departure. 'There's something I want to read to you.'

There were a few moments during which her back longed for the return of his hands. Then he appeared and read:

The very act of trying to see fish makes them almost impossible to see. My eyes are awkward instruments whose casing is clumsily outsized . . . Fish! They manage to be so water coloured. Theirs is not the colour of the bottom but the colour of light itself, the light dissolved like a powder in the water. They disappear and reappear as if by spontaneous generation: sleight of fish.

I am coming round to fish as spirit. The Greek acronym for some of the names of Christ yields Ichthys, Christ as fish and fish as Christ. The more I glimpse the fish in Tinker's Creek, the more satisfying the coincidence becomes, the richer the symbol, not only for Christ but for the spirit as well. The people must live. Imagine for a Mediterranean people how much easier it is to haul up free, fed fish in nets than to pasture hungry herds on those bony hills and feed them through a winter. To say holiness is a fish is a statement of the abundance of grace; it is the equivalent of affirming in a purely materialistic culture that money does indeed grow on trees. 'Not as the world gives do I give unto you'; these fish are spirit food. And revelation is a study in stalking. 'Cast the net on the right hand side and ye shall find.'

Still — of course — there is a risk. More men in all of time have died at fishing than at any other human activity, except perhaps the making of war. You go out so far . . . and you are blown or stove or swamped and never seen again. Where are the fish? Out in the underwater gaps, out where the winds are, wary, adept, invisible. You can lure them, net them, troll for them, club them, clutch them, chase them up an inlet, stun them with plant juice, catch them in a wooden wheel that runs all night — and you still might starve. They are there, they are certainly there, free food and wholly fleeting. You can see them if you want to; catch them if you can.

'Yes,' said Anna, after a pause. 'Yes indeed.' And she lay back on the couch and showed him where, just under her rib cage on the left-hand side, she should have her fish tattooed.

177

He swabbed down the area with some cotton wool; the spirit he used felt icily cold, just the patch where he rubbed it; the rest of her skin was warm and waiting. She closed her eyes and did not watch any more of his preparations, anticipating when the spear would pierce her side too and through the pain she would be united with Christ.

It hurt. It hurt an extraordinary amount. She had not imagined the degree to which it would hurt. Perhaps she had never known about real hurting before.

'Go into the pain,' he told her. 'Breathe into it, feel it. It always hurts the precise amount that you need and want it to hurt. Explore that pain.'

She felt as though she were on fire, being devoured by the clean flames of pain. And she went into that pain quite deliberately, because she believed that he was there as her guide and would walk with her. She should have looked for a proper spiritual director months ago.

Once he smiled and said, 'You know, it was only after Shadrach, Meshach and Abednego had walked all night in the fiery furnace that they were able to hear the voice of the whole creation and give back to the forests and mountain streams their tongues of praise. Don't however get over-ambitious; you are just having a tattoo on a Friday afternoon in London, of which your Reverend Mother would almost certainly not approve.'

She did not mind him teasing her. She had seen the three and the Holy One walk in the furnace through the night and she had never before even thought of daring to join them.

'I've been running away, you know,' she told him.

'There's a time for that too,' he said and went on releasing his bee stings into her side, wrapped in the silence of his own work.

It was a small fish, not more than two and a half inches long, watery blues and greens with neat overlapping scales. Its spine ran along just under the rocky cliff of her ribs and it was playfully headed downwards towards deeper waters. She knew that it was beautiful and she told him so. He covered the whole area over with antiseptic cream and a square of white gauze. 'Keep it secret and covered for three days,' he told her, 'like the sign of Jonah.' Now the job was over he was more detached. She paid him, faintly appalled at how expensive it was, wondering what on earth had come over her, but still inside the peace and the pain of it. They walked together through the outer studio and the waiting-room. He twizzled his 'Open/Closed' sign around again and let her out. 'Don't come back,' he said. 'It could get to be a habit with you. Find a masseuse next time it gets that heavy.' He touched her shoulder lightly and she walked away up the street.

After about a hundred yards the Fathers found her. She felt droopy and tired, in no mood for them.

'You are becoming a very odd nun if we may say so. And if we may not, then who may? We thought you were going to repent and turn back. You had better shape up. This was worse: necking in a battered old jalopy is one thing; seeking out masochistic sexual perversity is quite another.'

'It hurt. I let it hurt. It was my punishment.'

'But you wanted it to hurt. You enjoyed it hurting. You felt joy in that pain, didn't you? Didn't you? You daughter of foulness.'

'Yes.'

'Rose of Lima has nothing on you. And she produced the fruit of the spirit. You thought that you had grown out of that, didn't you? You wanted us to have grown out of that, didn't you? We listened to you telling that devil spawn, that scarlet whore all about cultural forms and appropriate modes for the twentieth century. We know you like your pain. We like it too. We inflict it. We worked his hands. You thought he was on your side. No one is on your side. He was laughing at you. He was feeling you up. You knew that, didn't you. Oh yes, we've got your number. Don't think we'll let you get away with it.'

The days imploded into formlessness.

She was sailing with Francisco da Orellana and the Companions down the great river and there was no end to it; the days and nights were undifferentiated, lassitude should have been a natural response, lulled in the sweaty darkness, but it was not. The darkness was shot through with blinding light, with fearful images. And under it all she knew that she had to decide, time was running out, and although she found it impossible to think clearly she had to make up her mind. Mother wrote reminding her that her time was up, she had to bring her boat ashore. She did not tell her that Kate was dead. That made her angry. It made it harder to think properly, since in the terms of her thinking she had to believe that Kate was still alive. She could not focus.

There were Karen's arms and her desire for them. She ached for them and woke hungry in the night, but she was too afraid. With Karen, in Karen's hands she would be at the mercy of every sensation, physical or mental, that happened to pass by. Karen would not protect her; Karen would with her own power break down all the walls, drive out the demons, smash into the silent places. Perhaps she could take the pain away, perhaps she could, but there would be a heavy price. 'The best lack all conviction, while the worst are full of passionate intensity' — and Karen would decide for that intensity at any price. That was her creed, despite her carefulness towards Anna, and Anna knew it. The carefulness was for stalking; once she was caught there would be no more delicacy. Karen offered her the whole conviction and its power, as a free gift. But it was non-negotiable. She believed that passionate intensity could authenticate itself; it required no balance, no frame, only consent. It was blind faith. And it was very dangerous to want too much.

There were the safe walls of the convent, reaching out to embrace her; there the Fathers would leave her alone and she would, each and every day, know what she had to do and do it. They would all be pleased with her. She had given her promise and keeping it would keep her safe; she had made a commitment, she had only to be faithful, faithful unto death and she would be given the crown of life. But that seemed an awfully long time to wait. Once it had been right. She knew that absolutely.

'Love must come first,' she had been taught. But what if the love was illegitimate? What when there was a choice of loves? What when two lovers both claimed the right of fidelity? How did one choose between them? Was the love of gut and instinct a sturdy warrior deserving of fealty and honour, or was it a whimpering of the flesh which she had once learned to subdue and yet now seemed to be rising in armed revolution against her military dictatorship.

And Kate was dead.

And she loved Caro, loved and heard the voice that called her towards a different freedom. But she did not know how to live out that calling. It was a way, a real way, but she did not know how to follow it. She could not imagine a life constructed in that structureless space and she was afraid. There were thousands of feet of freefall and no guarantee that the parachute would open.

She could not have her cake and eat it too.

There was no thread in this labyrinth.

She was paralysed with indecision. It flowed into the minutiae of her daily life. She could not bring herself to make the simplest plan for the next hour. All she wanted was to lie in her bed and escape the questions, comfort herself with her dark masturbatory fantasies and doze afterwards in a shameful peace. And that, living in a respectable convent, was completely out of the question. The bells brought her from troubled sleep to troubled waking and there was no place firm enough to rest against.

She was saved by Caro. By the circumstance of Caro. Fiona's father had quite suddenly to go into hospital for investigative surgery. Fiona's mother would therefore not be able to come to London for the birth; she would not be able to look after Caro while Fiona was in hospital having the baby. Stephen, strained tentative worried, knowing that Fiona would need him, remembering the horror of the time before, believing that Fiona could not survive without him there, asked Anna to help them.

'It's outrageous, I know, it's a lot to ask, but it's not . . . I can't ask just anyone. She knows you. Could you possibly come and stay, just for a few days, just from when we go to the hospital until Fiona comes home.'

It was a fixed point, and Anna accepted it with relief. She would not have to make any decision till then, until after that. It was a definite request and she could respond to it and afterwards perhaps she would know what to do.

Fiona was tired, mortally tired it seemed to the people around her. She had too many fears and she wrestled with them and that wore her out; she was exhausted too by the effort to protect the baby from the fears: fears about the birth, fears about Caro, fears about not being able to cope. She wrapped the unborn child away, crooning to it in a fear-free place, guarding it. She could not bear to be near Caro, and that sense escalated. She felt that the safety of the new child was her most important responsibility, and she sensed a malevolence in Caro now, a ferocity and cruelty.

She knitted frenziedly; through the clack-clack of her needles Stephen and Anna peered at each other, worried, seeking guidance. Fiona had focused away from them, turned her gaze inwards. She shut out all threats real or imagined to the baby.

One lunchtime Anna took Caro for a walk, out of the house in which there was now no room for their darkness and muddle and into the park. Stephen came, seizing a lunch break, and found them both.

'Anna, whatever shall I do? This just isn't going to work out. How's Fiona going to manage, I mean afterwards, when the new baby comes home? You can hardly come and live with us for always.'

'People have coped,' said Anna. She knew that she had no charity for Fiona now, she knew Fiona had refused Caro, turned away to a new project, and Anna was angry and bitter with her. She did not know how to frame herself towards understanding and affection.

'They have to want to cope,' said Stephen, 'and she doesn't. Not at the moment. Of course I understand; I think I understand; but even if she wanted to cope I don't think she can. The depression she had last time, after Caro was born, was bad, Anna, really bad. And Caro was in hospital then. I don't see how she'll manage.'

'Can't you take leave, can't you cope?' Anna challenged him, cross with him too for recognising his own limitations, even though he was not entitled to them.

'No,' he said, 'and I can't stand having to say it, but I don't think I can. Cope I mean.' He sat on the bench, his elbows on his knees, and looked very sad.

Anna said, in her best careful caring-nun voice, 'Then perhaps you should look for a hospital, a home, a place she can go at least for a couple of months when the baby is born. I'll ask the Catholic agencies if you like.'

A safe place. She had said it for him. They could put Caro away somewhere safe. She too could put herself away somewhere safe. She would go back to her order.

'Not for ever,' said Stephen, but it sounded like a question. 'I don't know, I just don't know. Why did we ever decide to have another one?'

'Don't ask me,' said Anna, but with a smile, a gentle joke. She and her sisters had teased her father like that when he had been depressed. It was their job, the daughters' job, to make the world more pleasant, to make the indigestible tasty for their men, in homes, in convents, in hospitals; all saying we can make it feel better, you can dodge the impossible, smooth out the wrinkles. Anna was skilled at that.

She felt a sudden weight. Caro was silent before her, would not speak to her, Anna had betrayed her. Not probably by suggesting the refuge but by making it easier and more pleasant for Stephen. Caro did not make nice for anyone or anything. She did not compromise. And the Fathers were silent too, she was being good and sensible. She ignored the fluttering of the fish's fins against her ribs: it was no time for tickling.

Stephen did not know how to approach the subject with Fiona. He had sought Anna out in the park and it had been the first time they had ever been together outside his house he realised. It made him feel edgy, guilty, as though he had somehow betrayed Fiona. He felt distanced from his wife as he had never been before. The sense of caring together that had survived even the worst times after Caro's birth, that had carried them through the shock of Fiona's post-natal depression, through the guilt and anger at Caro's disability, and through the grinding effort of Caro's Philadelphia treatment, had evaporated. He did not know where to find her when he went searching for her to try and discuss what they should do. He had wanted the new baby because he had wanted things to change and now they had and he was not comfortable. When he tentatively sidled up to the subject he was brutally rejected; he scuffed his toes on a solid wall of refusal.

'Of course I can cope, don't be silly. Other women have coped. You can bloody well take time off work, that's all. There is nothing to discuss.'

'Darling . . .'

'We've managed all these years, Stephen, don't be silly. I haven't got time for all this.'

If he discovered how she hated Caro he would never love her again. If he discovered that she could not cope he would never trust her again. She could not afford it. She must not admit even to herself what a relief that would be. She was not allowed to go near the idea of sending Caro away even in the secrecy of her own mind: she had to be the perfect mother so that the coming child could be perfect. The perfect mother never rejects her child. She was angry with Stephen for so much as hinting at it; her anger articulated itself forcefully in the only way it could find: men were so sexist, men had to learn to care for children; Stephen could just do his little bit and stop bitching. It was not she who did not love Caro, it was he who wanted to evade his responsibilities. She didn't have to put up with that, now of all times. She ran away from the conversation, from its implications and questions. Damn him. It was his turn. His turn to be so weary, to take so much care. She needed him to feed and tend her, to pour back into her the nourishment and strength she was pouring out into the baby.

And at the same time she moved with grace and fullness towards the birth; there was a certainty, a certainty and a mystery; she went bravely inside the chalk circle and he watched her with pride. She moved towards the centring point. The baby inside had turned downwards, poised for the journey through the strange gateway. Fiona was standing now, becoming the arch that holds the gate, and under all the fears and the tensions and the doubts and the tiredness there was something solid. The baby's head was pressing against her pubic bones and the feet were flexed upwards against the curve of the dome. She knew it; she knew that Stephen knew it; all their conversations went on in a different place. What she had to do required concentration. She could not make choices about other things now, she would not come away from this absolute moment and pay attention to details that were irrelevant.

And it could not matter to Caro. That knowledge was a relief. Caro could not and did not know what was happening, it could not make any difference to her. Anna was a relief, too, because she asked no questions, she did what was needed and went away again in the evenings. Fiona just wanted to sit quietly on the floor, to lean her back against Stephen's knees and not to think about anything difficult. She had given three whole years to Caro, now she was going to take some time for herself. Someone else could carry that burden. This time she had to get it right; this time she had to be ready, opening and giving. This time, not just for the baby but for herself, she was not going back into that maelstrom of pain and distress. She was not going to. She would hunt out every point of resistance and subdue it, so she could open up and float the baby down and out on a river of readiness.

Anna was outside this charmed circle. She knew she was and she did not mind; she had been cast out, neither mother nor lover. She was alone. It did not matter very much. She was tired and caring for Caro, taking the chores one by one through the day and having Fiona and Stephen accept that was good, was enough. Enough until the baby was born and then she would have to decide.

Kate was dead.

Karen had roared off into the night.

Caro was cowed.

But there were always some limits, limits of time now; the new baby was dictating the limits of Anna's time, and she welcomed the restriction and waited.

Fiona woke in the early morning with a feeling of anticipation and excitement. She climbed out of bed and went to run herself a bath. Stephen was sleeping and as she padded across the landing she could hear Caro's wheezy snores.

'Please God, please all the Saints, including St Jude patron of lost causes, let her not wake up when I turn the taps on. Just let her not wake up. Just let me have this bath, this quiet time on my own.' She sank into the bath and was comforted, relaxed, by the silence all around her. Anna would probably be waking up by now though, summonsed by a bell into consciousness in a cold convent. Eight months later and she still had no real idea who Anna was, she thought vaguely. She touched her taut stomach low against her pubic hair, cupping her hand round where the head must be. She'd know who this was very soon. She knew it would be very soon. When she climbed out of the bath and wrapped herself in a green towel she felt the baby move, an odd different movement, and as she walked downstairs to make herself a cup of tea her waters broke. She smiled. In a few minutes she would go and wake Stephen up, but first she wanted to be alone, to know she was in labour and to direct her whole attention to it. She was nervous, excited and completely calm. The details, the decisions, the things outside — ringing the hospital, ringing Anna, making breakfast — all those things had to be other people's business now, she was engaged elsewhere. The clock in the sitting-room said that it was twenty to seven, she made a mental note of that fact, wrapping the towel carefully round her so as not to seep more liquid on to the floor. At four minutes to seven she had her first contraction. She had arrived somewhere and it was a good place to be.

At eight she woke Stephen. Caro went on sleeping, oblivious or rejecting, Fiona neither knew nor cared.

'How do you know it's not a false alarm?' said Stephen struggling into consciousness, grumpy but endeavouring to catch up with Fiona so that they could travel together.

'I know,' said Fiona. 'Can you ring Anna?'

'It's too early.'

Fiona was irritated. 'She said to ring any time.'

'Sorry love, I didn't mean that. I meant she'd still be in chapel, she won't get out till half-past.'

'How do you know?'

'I asked her. I asked her every detail of her daily schedule, like how we could get hold of her at night. She said seven-thirty to eight-thirty was the only impossible time.'

He had taken care of her. She lay down on the bed beside him and relaxed. Stephen held her hand, stroked her shoulders, gently, not wanting to intrude, but wanting to say he was there, he was completely there for her. She rolled on to her side and tucked her legs up, assuming the same position as the child inside her.

'Do you want to get some sleep?' he asked.

'No, but to lie here and rest a bit.'

After a while he got up and left her lying there. She opened her eyes and said, 'Caro's still asleep.'

'Be grateful for small mercies. Perhaps she'll have a sleepy day.'

'I bet,' said Fiona still curled round her curled baby. Stephen was suddenly excited too, his mind busy with details. It would not be easy. It was a long journey but she would need him, need him to travel with her. He was going to have a baby. They were going to have a baby. This time it would be all right. It had to be.

186

Anna arrived shortly before ten. Soon after eleven Fiona and Stephen decided to leave for the hospital. The hour inbetween was strange. Fiona was buoyed up, her conversation punctuated by her contractions, and then gradually the other way around. Yes it hurt she told Anna, and Anna observing her excitement and containedness was filled with wonder. She was glad when they left though, it all seemed too complicated for her; and she did not know quite how to deal with the smugness hidden in Fiona's voice when she explained the feeling of the contractions.

But after they had gone Caro started to scream. Great waves of screaming that climbed up and up into huge crests and broke, broke over Anna's head and into her, and there was no pause or lull before the next wave; a storm of distress, of anger, of passion. Caro screamed for four hours without intermission, without rest. At first Anna tried to hold her against her own wails, tried to tuck her in and sustain her, warm her heart, be with her. But the anger continued. Caro seemed inexhaustible, empowered, mighty and dreadful in her wrath. The anger infected Anna like a disease, an invasion of bacteria against which there can be no resistance. Her own anger rose to meet Caro's and she cried too and screamed back, 'Shut up shut up.' She wanted to hit Caro, she wanted to carry her out of the house and dump her, she met her own anger in Caro and felt its power and its danger. She yelled at Caro and she screamed at Kate, 'How dare you, how dare you, you silly bitch. How dare you be so stupid and throw away so much love. How dare you leave me when I need you. What a stupid destructive idiotic thing to have done. Bitch. Bitch. You stupid violent despairing dangerous bitch. You deceitful treacherous shit.' Her anger flared. She and Caro were at the centre of the storm they were brewing up and they rode their broomsticks together across the dark face of the moon and exalted in their power and anger. Anna held Caro in her arms and walked her up and down, up and down the living-room while she screamed their anger and defiance to a world that had locked them both up, trapped them in its own puny causality.

'And as for you Karen, what the hell did you think you were doing? Who asked you to wander all over my life and inflict me, conflict me with your certainties? Even when Kate died you were thinking about how you could fuck me. Well fuck you sweetheart.

God damn. God damn you.' Anna knew now how she had never been able to answer Karen, never been free to contradict her; she had been powerless before Karen's naming of the universe; she had played Eve to Karen's Adam — it was not good in her but it was no better in Karen. Karen allowed space only for certainty, she took no account of tentativeness. 'Get out. Leave me alone. Get out of my dreams, get out of my life. Your way is not the only way. I can find my own. Shut up.'

Now battered by exhaustion and by Caro's screams, Anna was beaten down into a new anger and a new reality. She knew that the dark is not an impossible place to be, but only a difficult one. It is possible to travel, though slowly, through the night. And in this knowledge Anna turned on the Fathers. Now it was time for the wrestling match with them, like Jacob. Now in the glow of Caro's rage and the power of Fiona's contractions, here in this women-place the Fathers were vulnerable, vulnerable to her anger. Hunted too long, she turned now wild and frightened and lethal. Still holding the screaming child in her arms, still pacing, dandling, dancing her, Anna summonsed the Fathers.

'OK,' she shouted, 'come here. By the power of the Holy Virgins I summon you; by my own power I command you. I gave up my magical powers for you. Of course I am afraid, but I shall chew on the energy of that fear and it will nourish me. It is bitter herbs but I will not spit it out. I shall use it. Tell me what you have given me. What you have ever given me?'

And they come: called, they come because they must. Very loud and very fierce, but not so loud or fierce as Caro's screams.

'How dare you question us? You may not question us. We can destroy you, we can take everything away, if we have to we will blast the creation away.'

'Before there was creation there was chaos. And afterwards again a new creation.'

'What about hell? We can damn your soul and feed it to the fires for eternity.'

She almost wavered. 'I don't think you can. I have chosen another: the mark of the fish is upon me, I am branded in his love. The fish tail undulates on my flesh; the virgin's son, the virgin's lover will protect me.'

'Oh no; the son is on our side.'

'Wrong wrong. The virgin's son is not on the side of the Fathers. The virgin's lover is on the side of the lesbians.'

'Stop. Stop this now. We can punish you and we will. We will drive you mad and everyone will cast you out on the mountain-side, food for the scavengers and worms.'

'But you are doing that anyway. I am alone, I am crazed and rejected. You punish me anyway. That's where this deal has come unstuck, I now realise. I have been a good child of the Fathers for thirty-six years, three years longer than Christ put up with it, and what have I got out of it? You don't deal straight do you? What have you given me? Dear God, I've done my bit, haven't I?'

'Obviously not. Justice we deal in. Virtue we reward. But you have cheated. You have kept company with whores and mad children, with filth and perversion. We will break up the words. You speak only because we let you. We are the Eternal Word.'

'Rubbish. I refuse. Your voices are mine. You have no more power over me than the power I have given you. And I have given you a lot of power, the power of my fears and frailties, my weakness, my stupidities, my evasions and dishonesties. You've glutted yourself on that, and waxed fat and grown strong. I know I can't have it back, just for the asking, just easy and simple. But now I know that you have only the power that I have handed you on a plate. You have none of your own. You need me. I know that. And I know too that however powerful you are, then that is how powerful, how strong I can be. I will not, I do not pay any more.

'See, I can make you turn. I can call you and you have to come. I shall hunt you down, a great slobbering running bitch. I shall hunt you down even to hell if I have to. I shall tear into you as the mad women tore into Pentheus, and I shall eat your flesh and grow strong. I shall thrust myself upon you as Jael banged in the tent-peg. I shall chop you small as Medea chopped her stepson. I shall grind you down and spin you out as all the women always have. I shall use the women's power, mine and Caro's and Kate's and Karen's and Fiona's: the power of hands and bodies and blood and birth and madness. And I shall use your power too, because I've served in your courts and know your ways; the ways of words, and bright skeins of discourse and cleverness. I shall unknot your threads and reweave them my own way. I shall be patient and I shall be fierce. But, before God, I will not cower before you anymore. I won't. I won't. I won't.'

'This is a temper tantrum. Temper tantrums must be punished. Do you remember that? You do remember that. Our faithful slave, your father taught you that. Loss of control must be punished by our losing control. He taught you, didn't he? Do you want that again, do you want that again?'

Whipped in a new remembering, she panicked suddenly and retreated.

'No, no please. Not that.'

'You are bad.

You are bad and mad and disgusting.

You are not lovable because you are not good.

If you don't behave we will lock you up, for your own good.

You are crazy. Bad. Mad. They rhyme, they are the same.

'You want us to break you, you do really. You are provoking us for your own delight. Shall we spank you, spank you till your buttocks are red and raw. Shall we beat you. Shall we beat you with belts and whips. Women cannot be trusted. Unless they are disciplined they will run away. But you will not escape. Beg, beg and grovel. Ask us to punish you, ask us to make you good. Ask us and we might help you.

'You are disgusting. You are a woman. You are bloody and bad. You are foul. You are unclean. You are mad. We can keep you safe if you will let us break you. You need us. You are horrible. What are you?'

She was whimpering, 'I'm bad. I'm a bad woman, a bad girl, a bad nun. I am wicked and filthy. I am shit. I am horrible.'

'Are you disgusting? Are you foul. Tell us how foul you are. Tell us. Say it. Say it. Say it or we'll make you.' But miraculously Caro's screams were louder, Caro's chaotic flapping arms, shapeless and strong, beat hard against the voices in her head.

She said, with what little boldness she had left, 'No. I am not going to play those games again. Never again.'

'But you want to, don't you? don't you? Don't you? You want that don't you.'

'*Yes*,' she shouted now, finding her rage and holding it, clasping it and Caro close in her arms. 'Yes, yes I do. Yes I want to be punished. Yes I am frightened and ashamed by the humiliations and pains I have suffered at your hands. Yes I am scared of internalised violence, and sexiness inside me. Yes I am frightened by the emotional storms you have brewed up for me. Yes I have a deep craving, a need even for all sorts of horrible, deranged and unnamable things. Yes I am terrified to look inside myself and see what you have made there. Yes, I have accepted your rules and demands and paid my blackmail money and my protection money and my blood money all these years. So what? Yes and yes and yes and yes and finally also and resoundingly no. No, I will not consent any more. No, I reject your lousy rewards for my so-called good behaviour. No, I don't know what I want instead. No, I can't answer all your hurtful questions. No, I don't know how I will live without you. But I don't care. I don't bloody care anymore. You've pushed too far. You've had it. I'm coming out to fight you. I will name you and learn who you are and eventually I will fight it out with you, on the planes of destruction if necessary. You are the old power of the fathers. I may even have uses for you. But I won't tolerate this way of living any more. I've had it. I won't. I won't. I won't. Look, look here, look at me and Caro. We're having one monumental, grade A tantrum. We're behaving like lunatics, we're shouting and yelling and screaming in a respectable London terraced house. Look, she's shitting. We've got shit all over both of us. Look, this is a tantrum. And what the hell can you do about it?'

When she stopped shouting there was still no silence, because Caro went on screaming, indifferent and loud, and Anna was glad of it. The Fathers could not cope with the senseless enormity of noise, the roaring of pre-words out of the void. The crashing of the vastness of emptiness filled Caro's small body and crashed on outwards through Anna and into the ordered world.

The phone rang. Anna answered it quite calmly and efficiently. Over Caro's still continuing screams, she heard Stephen's voice. 'Anna, we have a son. He's fine. He's lovely. Fiona's fine too. It was good. A wonderful birth. How's things?'

Anna laughed shakily. 'Well, you can hear. We haven't had the best possible day.'

'Can you hang on?'

'Stephen, of course. Give Fiona my love.'

'Will do. See you later, OK?'

'Yes of course, goodbye now.'

She put down the telephone receiver and said to Caro, 'Well, you have a brother.' But Caro was not pacified. She was not even interested. She went on screaming and screaming. But underneath the screams she talked, too, and Anna heard her voice.

So what? So what? We send the Fathers packing. But where are the mothers then? That's what I want to know. You blame the Fathers but I have to ask, where are the mothers then? The mothers are rats, crawling in the sewage works. They are treacherous. They gnaw through the cord too soon. They ought to wait, but they do not. The rat mother cannot wait to betray the baby. They chew through the cord and hand us over to the Fathers. They forsake us. They let us be snatched up to heaven, to the courts of the Fathers, to the bright glory. The mothers are crowned with the stars and the sun and the moon are at their feet, but we are the price they pay for their honour; they pay the Fathers with the flesh of the daughters.

The mothers prefer the Fathers; they desert the daughters.

The mothers hand us over into the slavery of the Fathers.

The mothers bind the daughters' feet.

The mothers rip out the soft labial flesh.

The mothers cut away the clitoris with broken bottles.

The mothers scar the daughters' skin so the Fathers may know their own.

The mothers cripple the daughters and sell them into whoredom.

The mothers teach the daughters the new rules.

The mothers desert the daughters. They sell us to the Fathers, over and over again. They run away. They keep silence. They explain and they apologise. They protect the Fathers from the anger of the daughters. Where are the mothers? They are busy gnawing through the cord so they can sell us off, and their price is cheap. I hate them. I hate them. They go away. They ought to stay with the daughters but they go away.

The two of them, Anna and Caro, flopped worn out into the sofa. Caro's screams trailed off; she was stained pink and blotchy by them. She curled foetally in Anna's lap, her drooling mouth found the back of her own hand and she mouthed and slobbered on it and drifted into sleep. Anna too, half waking, sat there cradling her; weary, travel-stained from a long journey, home again, but with new maps of the interior, new plans for further explorations. She would have to go again.

Later she fed Caro, washed her and put her to bed. Caro's calm continued as though she were drained. She was limp and unresisting, and, when cleaned, warm and sweet-smelling. Anna came downstairs again, gentle and blank inside herself; she started to cook, pottering in the kitchen, feeling normality seep softly back. It was not yet time to think about what had happened. It was time for the solid and material; bread and cheese and milk and vegetables. Cutting and cleaning and real things.

She thought suddenly and vibrantly of Karen; it grabbed her as a loss, the beauty and warmth of Karen. Her enthusiasm and, sweet Lord, her love. Laborious, patient caring. Her willingness and generosity. It was she, Anna, who had been in too much of a hurry. She had been the baby who had resisted its own birthing and then surged out in fierce and wild panic. She could feel Karen quite vividly, her backings and advancings, her strategies and determinations, her elegant rapier phrases disarmed by the ironic grin. Anna thought, almost, that she would ring her up, but even as she considered it she heard Stephen's key in the door. It could wait, she thought, it would wait, but she would have to return there. She went out into the hall to welcome Stephen home and congratulate him. But he was not smiling, instead he looked drained, tired, defeated.

'Are they all right?' she asked him fearfully.

'What? Oh yes, yes they're fine, beautiful. Oh dear, is it that obvious? I've been walking in the park for the last hour trying to make it less obvious. Anna, get me a drink would you, please.' He slumped into his chair, his legs long and skinny in front of him. Anna gave him a glass of wine and stood interrogatively before him. 'Anna, she wants Caro out of the house.'

'What, now?'

'She says she won't come home until Caro is somewhere else.'

'She doesn't mean it, not really; it's just shock and exhaustion, surely?'

'I don't know, Anna. It was a good birth, given her fear and last time and everything, it was magic, really magic. I was filled, well filled with awe. But there was a difficult patch, a hard time they call the transition phase. So they gave her some pethidine and she got a bit woozy. She talked about Caro, and about hating her, and how she feared she would damage the new baby, about her being malevolent and impossible, and how there would not be time for both of them in a single day. She muttered on and on. I didn't know what to say, I felt I had to be on her side then stay with her, be there only for her, I couldn't argue with her. The midwife was marvellous, very comforting; I felt guilty using up so much of her time. She said that Fiona didn't know what she was saying, that pethidine had odd effects on people and they said all sorts of things and that it didn't matter. I couldn't help hearing her though. And then she came round and got back to work and he was born and it was wonderful, exciting, and we were high on it, you know. And Fiona seemed happy and proud, though tired of course, and we looked at him and she fed him and stuff and then I came and phoned you and our families and all that. Afterwards we had a cup of tea and everything seemed absolutely normal and good. Then we all went up to the ward and they said Fiona and the baby should sleep and I should go. So I kissed her and everything and went to the door. And she called me and I turned round and she said quite calmly, ''I did mean it you know. I'm not letting her near him. I'm not coming home till she's out of the house.'' Then she closed her eyes and smiled and blew me a kiss and said, ''See you tomorrow darling'' as though that were the only thing she'd stopped me for.'

Anna was silent, wondering, thinking.

Stephen said, 'The thing is, I have to do something. I have to take some action. Either I have to argue with her, make her discuss it, or I have to take her at her word and do something. Either way I have to take sides. And she's right in a way. At least for a little while it would be easier, better, and it's hard to believe that Caro would mind, would mind that much. Do you think she'd mind?'

Anna thought. About how to say it, how to be gentle but not let him off his hook. 'Yes, yes, I do think she would notice. I think she would mind. But that's not necessarily a reason not to. I thought before you should think about it. I told you. But not because she wouldn't mind, wouldn't notice. And, Stephen, this may sound odd, but she might hurt the baby. Not physically but psychically. Fiona's right, she might use up too much time and energy. But more than that; she was so angry today, so angry from the minute you left until after you phoned, I've never seen anything like it. Pure rage, and despair and hatred and fury.' Like Kate, like Karen, why did she have to love these fierce women?

'It's too sudden,' said Stephen. 'This isn't the right way to do it. I think Fiona needs some help, professional help to work this one out. Oh God, Anna, what the hell am I going to do?'

'I can't help any more, I can't advise you. I have identified with her too much. What you decide will help me decide about me; we are both caught she and I inside the dark shadow of habits.' Anna was rather impressed at herself for so smooth a pun even here; Karen had given her more than she had realised.

Stephen and she went upstairs. They did not even speak about what she had said. At the door of Caro's room they both took their shoes off and tiptoed in; her strange grunting noise filled the whole room, the shadow of her sleeping self swelled up and there was no space for them to talk. They watched her for a while, listening to her, listening through her breathing to what they should do, what would be right. Caro had nothing to say to Anna now and Anna did not expect to hear her.

Afterwards they sat on the stairs, Stephen leaning against Anna, weary.

After a while he said, 'You see, she is my quest, my Rapunzel; it is about her that I am romantic. I feel that I have to rescue her from the tower, or never carry myself with honour again. But the only way through to her is herself, she has to let down her hair and let me in. I have to find the words of the song and only the witch and she know what they are. I can't do it on my own. Fiona says she is Sleeping Beauty and that we must cut through, we can cut through and kiss her into life. But I know that she isn't passive like that, waiting, sleeping; I don't experience her as passive in that way. She has to want to come out, she has to work. She has to want the prince as much as she wants the witch. The doctors say and I believe them that it isn't like that; that it is a physical thing only. But if you live with her. . . . She has taken all my tenderness, I had none left for the new baby, none to spare for Fiona. I could be there, but I couldn't feel it. They were radiant tonight, a radiant madonna and child, so beautiful, like a painting. The whole experience was beautiful, Fiona was so strong, so confident, so utterly present. Not like when Caro was born, then it was dreadfully awful and horrible, but she needed me. Tonight I said, "Darling, you are beautiful," and I knew she had gone into a picture. Raphael, madonna and child. I felt she had left me behind with Caro in the darkness and that was where I wanted to be. I am pledged to Caro, you see, I think there is no space left for anyone else.'

Later he added, 'But you know all too well that this is a cheat. Caro is kept here by Fiona; Fiona puts in the sweat and tears and if Fiona pulls out then Caro will have to go away because I can't do it. I know I can't do what Fiona does. Lugging her about, changing her filth, wrestling with her, keeping her alive; the constant endless cramping constraining caring. And I come home in the evening and read her fairy stories which she cannot understand and say that I am pledged to her. Fiona says I'm sexist and perhaps I am; yes I am; but there's a shining energy in Fiona, there always has been, and I can't match it, can't match that sort of determined devotion.'

'Perhaps,' said Anna tentatively, 'perhaps Caro is a Cause for Fiona; she needs causes. Fiona's a knight on a white charger, a saviour of maidens from dragons. But sometimes just occasionally the maiden doesn't want to be saved, or is already in love with the dragon or something. I was one of those once, so I know, a missionary burning with missionary zeal. But there is another way: loving the dragon, loving what, who Caro is now, just as she is, and being content, no — exulting in that. I never meant to fall in love with Caro. It is perilous loving Caro, it takes you to strange places and you have to be careful not to be sucked into doing good, working on her and feeling virtuous. I never meant to fall in love with Karen either; perhaps loving itself is a perilous place. You have to go in and in, and still not know if there will be a way out.

'We've sentimentalised. Because of the Resurrection, I suppose. But the Minotaur was a monster, really was, remember. You went in and in and then he ate you up.

'You have to love the monster. Kiss the monster. For love alone, not knowing if it will turn into a prince, not even hoping, not thinking about that.'

Stephen was not really listening to her and she knew he wasn't; far from being hurt that seemed exactly right. They had both been on very long journeys that day, and seen new lands far away. She had said out loud that she had loved Karen and loved Caro and Stephen had not noticed. And she was glad.

After another while he said, 'I have a son. We should be celebrating.' So they went downstairs and ate the dinner she had cooked. Stephen drank most of the wine and fell asleep on the sofa. Anna went upstairs, glad she was staying the night, that she did not have to leave the house yet. She noticed their two pairs of shoes outside Caro's door. 'Take off your shoes for the ground whereon you tread is holy ground.' She went back into Caro's room and watched her again in her sleep. Caro's growling voice came forth low and deep beneath the chesty breathing.

When the true son comes the slave woman and her child are driven out into the desert. You are the slave. I am the wrong child. We are driven into the desert. In the desert it is very bad, our skin is burned, flayed off by the sun. Beaten by the sun. The Fathers beat us unmercifully. The father drives out Hagar and Ishmael so they cannot distract attention from the true son who must shine in singleness. In the desert it is very fierce. The sand scours your skin, it strips you down to the thinnest layer. You are punished, stripped and scourged for being the wrong kind. Hagar was sexy and foreign and bold, not a wife. Ishmael was wide-eyed and hasty, not the right child. We are gone into the desert, you and I.

In the desert, they tell us, you will die. You will die parched and alone and the sand will grind your bones to powder, you will blow in the wind and find no resting place. It is worth being charming, worth remaining in slavery and paying the price. But I know a secret. I will tell you my secret: in the desert when everything has gone, even your skin has gone and your bones are shrivelled, then in the desert you will see God and live.

Anna smiled; Caro's voice was so low and conspiratorial, her body so tiny, just a humped darker blob in the darkness, so different and frail compared to the great anger of the daylight. But she is telling Anna a great secret. She is chuckling now. She knows they must part and this is her gift for the road.

I'll tell you another secret. They say if we are bad they will throw us in the lions' den and the lions will eat us up. The lions are hot and filthy, they stink and prowl. The lions' den is underground; it is dark and damp and fetid. But I know the secret. The lions' den is a womb. We can dance with the lions. Daniel did, dancing whirling and making music with the lions all through the night. If you are not afraid of the lions you can dance with them and they will dance with you. Then they may eat you up but it will not matter very much because then you will love the lions. You have to love the lions, you have to love the womb, you have to dance with the lions not afraid. Hagia Sophia, I have told you, danced on the void before there were words. I know all about it. She danced in the womb of darkness, in the place of the sounding waters. You can dance on the waters, if you know that you may drown, but you do not mind too much.

She whispered now. Anna leaned right over her cot to hear her.

Lions are very very ticklish.

Anna was too tired now. There had been too much of this day. All she wanted was to go to sleep. It was nice, she thought, just for once to know what you really wanted and be able to have it.

Anna stayed for eight days looking after Caro. She did not go to the hospital to see Fiona, offering Caro's need of her as an excuse. But she did not want to go, she did not want the final treachery of admiring the golden son who had replaced the dark daughter. To help Stephen she telephoned and talked and argued with social workers, health visitors and children's homes. She and Stephen told each other that it was only a temporary expedient, till Fiona recovered, till Fiona was able to decide what should be done. People were sympathetic, though everyone kept saying they should have thought about it sooner, that nothing could be arranged that quickly. Fiona was kept safe, kept away from it all, enshrined in the gleaming white temple of maternity up on the hill. No one seemed to find it strange that now she had a son she should want the daughter removed. Anna found it very strange. She found it difficult, painful; she wanted somehow to explain to Caro, to try and show her why; that they were sending her away to keep her safe. She, Caro, had not wanted to come out of her dark place, had not wanted to join the world of sunshine, logic and cleanliness. They would send her now to a place that would protect her from all that; no one would make her quest or cause any more. She would be all alone and safe in her hole.

But for herself Anna was no longer tempted. She had seen the light and did not want to go back into the dark. Caro's voice tried still to urge it upon her, but she had lost the glorious lyricism, had descended to monosyllable and plainness:

Choose mad, choose me, choose the dark and me. Come with me, Anna, come to the safe place. Come to the place where I am. You are me. You are like me. So come on. Come where you can be who you want; where you can be child, come back to the womb. Come. Come in to the dark. Come please. Come on.

And for the first time she answered Caro's voice directly. She had barely noticed that while she had argued with the Fathers, she had listened, only listened, to Caro. Now she said, gently, passionately, lovingly, 'Caro, I love you. I love you and you know I love you. I accept your love. But we aren't the same. I may be retarded, but not damaged, not really cracked and damaged. Those painful exercises in normality are appropriate for me. I do want to be a grown-up, you see, that is what I have chosen. You have given me a love gift, a new part of myself, a new way, but I don't have to come all the way down with you. I love you but we are not the same. Do you understand that?'

Caro growled and sulked but she understood.

Anna wore the habit that week; it gave her the right to meddle in other people's lives. It gave her negotiating power. Part of her smiled bitterly, knowing truly that the garments of poverty and humility gave their wearers power and authority. She felt a little uncomfortable and silly, putting on the uniform again and doing good works. But by and large she was calm and still. Not forever; it would not last forever, this calm, and she would not want it to. But her head was cleared; cleared of noise and voices, as it had been briefly on the hill above the joyful, moving horse. For too long she had lived with a buzzing cacophony between her ears, like a badly tuned radio; now she was clear of fear and interference. She could wait.

The last evening she sat with Caro on her lap. Her voice was all gone, too; there was just a small brain-damaged toddler, a source of effort, grief and joy. The child was also calm, sprawled across Anna's lap, her blanket twisted round her hand, at ease. Anna knew that this was the only child she would ever have as her own, and there was a rightness to that. She would never have been able to learn how to mother a normal child. She did not know what a normal mother was. Stephen came in from the hospital and said again as he had said before how alike they looked. He still seemed puzzled by this.

'I can't', said Anna, 'apologise for loving her, it is as obvious and essential to me as breathing. Like breathing it has kept me alive; but I can't help wondering if my loving her, my being able to love her so much took something away from Fiona. What happens when two princesses both want to kiss the same frog?'

Stephen smiled comfortably. 'I don't know Anna. It's something we'll all have to talk about I suppose, you and Fiona and me. The whole thing about what you have meant to us, we'll have to work it out.'

'No. Not me.'

'What?'

'Not me. You and Fiona. I'm going away. You've been a catalyst for me, and perhaps me for you two. But I'm off. My time is up.'

'Are you going back to Santa Virgine?'

'I doubt it.'

'Are you all right, will you be all right?'

'Yes, I believe so.'

He asked no more questions; she knew he trusted her. Caro slept on her lap. She would be sorry to say goodbye to such friendly acceptance.

'Well, I'm not going tomorrow,' she told him, 'but soon now. I'll see you all before then. Stephen, there is something that you must make clear to Fiona. I don't know much about how it is in a house with a new baby. I've heard it's quite chaotic and difficult, but Fiona has to know that I can't help her with that one. That's hers. Of course this was for her too, taking care of Caro, because she's my friend; but it was also for Caro and especially for me. Do you understand?'

'No,' he said. 'No, not really, but it doesn't matter. I believe you. It's OK. I can imagine that new-born babies would be difficult for ou now.'

It was not that, she knew it was not that, she would not be jealous or broody or repining, but she owed Caro some fundamental loyalty. Somehow it was too difficult to explain and it did not matter.

When Stephen took Caro off in the car the next morning Anna kissed her and waved goodbye from the doorway. It was over. On an impulse she borrowed a bathing suit of Fiona's and went swimming. The pool was quite empty, mid-morning, and she swam up and down until the muscles in her wrists ached and she began to feel cold. She swam and did not think about anything except that she was getting very unfit and that the water felt wonderful and firm against her effort.

The shower was hot and comforting. She was tired and knew it. Looking after Caro was tiring; she understood Fiona better for those eight days. She wondered, as the hot water crashed over her short hair, if she was exhausted too from the wrestling match with the Fathers. But she had secured some victory, she had driven them off; she had created time for herself to prepare to go hunting. Next time she would be able to pick the ground. She could not linger in this hot shower for too long; they would rally themselves and return in force, and she doubted if she was strong enough at that moment to do it again. She had to equip herself, make up her mind, move forward again. Today she would take off, but tomorrow, tomorrow she would stiffen the sinews, summon up the blood. She laughed at herself and stepped out of the shower, suddenly pleased and joyful. Challenged. She had not felt challenged for years. As she towelled herself and caught the eye of the changing-room attendant staring at her tattoo she was almost laughing. She found herself humming a hymn tune and worked out fairly quickly what it was:

> *Dear God hear the prayer we offer,*
> *Not for ease our prayer would be,*
> *But for strength that we may ever*
> *Live our lives outrageously.*

She knew that wasn't quite right really. 'Courageously' was right. She giggled.

> *Not forever by still waters*
> *Would we idly rest and stay*
> *But would strike the living fountains*
> *From the stones along our way.*

'Hello God,' she said with surprise. And there was no answer. Which was comfortable.

At Mass the next morning:

'Listen, oh daughter, give heed to my words; forsake your people and your father's house.'

It was the psalm response for the Common of Virgins. They had sung it, she remembered vaguely, at her own profession, a great and passionate love song. It had seemed then a call to love and freedom and now it was again. She heard the words with a limpidity which surprised her; they were separated from their context and it was as though she had never heard them before; a summons, a permission. No, a promise.

'Listen oh daughter, give heed to my words; forsake your people and your father's house.'

The time had come for decisions. She stuck a little label on her chest which said 'I am in Retreat', so no one would talk to her. She went to the chaplain's office to make her confession, did these things methodically, old custom taking over easy and reassuring, strong and sweet. But tinged she noticed with nostalgia. She had to wait in the priest's reception room, she had not thought of that, but it was comfortable and she had lots of time. On the low table in the middle of the room was a big square book, called *The Sign of the Tree*. She picked it up, it was a

202

picture book, black and white, vibrant leaping pictures full of bottomless black holes. She skimmed them, noticing idly that the artist was a Benedictine nun. It fell open at a picture, strange semi-abstract and slightly Japanese somehow, curved and shady; 'The Garden of the Mother' she read, and then:

Shortly before his sudden death Pope John Paul I, speaking about God at a Sunday Angelus blessing in St Peter's Square, said, 'God is Father. Even more, God is mother.'

We worship our mother in solitude, seeking the secret places to be with her. She lives in the secret garden, in the dark places of deepest interiority. Everything in the garden magnifies her presence because everything there pours from her source. The garden flows with her white milk and golden honey and all her children are fed. Everything participates in her being. Everything is holy.

Haunted by her mystery, we are roused to enter the garden where she is always waiting for us to arrive. Searching for our mother, we run through trees, lifting stones, kneeling at every pool and animal's hollow, looking into every cleft and beneath birds' wings. We are overwhelmed when we find her. Welcomed we enter into her tender matrix, enclosed in the grotto of God's eternity.

And her darkness was ablaze with light. It was not a question of whether she believed that exactly, but she was willing to suspend her disbelief. It was all perfectly simple; she had never gone far enough. It was as simple as that. She thought she had left her father's house when she had travelled up the Hudson Valley to the Mother House, but that had only been a way-station, a safe little place where children might play while they were growing into their full strength and discovering their true stature. It was not meant to be the journey end. If she had realised that sooner she could probably have used it as a base camp for always. But now she would have to go travelling unprotected, commit herself to the great river and float down into the dark interior; she had to go and seek the country of the Mothers. She had to explore the lands and exorcise the ghosts.

'We worship God our mother in solitude.' The only way. Kate

and Karen had been ways in, but both impossible for the mother-less child. Until she found her mother she could not love her sisters because she could not tell who they were; until she learned that she could not go courageously out into the jungle and hack through the entangled branches of dreams until she came to the white city where women knew their own power.

'We are roused to enter the secret garden.'

The Fathers do not want the daughters to leave them; they make it hard by bribery and blackmail. Her father did not want his daughters to go searching for their mother.

Her mother had not searched for her.

The virgin mother searched for her child in the temples of men, in the great halls of the power of the Law; she had searched for the fruit of her womb, sorrowing and weeping. But later she had sent her child out into the desert to wrestle with the powers of hell. After he had known her and been at home with her, obedient to her. Then she had sent her child out full of wisdom and stature. And the angels had ministered to him.

Demeter searched for her child: for six months she had refused all consolation, searching for her daughter. But after she had found her and embraced her Persephone was free to come and go between the two places; the maiden can stroll easily between heaven and hell and gather flowers safely wherever she desires.

To Anna it was gloriously simple, not easy but simple. She must go back to the womb and be born again in the power of the spirit. She must go back to the beginning to the place that Caro has invited her, not trying to graft the formlessness on but stripping naked to meet it. She must go back to the dark damp belly. She will go back to the Amazon valley where she has once been with Kate. She will go to the headwaters and float down the great river until she comes to the land of the mothers and she will stay there and learn to be a grown-up woman.

She made her confession. She confessed to the sins of cowardice, spiritual blindness and a lack of self-knowledge and authenticity. She confessed to imposing limits on the goodness of God and to a weakness of faith. She confessed to cheating Karen, but not to desiring her because she did not believe any more that that was a sin. She accepted the forgiveness flowing in blood and water from the side of the virgin's son and in milk and sweetness from the breasts of God. She did not speak to the priest of her wrestling match and her decision, because at that point it seemed to belong to her alone.

Later she realised the enormity of her task and the loneliness of her way. She felt weary but unafraid.

Dear Mother (she wrote)

Thank you, as ever, for your last good letter. You are right and it is time for a decision; perhaps there is part of me that would like to put it off, because I kept hoping to find some way that would make it possible for me to do what has to be done *and* stay with the community which has been my family for so long. I don't know — but I'm grateful to you, both for giving me this time and for forcing the issue now. You will gather from all this that I recognise that it is impossible for me to return to the community. I'm not sure at this point what I will do in the long run, but immediately I'm planning to return if possible to South America, to try and spend some time in contemplation and to work out how I can best use the second half of my life.

Because I like to do things tidily — you know me — and because I want to remain within the charity of the Church, I would be grateful if you would prepare the paperwork for my application for dispensation from vows. But knowing where I am, it does seem silly for me to wait until they are processed: a waste of my time and disruptive for the rest of you, particularly as I have been living outside the community for this time. However I would like your advice on this. I think it would be easiest for both of us if you applied on the grounds that I have had a nervous breakdown and am not likely to be fit for community life for some time to come. I think this is probably true anyway.

I'm not really explaining anything, am I? I shall be travelling via the USA anyway, to see my family and try and organise some way of feeding myself — perhaps an advance on a book based on my work here, perhaps some field social work for the time being (it is important to me not to be supported in any way by my father at the moment). May I come and see you then and try and explain what has been happening to me? I would like to do this, but it is too difficult to write down just now.

I want you to know how much I love you all and how precious to me my time in the order has been; there is no question of thinking the whole thing a mistake. It wasn't. It was right then, and now it isn't, and I want to go bravely.

with love, Anna.

And then that was not quite enough, it was too distant, too clear. She added a postscript:

Mother. This hurts me. I understand why divorce makes people bitter; it is the taste of sorrow in the mouth. You ought to have told me about Kate; I read it in the newspapers here. I think that was not honest of you. I don't think it would have made any difference but you should not have kept it from me. Nonetheless I do love you. Anna.

She thought it would be impossible to write to her father. She sat numb with pity at the task. Then she thought she would not leave the order after all because she could not bear to tell him. She breathed upon the thought of staying and knew it was impossible. It was too late for honesty from her now, too late even for too much kindness, but she had to tell him. Her hand was shaking so that she could hardly form her letters; they were shaking, she realised abruptly, not with compassion but with fear. Damn him, she thought, and wrote:

Dear Daddy,
You will not like this letter very much. I have today asked Reverend Mother to seek a dispensation for me as I have decided to leave the order.

Oh God, it was not possible. His fury would find her across the seven seas, 'yea though I take the wings of morning and fly to the uttermost ends of the seas'. She could not afford to care any more.

I know you will not be happy about this. I'm not so happy

206

myself, but no one is perfect. I ought to have tried to explain to you when you were in London that last time, but then I did not know and I did not see any point in worrying you unnecessarily; a mistake. I'm sorry.

I leave for New York in a few days and will let you know my plans when I have some. In the meantime you can find me care of Claudia, I think.

Daddy, please try not to be angry or sad. I am sure that this is what God wants me to do, even if we do not understand it altogether. Take care of yourself, I'll hope to see you soon.

love and kisses, Anna.

She did not want to put the kisses in, but decided that would be mean. He could not help being who he was.

Then. My beloved, she wrote, but threw the piece of paper away; it was not a phrase that came naturally to her and she did not want to raise Karen's expectations.

My dearest Karen,

This one is overdue. I owe you all sorts of apologies, but not I think the ones you want or expect. It was more simple than I let it seem, I think. Just sexual passion is not appropriate to a pre-adolescent, and in emotional terms that is what I am. I can almost sympathise with some guy hauled up for statutory rape saying that he just didn't know the kid was under age. The problem was that I didn't let on; I carried on like a grown-up, like superwoman in a nun's disguise. I didn't allow you to see enough of the holes and the craziness and the damaged child inside. You offered to hear it and I failed finally to take the risk. I thought that sex might be a way out, but obviously on those terms it couldn't work because you were offering real love. I was not paying enough attention to you, and using you as a way to get out.

I'm sorry because I now know that I really loved you, and I suspect we could have loved each other; and we blew it.

I'm not going back to my nunnery. It doesn't seem like a place where a child should grow up, although it has kept me safe for years. I am going back to South America though, as soon as I can get organised — sort of in search of Kate, though not literally. In search of growth and understanding about how the lines of friendship and love might lead. Perhaps I will come back sometime — I sort of suspect, things being what they are, that I will end up either as a radical lesbian or as a contemplative nun. I'm not planning on either, just on finding out what it means to be a free woman. I know you won't approve of my methods; I know you think the body is the only way in, but I'm not you and come from a different place.

Please thank Sybil, for lots of things, but the loan of her car will do. Tell Judy that I have a tattoo more beautiful than hers (honestly) and that I wish I could be with you all again sometime.

I love you very much. Take good care. Anna.

It was done. It was not good enough, but it was the best she could manage for now. She had an obligation to Karen, of duty and love, but she did not know how she could fulfil it. She would try again later. Now it was too delicate, too dangerous to try and explain.

Inside her there is something silent. Silent, almost sullen. Stubborn, pig-headed. There comes a point, she discovers, where words become impossible, even dangerous; a point when all the words are taken over and belong to other people and you are left with none of your own. At that point you know that only sullenness will pay. Where the sulking child has to take over from the grown woman. Where even the toughest woman has to lean on the mute strength of the sulking child. Caro has lent her this knowledge, the power of not coming out to play. To use it is the best way she can thank Caro now. Caro knew and showed her that they can punish you, yell at you, cajole and tempt you, and even if they want to they can kill you. But in the end they cannot make you consent. They cannot make you obey. There comes a time when you just have to hunker down in a grim sullenness, not answer back, not try to explain, not respond. A place where love is as dangerous as hostility; where offers of help are as cruel as threats of torture.

Anna has stepped freshly outside her own conditioning, out of her carefully constructed skin. She is frail, vulnerable and cold; she must not let anyone come too near her, not now, not yet. It is an enormous effort laying claim to new possibility. She has had to burrow deep inside her own silence and hug herself there, because there is nothing else. She has to cling to the heavy, implacable unmovable weight of her own sullenness. It will be enough, just. And it will be everything.

She is ready to go travelling; that is all.

At about eight forty-five most nights, Sr. Katherine Elizabeth walks up the pitted track which leads from the shanty-town to the house above it where the nuns live. She has still not entirely worked out how to forgive the rapists without minimising the rape, not just her rape but the possibility of the rape of all women everywhere. But for herself, gradually, something has happened. Rather two things have happened, closely connected but different. Her protection has been stripped away, her privilege and her protection, and that she cannot entirely regret. She has something in common with all women everywhere, and something in common with her friend and brother on the cross. She knows that if it ever happens again she will not shout and yell in English, because the rape of an American nun is no different from any other rape; they are all unspeakable. But something else has been stripped away too, her purity and choice made clearer by losing its symbol; the Church, the western civilisation which is meaningless here had given her her virginity, but she has given herself back her purity, has reclaimed her chastity, and it is all her own. She prays for Kate with immense compassion, for Anna with considerable sadness and some curiosity, for her community with a certain wry affection and for Santa Virgine and its people with total commitment. For herself she knows that she still has to wrestle not with her anger which is legitimate, fierce and right, but with her guilt which is pointless, destructive and wrong.

She would like, she thinks, to stay out late tonight and play with the white unicorn who comes to her dancing down the trail of the bright stars, seeking with love the milk from the breast of this pure virgin. She would like that; not to go home but to ride the sides of the steep mountain and sing until dawn. But she knows that her sisters would worry enormously, especially, if she were late for Compline, so she trudges on up the hill towards the women's house where she lives.

Also by Sara Maitland

DAUGHTER OF JERUSALEM

'A novel full of brilliant observations which seldom fail to hit home' – *Emma Tennant*

WINNER OF THE SOMERSET MAUGHAM AWARD

For five years, Elizabeth and her husband Ian have unsuccessfully attempted to have a child. Tests have shown inescapably that it is Elizabeth who is unable to conceive. However, her gynaecologist believes it to be a psychological, not a physical barrier that is preventing her from becoming pregnant . . . This perceptive and sensitive novel, first published in 1979, is more than a tale of one woman's struggle to have a child. It is an intelligent, intensely felt examination of the conflicts and choices that have always faced women. Infused with truth and warmth, it is, ultimately, a compassionate, understanding celebration of the love that makes hope possible.

THREE TIMES TABLE

'A rare blend of erudition and flamboyance' – *Sunday Times*

'Original and compelling . . . consummate storytelling
. . . weaving a sensual realism across the exhilarating,
fantastic myth-making' – *New Statesman & Society*

Three women – Rachel, her daughter, and her daughter's
daughter – share a house, but inhabit different worlds. Fifteen-
year-old Maggie flies with her dragon over the rooftops of
London to a secret world; Phoebe, her mother, who has carried
the values of the sixties into the harsher world of the eighties, is
caught up in a private dilemma and confronts difficult truths
about love and honesty; Rachel, the grandmother, an eminent
paleontologist, has to reconsider the theories she has fought for
throughout her professional life. Sara Maitland's remarkable
novel focuses on one strange and wakeful night in which Rachel,
Phoebe and Maggie find themselves facing the illusions of their
own pasts. This is a powerful, magical novel about the shaping
of women's lives – their work, their friendships, their mothers
and fathers, the extent of their freedom and the boundaries of
their experience. Rich and deeply perceptive, *Three Times Table*
re-examines familiar issues and gives them a very contemporary
turn.

WOMEN FLY WHEN MEN AREN'T WATCHING

The breadth of Sara Maitland's interests and inspiration are brilliantly displayed in this gathering of tales old and new: from folk-stories in 'True North' to classical mythology in 'Cassandra'; to Christian heroines like Perpetua in 'Requiem'. And as she intertwines the everyday and the inexplicable to witty or disquieting effect in 'Greed' and 'The Loveliness of the Long Distance Runner', her wildest flights of fantasy remain anchored in a consciousness of the oppression of women, overlaid with a wickedly ironic humour.

VESTA TILLEY

Singer, actress, male impersonator, and one of the greatest of the 'gender benders', Vesta Tilley (1864–1952) was for forty years the toast of the British music hall. Hers was a rags to riches story: born to a poor working-class family in the Midlands, she died a stage idol, a much loved philanthropist, the wealthy and respected widow of a Conservative MP. But behind the fairytale path to fame lay not only a formidable talent but also a wit and daring that saw her not so much mimic male fashions as create them. At a time when the issue of gender and its meaning were changing radically, she played with the limits of sexual differentiation to create a series of stage personae which raise fascinating questions for us now. Sara Maitland's intriguing examination of Vesta Tilley's life and artistry takes in both specific and general discussion of the meaning of cross-dressing and acting as the other sex, the performer's relationship to the men and women of her audience, class mobility and women's professionalism and self-determination. It is a fascinating account of a remarkble woman and her still vibrant legacy.

VERY HEAVEN

Looking Back at the 1960s

'Truly, it felt like Year One, when all that was holy was in the process of being profaned' – *Angela Carter*

When the Beatles hit the charts and the mini skirt hit the streets, the world changed. Or so it seemed. Twenty years on, twenty-five women look back on their lives during the decade known as the 'swinging sixties', to the challenging days of protest and pop, and the first stirrings of the Women's Liberation Movement. Their engagingly personal memoirs describe the sheer fun and excitement of those heady times as well as the euphoria – and the uncertainties – of the new freedoms, new struggles: the 'it-changed-my-life' liberation of the Pill; Barbara Castle's days as a Cabinet Minister; trying to be a Twiggy look-alike; the eruption of the underground press with *Oz* and *Ink*; Paris and Derry in 1968; Julie Christie recalling *Darling*. For many women, it was also a decade of not belonging, of outsiderness: here are Terri Quaye's and Lee Kane's accounts of being Black in Rachman's London, and, in Uganda, Yasmin Alibhai's realisation that Britain wasn't 'home'. For Michelene Wandor 'the sixties was a time when many people went to pot/except for me/I did not/. . . I yearned a lot'. These fascinating pieces, combined with Sara Maitland's perceptive and witty introduction, make *Very Heaven* a wonderful social document.